OFF-THE-WALL SKITS WITH PHRASAL VERBS

By Bonnie Trenga

Joan Ashkenas, Editor

Illustrations by Richard A. Goldberg

 JAG Publications

DEDICATION

To my son Jake, for giving me the time to nurse my idea.

Copyright © 2003 JAG Publications

Published by JAG Publications
11288 Ventura Boulevard #301
Studio City, California 91604
Telephone and Fax: 818 505-9002
E-mail address: info@jagpublications-esl.com
Website: www.jagpublications-esl.com

Illustrations by Richard A. Goldberg
Composition by Jack Lanning

Library of Congress card catalog number 2003101417

Printed in the United States of America

10 9 8 7 6 5 4 3 2 1

ISBN 0-943327-28-8

TABLE OF CONTENTS

TO THE STUDENTS

If you've just opened this book, you're probably wondering what "off-the-wall" means. Well, it's an adjective that means "unusual," "strange," "a little silly." As the humorous illustrations suggest, *Off-the-Wall Skits with Phrasal Verbs* will be different from most books you've used in the ESL classroom. Here, you can pretend to be someone else—someone who is a little odd—while you improve your conversation ability. You'll meet unusual characters such as Madame Soufflé from Chapter 1. This granny likes to drive a little faster than the average grandma (we don't suggest that you drive like she does). Say hello to Constantine from Chapter 6. He's a weatherman who likes to wear slippers at work. When you pretend to be this forecaster, don't forget to bring your own slippers to class. The ones with the rabbit ears will be fine.

While you're laughing with your classmates as you perform the skits, you'll be learning some phrasal verbs too. A phrasal verb is a combination of a verb and a preposition (or prepositions) that often means something unexpected. For example, "work out" (from Chapter 7) has nothing to do with the idea of working. "Work out" means "exercise." Thousands of phrasal verbs are used in both formal and informal English. *Off-the-Wall Skits with Phrasal Verbs* covers just one hundred and twenty essential ones, but it will help you make your English sound a lot more natural. It may sometimes be hard to remember which preposition you need to use, but this book offers plenty of oral and written practice with each phrasal verb. You'll be a pro soon.

So, open your books to Chapter 1 and start exercising your laughing muscles!

—Bonnie Trenga

TO THE TEACHER

Welcome to the unusual world of *Off-the-Wall Skits with Phrasal Verbs*. This book is probably different from any you have used before. Its premise is simple: get your intermediate and advanced students talking in more natural English, laughing, and remembering one hundred and twenty phrasal verbs.

Elements of the Book

The book is arranged into twenty subject-oriented chapters of six phrasal verbs each, and each phrasal verb is covered on one page. Each page offers multiple opportunities for students to see the phrasal verb used in context and to practice it themselves:

- *A sentence in a box*—This sentence gives students a quick look at how the phrasal verb is used.

- *Two short introductory conversations that set the stage*—Your students can read these aloud to practice intonation and pronunciation.

- *Two skits to perform*—Students will put themselves in character as they practice the target phrasal verb. Each skit has at least two roles.

- *Written exercises*—Four questions at the end of each page reinforce the phrasal verb as well as the bonus words in italics (defined in the Glossary of Bonus Words at the back of the book). Be sure to have your students use the Glossary of Bonus Words often. It defines both the bonus words in italics and the idiomatic chapter titles.

In addition, written exercises at the end of each chapter reinforce the six phrasal verbs covered within that chapter.

Things to Remember When Using This Book

- *Phrasal verbs can have multiple meanings*—Some of the phrasal verbs have many meanings but only one of them may be explained in the book. On the other hand, a few phrasal verbs in the book appear as many as three times. To avoid confusing your students, it's probably best to discuss only the meaning explained on the page you are teaching. If students are curious about alternate meanings, feel free to explain other usage.

- *Previously covered phrasal verbs are reinforced*—As you move through the book, you'll notice that previously explained phrasal verbs appear here and there. Encourage students to practice both the new and old ones. It is suggested that you start with Chapter 1 and end with Chapter 20.

- *You'll meet many silly characters*—Not all characters introduced in the conversations appear in the skits. Likewise, not all characters that appear in the skits are introduced in the conversations. However, no matter where you meet them, characters like June, the motorcycle-riding ESL teacher from Chapter 1, will keep your students—and you—entertained and involved in the lesson.

- *Students will speak only a short time at first*—When your students open their books for the first time, they will probably not be very confident. This is to be expected. Encourage the students to use complete sentences at first and to speak in their roles for a minute or two. As they improve, you can let them use incomplete sentences where appropriate, and after a few chapters you will find they can probably prolong a skit for several minutes. Encourage them to be as imaginative as possible. Nothing is too silly here.

- *This book can be used as a supplement or as a main text* —You can use *Off-the-Wall Skits with Phrasal Verbs* once in a while or you can use it every day as a basis for your conversation class.

Tips for Having Fun with This Book

- *Being a little silly*—If you encourage students to allow themselves to be a little silly, they may feel more relaxed and willing to participate. Feel free to be a little silly yourself! However, if some students don't want to be silly, that's OK. The main point is for them to concentrate on understanding the situation at hand so that they can practice using English more naturally.

- *Using different voices and adding actions to words*—Encourage the students to adopt appropriate voices when doing a skit. If a skit is for two male characters, for example, two ladies could do the skit using deep voices or stroking a mock beard. Using silly voices might help tense or shy students loosen up. Also, encourage the students to move about the room and do what the characters in the skits would be doing.

- *Using props*—If it's feasible, bring props to use in the skits. Or, you can use anything in the classroom as a prop. For instance, when you are preparing to teach "get across" in Chapter 9, you may want to bring a few rocks. Likewise, some earmuffs may come in handy when you get to "look out for" in Chapter 14.

How to Get the Most out of This Book

This book is flexible, and you can use it in many ways. Each section of the page gives a suggestion about what to do, but feel free to use the book however you imagine. Here are a few suggestions:

- Students can practice their reading and pronunciation skills by reading the conversations or skits aloud while others (who have their books closed) practice their listening comprehension.

- Students not participating in the current skit can critique it when it's over; encourage students to listen for mistakes so that after the skit is finished, you can discuss incorrect grammar or vocabulary.

- You could assign the students to read one page as homework to prepare for the next class.

- Pick a grammar construction used in an introductory conversation or skit. Then, after the students perform the skits, use that construction as the basis for a lesson.

Ready, Set, Go

So, now it's time to have your students "speak up" (Chapter 9) and "hang out with" (Chapter 13) some fun characters. I hope you all enjoy it.

—*Bonnie Trenga*

USING PHRASAL VERBS

Although *Off-the-Wall Skits with Phrasal Verbs* is humorous, let's get a little serious about usage and grammar for a moment. This book explains how to use each phrasal verb. This usage information appears in *italics* under the definition of each phrasal verb. Here is an explanation of the usage information you will see here:

1. *Does not take an object*—This means that the phrasal verb stands alone in the sentence. No object is used. Another way of looking at it is to say that you could create a sentence by using just a subject and the phrasal verb. For example, you could say, "The whole family **ate out.**" ("Eat out" is covered in Chapter 20.)

2. *Can take an object between the verb and the preposition*—This means that the phrasal verb does not stand alone in the sentence. An object must appear somewhere, either between the verb and the preposition, or after the preposition. For example, you could say, "I **looked the information up**." You could also say, "I **looked up** the information." ("Look up" is covered in Chapter 3.)

3. *Is followed by a noun phrase or pronoun*—This means that the phrasal verb does not stand alone in the sentence. An object must appear, and it comes only after the preposition. For example, you could say, "He **came down with** the flu." ("Come down with" is covered in Chapter 7.)

4. *Is followed by a noun phrase, pronoun, or verb phrase*—This means that a noun phrase, pronoun, or verb phrase must come after the preposition. For example, you could say, "I **am looking into** running for president." You could also say, "I **am looking into** it." ("Look into" is covered in Chapter 10.)

5. *Is followed by an adjective or noun phrase*—This means that an adjective or noun phrase must come after the preposition. For example, you could say, "She **comes across as** smart." You could also say, "She **comes off as** a smart person." ("Come across as/come off as" are covered in Chapter 8.)

6. *If not followed by "of," does not take an object; if used with "of," is followed by a noun phrase or pronoun*—This means that you have two choices with the phrasal verb. "Run out (of)" (covered in Chapter 5) is a good example. You could say, "I **ran out.**" You could also say, "I **ran out of** paper."

7. *Always takes an object between the verb and the preposition, and is then followed by a noun phrase or pronoun*—This means that you must use an object between the verb and the preposition, and then you must use a noun phrase or pronoun after the preposition. For example, you could say, "She **ran it by** me." ("Run by" is covered in Chapter 9.)

8. *Mean the same thing*—This means that the two listed phrasal verbs have an identical meaning. "Hand in/turn in" are examples (covered in Chapter 3).

9. *Mean about the same thing*—This means that the two listed phrasal verbs have a very similar meaning, but you can't always use them in exactly the same way. "Come by/stop by" are examples (covered in Chapter 13).

CHAPTER 1

BEHIND THE WHEEL
(DRIVING)

Break Down   Stop working

Usually applies to a vehicle or a complicated machine; does not take an object

You may hear it used like this: The tour bus **broke down**, so the group was *stranded*.

It's time to meet some of our characters. Read these conversations aloud.

Svetlana (25, a young lady): "Mark, I thought you were planning to take your ducks Bill and Will to the park today."

Mark (40, Svetlana's friend): "Yeah. I was going to, but my car **broke down** this morning. Could you give us a ride?"

A while later . . .

Mark: "Thanks so much for taking us. I'm sorry about all the feathers."

Svetlana: "That's OK. I had fun. But next time you **break down**, please call someone else."

Let's perform the skits. Take roles, add your ideas, and practice the phrasal verbs.

Skit 1   Two weeks later, Mark's car **breaks down** while he is *running errands* with his ducks, Bill and Will. Mark calls a tow truck for help. He tells Mrs. Hobson (50, the towing company representative) where he **broke down** and where he was going. (He was on the corner of Walnut Street and Pine Avenue and was going to buy grain at Duck Land.) Mrs. Hobson is *hard of hearing* so she asks Mark to repeat what he said.

Skit 2   Bill and Will were with Mark when the car **broke down**. Bill was asleep and is now wondering why the car has stopped. He asks Will to explain what happened. Will tells him that they **broke down** and are waiting for the tow truck. Bill then wants to know what time it is and when he can have a snack. Don't forget to *quack*!

Write sentences using the phrasal verb and bonus words in italics.

1. What were Mark, Bill, and Will doing when the car broke down?

_____

2. What did Mark do after the car broke down? What did the ducks do?

_____

3. Is it better for a car to break down on a big street or a small one? Why?

_____

4. Has your car ever broken down? Were you stranded?

_____

Cut Off   Go in front of unexpectedly in a vehicle
Can take an object between the verb and the preposition

> You may hear it used like this: Hey! That *jerk* **cut me off!**

It's time to meet some of our characters. Read these conversations aloud.

Sam (21, a passenger): "Diane, your grandma sure drives faster than most people."
Diane (22, Sam's girlfriend, also a passenger): "Yeah, I know. My granny loves **cutting people off**—
    especially truck drivers."

A while later . . .

Madame *Soufflé* (69, the grandma): "Diane, dear, would you or Sam like to drive? We are alone
    on the road now, so I can't **cut anyone off.**"
Sam: "Yes, yes. Please let me drive. I was about to have a heart attack!"

Let's perform the skits. Take roles, add your ideas, and practice the phrasal verbs.

Skit 1   Jack (26, a police officer) saw Madame Soufflé **cut off** lots of cars. He plans to give her a
ticket for driving dangerously. He tells her how many cars she **cut off** (six) and how many of them
slammed on the brakes (five). Madame Soufflé tells him she always drives like that because it is a
good way to meet policemen. Jack then notices her beautiful *puffy* hair. He wonders for a few
seconds if he should give her a ticket or ask her to go to the movies with him. Then he decides.

Skit 2   Jack has finished working and is relaxing in a restaurant with some other police officers. He
and Akiko (24, a policewoman) chat a while. She says her police car broke down earlier in the day.
Jack asks her for a few details. Then he tells Akiko about seeing Madame Soufflé **cut off** so many
cars. Akiko asks what kind of cars she **cut off**. She also wants to know if he gave her a ticket.

Write sentences using the phrasal verb and bonus words in italics.

1. What did Jack do when he saw Madame Soufflé cut off six cars?

_____

2. What happened to Akiko? Was she cut off?

_____

3. Does your father get mad when someone cuts him off? Why or why not?

_____

4. Would you prefer to break down or be cut off?

_____

Drive Around   Drive to nowhere in particular

Does not take an object

You may hear it used like this: I have nothing to do, so let's just **drive around**.

It's time to meet some of our characters. Read these conversations aloud.

Silly Brother (17): "What do you want to do this evening? I'm *tired of* looking for change under the couch."

Silly Sister (16): "I don't know. Let's just **drive around** and count how many *bats* we see."

A while later . . .

Silly Brother: "*Darn*! That was a *waste of time*. I thought we would see at least one bat while we were **driving around**."

Silly Sister: "Me too. I guess we should have brought a flashlight."

Let's perform the skits. Take roles, add your ideas, and practice the phrasal verbs.

Skit 1   Silly Daddy (40) and Silly Mommy (42) are having dinner. Dad says he saw Silly Brother and Silly Sister earlier and they looked a little sleepy. Mom asks why they were tired. Dad explains what Silly Sister told him about **driving around** looking for bats. Mom asks Dad for more details. Why did they do that? (They were bored.) How long did they **drive around** (four hours)? How many miles did they drive? (Not many, because they just drove up and down their street.)

Skit 2   The next evening, Silly Brother and Silly Sister discuss whether they should **drive around** again tonight. Silly Sister says she would be happy looking for change (she found a nickel and a quarter yesterday), but Silly Brother wants to try **driving around** again. The two of them discuss what they could count and where they could **drive around**. At first they have different opinions but then they agree.

Write sentences using the phrasal verb and bonus words in italics.

1. Why did Silly Brother and Silly Sister drive around and what did they see?

_____

2. Where do you think Silly Brother and Silly Sister are going to drive around tonight?

_____

3. Do you think it's fun or boring to drive around?

_____

4. How often does your family drive around on weekends?

_____

Fill Up/Gas Up   Put gas/fuel into a vehicle

"Fill up" and "gas up" mean the same thing; can take an object between the verb and the preposition

> You may hear it used like this: He should **gas the car up** before he leaves for his trip.

It's time to meet some of our characters. Read these conversations aloud.

Tina (45, an ESL teacher on a motorcycle): "Hello teachers! Let's all get ready to ride to the *Ninth Annual* Grammar *Convention* together."
June (38, another ESL teacher): "Yeah! Let's **gas up** our motorcycles and go!"

A while later...

June: "Wow! All those phrasal verbs were so interesting! But I guess it's time to go."
Tina: "You're right, we should be on our way. Have you **filled up** yet?"

Let's perform the skits. Take roles, add your ideas, and practice the phrasal verbs.

Skit 1 June went to the grammar convention and really enjoyed herself. When she returns to the classroom, Pierre (22, one of her students) asks her a lot of questions about her road trip. How long has she ridden a motorcycle? How many times did she have to **gas up** on the way to the convention? Did anyone's motorcycle break down? Was she cut off? She answers most of the questions enthusiastically but is not very happy when talking about how she was cut off.

Skit 2 Gus (24, a gas station attendant) has *had a long day*. After work, he has dinner with Linda (24, his girlfriend). She asks him if anything interesting happened at work today. He tells her about all those crazy ESL teachers who **gassed up** at the *pump* on their way to the grammar convention. Linda then asks what they were wearing (all leather) and if he helped any of them **fill up**. Gus tells her about June, the pretty teacher he helped. Linda becomes angry.

Write sentences using the phrasal verb and bonus words in italics.

1. Where was June going when she gassed up at the gas station where Gus works?

_____

2. Why is Linda mad that Gus helped June fill up?

_____

3. When you fill up, do you prefer to pay at the pump or pay inside the gas station?

_____

4. Do you always gas up at the same station or do you drive around until you find the best price?

_____

Run Over   Hurt or kill someone/something with a vehicle

Can take an object between the verb and the preposition

You may hear it used like this: Help! That car just **ran over** my dog.

It's time to meet some of our characters. Read these conversations aloud.

Darren the Dog: "Doctor, last night I had a terrible dream that my owner **ran over** me *on purpose!*"
Doc *Dalmatian* (also a dog): "Oh dear! That sounds like an awful nightmare. Maybe you should stop
    biting him during the day."

A while later . . .

Oscar the Owner (64, Darren the Dog's owner): "Darren, I wish you would not bite me!"
Darren the Dog: "*Woof*, woof, woof." (Translation: "Well, I wish you would not **run me over** when
    I'm asleep. I feel better now.")

Let's perform the skits. Take roles, add your ideas, and practice the phrasal verbs.

Skit 1   Doc Dalmatian is leading a *support group* for unhappy dogs. Doc asks Darren to tell the
others about his nightmare. Darren is shy, so he is afraid to speak in front of everyone. Doc helps
Darren tell the story by asking him questions about his dream. He asks him what street he was on
when he got **run over** in his dream, and what time it happened. He also encourages the other dogs
to ask him questions. Several of them do.

Skit 2   The following week, Doc Dalmatian notices that one of the dogs, Amy, looks sadder than
usual. He asks her why she is so unhappy. She explains that she had a nightmare. In her dream, her
owner bit her and then **ran over** her pet cat. Doc asks where the owner bit Amy (on the left ear)
and what kind of cat she has (Siamese). Darren the Dog says something nice to her to make her feel
better.

Write sentences using the phrasal verb and bonus words in italics.

1. Who ran over Darren the Dog in his dream?

_____

2. Where is Amy when she talks about her cat getting run over?

_____

3. If you saw someone run over a cat or dog, what would you do?

_____

4. Have you ever had a nightmare that you were run over or that your car broke down?

_____

Speed Up   Go faster, step on the gas
Can take an object between the verb and the preposition (sometimes "it")

Slow Down   Go slower, step on the brake
Can take an object between the verb and the preposition (sometimes "it")

You may hear them used like this:	Can you please **speed it up?** Would you **slow down** a bit?

It's time to meet some of our characters. Read these conversations aloud.

Mr. Carter (40, a driving teacher): "Welcome to the *Get out of My Way* Driving School. We will be teaching you how to have fun while **speeding up** in your cars. We will not discuss **slowing down** because that's not much fun."
Lou E. Gee (19, a student): "Mr. Carter, will you tell us how to avoid getting a ticket?"

A while later . . .

Lou E. Gee: "Mr. Carter, you're talking a little too fast. Can you please **slow down?**"
Mr. Carter: "No. You'll have to **speed up** your brain."

Let's perform the skits. Take roles, add your ideas, and practice the phrasal verbs.

Skit 1   Lou E. Gee has just won the school's Best *Backseat Driver* Award. He decides to practice on Caroline (20, his friend), who is driving him to the mall. At the beginning of the ride, Caroline asks Lou E. Gee some questions about his driving school (the name and its location). The trip seems like it will be fun. However, Lou E. Gee then tells her, "**Speed up!**" and "Don't **slow down!**" every minute. Caroline becomes unhappy and tells Lou E. Gee to be quiet.

Skit 2   Lou E. Gee is back from the mall and Francisco (49, Lou E. Gee's father) has asked him to vacuum the living room. Lou E. Gee doesn't want to but then agrees. He starts vacuuming very slowly, so his dad asks him to **speed it up**. Lou E. Gee then realizes that vacuuming can be like driving, so he **speeds up**. He also starts to sing his favorite song: "A, B, C, D, E, F, G. . . . " Francisco now thinks he is vacuuming too fast, so he asks Lou E. Gee to **slow down**. He **slows down** his vacuuming but **speeds up** his singing.

Write sentences using the phrasal verb and bonus words in italics.

1. What did Caroline think when Lou told her to speed up and not slow down?

_____

2. Why did Lou speed up his vacuuming?

_____

3. When you see a yellow light at a traffic signal, do you speed up or slow down?

_____

4. How often do you ask your teacher to slow down when he/she is talking?

_____

Chapter Review Questions

Rewrite each sentence using the correct phrasal verb. Choices: **break down, cut off, drive around, fill up/gas up, run over, speed up/slow down.**

1. Instead of reducing his speed, the driver went in front of me.

   _____

2. Laurie's car didn't have any gas.

   _____

3. The baseball players couldn't play their game because the bus had trouble.

   _____

4. My boss wanted me to do it more quickly.

   _____

5. The ice cream truck visited many streets in the neighborhood.

   _____

6. The mailman wasn't trying to hurt the dog but he did by accident.

   _____

7. The driver went less quickly because she saw a police car.

   _____

8. She ran more quickly because she thought the truck was going to kill her.

   _____

9. The policeman went in front of the criminal's car.

   _____

10. His van needed more fuel.

    _____

11. My car had a problem in the middle of the street.

    _____

12. Angie drove up this street and down that street because she was bored.

    _____

CHAPTER 2

ON FOOT
(WALKING)

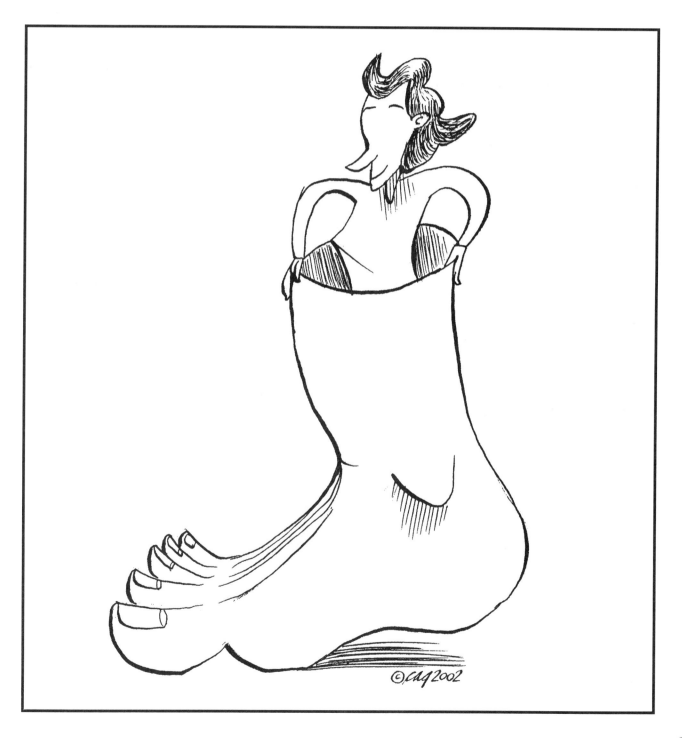

©cag 2002

Catch Up (To)   Go faster so you go the same speed as someone else

If not followed by "to," does not take an object; if used with "to," is followed by a noun phrase or pronoun

> You may hear it used like this: I tried to **catch up to** my friend but he was too fast.

It's time to meet some of our characters. Read these conversations aloud.

Katie (12, a young lady): "Lizzie, I'm so glad you joined The Hoppers. Are you ready to start our one-mile *hop*?"

Lizzie (11, Katie's friend): "Yes, but if I'm slow, don't wait for me. I probably won't **catch up to** the rest of you. I may even *fall flat on my face*."

A while later . . .

Phil (30, a *paramedic*): "How did you hurt yourself?"

Lizzie: "I was trying to **catch up to** my new hopping friends, but I was too *clumsy* and fell down."

Let's perform the skits. Take roles, add your ideas, and practice the phrasal verbs.

Skit 1 Your ESL teacher is a member of The Hoppers. Your teacher and one student in your class will now have a sixty-second race. Use a big space in the room. At first, the teacher hops faster than the student. Another student in your class enthusiastically encourages the hopping student to **catch up to** the teacher. The hopping student says it is impossible to **catch up**. The other student keeps encouraging until the race is over!

Skit 2 The Jumpers and The Hoppers have decided to have a competition, which will be shown on television. Two television announcers (Ann, 42; Van, 28) are discussing the race before it begins. One thinks The Hoppers will win, starting slowly but then **catching up**. The other thinks The Hoppers will never **catch up to** The Jumpers. The race starts, and Ann and Van speak into their microphones as they talk about the two teams.

Write sentences using the phrasal verb and bonus words in italics.

1. Why couldn't Lizzie catch up to the rest of The Hoppers?

_____

2. Which announcer was right? In your skit, did The Hoppers catch up to The Jumpers?

_____

3. If you rode a bicycle, could you catch up to an Olympic runner in a race?

_____

4. When a lion chases a zebra, how long do you think it takes for the lion to catch up to it?

_____

Head Out (To)   Leave to go (somewhere)

If not followed by "to," does not take an object; if used with "to," is followed by a noun phrase or pronoun

> You may hear it used like this: We're **heading out** now. We'll see you later.

It's time to meet some of our characters. Read these conversations aloud.

Gianni (48, a pet owner): "Hi, Kenji. I'm **heading out to** the pet shop now. Would you like to come with me?"

Kenji (42, Gianni's friend): "Sure. I need to buy some *diapers* for my monkey, Keith."

A while later . . .

Kenji: "Hey, Gianni. I need to **head out to** the pet store again. I forgot to buy *wipes* for Keith. Will you come with me?"

Gianni: "OK. I suppose I can go with you and buy some cans of food. It's nearly dinnertime and I need something to eat tonight."

Let's perform the skits. Take roles, add your ideas, and practice the phrasal verbs.

Skit 1   Earl (20, Kenji's son) has a date this evening. Kenji asks him what time he's planning to **head out** (7 p.m.). He also wants to know where Earl and his girlfriend plan to go after the ballet. (Earl thinks they will just drive around for a while.) Kenji tells Earl to be home by midnight because they have to **head out** early the next morning. He reminds Earl that they are going to see his grandparents perform at the circus and that Kenji needs to gas up before they leave.

Skit 2   Kenji and Gianni are having lunch in their favorite restaurant. Gianni reminds Kenji that he has to leave soon. Kenji has forgotten where Gianni is going. Gianni tells him he is **heading out to** work at the *fruit stand*. Kenji asks him various questions about the bananas, his favorite fruit. How much are they per pound? How many can Gianni eat in one minute?

Write sentences using the phrasal verb and bonus words in italics.

1. Why does Kenji have to head out to the pet store?

_____

2. What does Kenji need to do tomorrow morning before heading out to the circus?

_____

3. When you have a picnic, what time do you usually head out?

_____

4. Do you like heading out early when you go on a vacation?

_____

Hurry Up   Do quickly

Does not take an object

You may hear it used like this: **Hurry up!** *I don't have all day*!

It's time to meet some of our characters. Read these conversations aloud.

Danielle (39, the company president): "Welcome to the company's annual *three-legged race*.
    It's time for all partners to tie their legs together."
Dan (46, the company vice president): "Danielle, I want to be your partner! **Hurry up** and come
    here so we can get ready!"

A while later . . .

Danielle: "We can win this race, Dan. Let's **hurry up** a bit."
Dan: "I'm sorry but I can't speed up. I just ate six hamburgers and I have a stomachache!"

Let's perform the skits. Take roles, add your ideas, and practice the phrasal verbs.

Skit 1   George (47, the trophy presenter) is giving the trophy to the slowest team, Dan and
Danielle. Danielle accepts the prize because Dan is still trying to *catch his breath*. George interviews
Danielle about the race. Why couldn't they catch up to the other runners? What did she say to Dan
to try to make him **hurry up**? Will they run together in next year's race?

Skit 2   Dan spent the afternoon at the movies because he was so tired after the race. At 7 p.m. he
comes home and hugs Laura (45, his wife). She notices he seems very tired. She asks him why. Dan
tells her about the race and that Danielle tried to get him to **hurry up**. Dan then realizes that he is
very hungry although he ate a lot before the race. Can Laura **hurry up** and make dinner? She tells
Dan to make it himself because she's just about to head out to a *double feature*.

Write sentences using the phrasal verb and bonus words in italics.

1. Why couldn't Dan hurry up while running in the three-legged race?

_____

2. Why didn't Laura want to hurry up and make dinner?

_____

3. Do you want to hurry up and learn English or do you want to learn it slowly?

_____

4. Do you usually have to hurry up to be on time?

_____

Run Off (With)   Leave in a hurry

If not followed by "with," does not take an object; if used with "with," is followed by a noun phrase or pronoun

| You may hear it used like this: When he showed her the big spider, she **ran off** in fright. |

It's time to meet some of our characters. Read these conversations aloud.

Young man (19): "Hey! That old lady **ran off with** my wallet!"
Policeman (46):   "Attention all units! *Suspect* is an old lady in a *polka-dotted* dress."

A while later . . .

Ginger (80, the old lady who took the wallet): "So, Stella. I **ran off with** a young man's wallet
         today. How much money did you **run off with**?"
Stella (75, Ginger's *accomplice*): "None, unfortunately. I took only one purse, and it was full of bees!
         I *got stung* fifty times!"

Let's perform the skits. Take roles, add your ideas, and practice the phrasal verbs.

Skit 1   Doctor Stapleton (56) is treating Stella for multiple bee stings. He notices that his patient seems quite healthy for a 75-year-old, although she is wearing a lot of make-up and a red nose. He asks her what she does for exercise and how often she does it. She tells him about how she and her friend **run off with** things (purses, wallets, and shoes) three times a week. The doctor asks her if she has ever worn the shoes she steals. She shows him the clown shoes she is wearing.

Skit 2   Nat (83, an old man) sees Stella and thinks she looks friendly. He introduces himself and tells her his name and profession. He then asks her about her hobbies. (She likes eating lettuce and **running off** unexpectedly.) Then he wants to know what kind of books she reads. (She prefers ESL books.) After answering these questions, Stella suddenly **runs off**. Nat quickly catches up to her and shouts, "Don't leave! Let's go on a date!" Stella must then decide if she should continue running or go to the theater with him.

Write sentences using the phrasal verb and bonus words in italics.

1. How did the policeman describe the person who ran off with the wallet?

_____

2. What happened when Stella ran off with the purse?

_____

3. If someone ran off with your purse or wallet, would you try to catch up to him/her?

_____

4. What would a mother do if her child ran off without her permission?

_____

Take Off   Leave quickly or immediately

Does not take an object

You may hear it used like this: After the car nearly ran him over, it **took off**.

It's time to meet some of our characters. Read these conversations aloud.

William (15, the club's president): "Welcome to the Teenagers United meeting. Today's topic is how to avoid doing *chores*."
Charles (14, a new club member): "This lecture is not interesting. I'm **taking off!**"

A while later . . .

William: "That's exactly what this meeting is about, *folks!*"
Enrique (13, the club's vice president): "That's right! We all hate boring meetings, just like we hate chores. So, everybody **take off** before William starts his lecture!"

Let's perform the skits. Take roles, add your ideas, and practice the phrasal verbs.

Skit 1 Fred (41, William's father) asks William what he liked best about school today. William tells his dad that the students in his Spanish class didn't want to take their test. They all **took off** when the teacher came into the room. Fred asks his son for more details. What time did they **take off** (1 p.m.)? What did the teacher do? (Mrs. Garcia **took off** too because she wanted some ice cream.) Fred asks William what he did after he left Spanish class. William tells him something he doesn't expect.

Skit 2 Fred doesn't feel like working hard today. His boss has just told him to come into his office for an assignment. Before getting his assignment, Fred approaches Julian (46, his co-worker) and *makes small talk*. Fred then mentions how his son's Spanish class **took off** to avoid taking a test. He wants Julian's advice. Should he **take off** instead of meeting with his boss? Could he *be fired*? Julian gives Fred some good advice.

Write sentences using the phrasal verb and bonus words in italics.

1. Why do the members of the club want to take off when William starts speaking?

   _____

2. What could happen to Fred if he takes off before he gets his new assignment?

   _____

3. If a bee flew near you, would you take off?

   _____

4. If you were at a boring party, would you take off or stay?

   _____

Walk Up (To)   Approach

If not followed by "to," does not take an object; if used with "to," is followed by a noun phrase or pronoun

> You may hear it used like this: She **walked up to** him and asked him the time.

It's time to meet some of our characters. Read these conversations aloud.

Amanda (16, a girl at a dance, who is talking to a friend): "I hope someone cute will **walk up to** me soon and ask me to dance. This party is not much fun."

Roy (15, a boy who approaches Amanda): "Hey, are you hungry? Wanna eat this *bug*?"

A while later . . .

Melinda (18, Amanda's sister): "How was the party?"

Amanda: "Awful! This *weirdo* **walked up** and asked if I wanted to eat a *roach*!"

Let's perform the skits. Take roles, add your ideas, and practice the phrasal verbs.

Skit 1   Roy becomes *tongue-tied* when he talks to a pretty girl. He wants Mikhail (40, his father) to give him some advice about girls. Roy asks Mikhail what he should say when he **walks up to** a girl, and what he should wear. After answering his questions, Mikhail suggests they practice. Mikhail will be the girl and will use a high voice. Roy **walks up to** Mikhail and starts a conversation.

Skit 2   Mikhail is telling Katya (37, Roy's mom) about how he and Roy practiced starting conversations with girls. He tells her what Roy decided was the best thing to say when **walking up to** a pretty girl. Katya then asks Mikhail if he remembers what she said to him when she first **walked up to** him twenty years ago. He remembers that she said, "I like your eyebrows." Mikhail reminds her what he said next: "I like your toenails."

Write sentences using the phrasal verb and bonus words in italics.

1. What do you think Amanda did when Roy walked up to her at the dance?

_____

2. What happens to Roy when he walks up to a girl?

_____

3. What do you normally say to someone good-looking when you walk up to him/her?

_____

4. Are you confident enough in English to walk up to someone and ask the time?

_____

Chapter Review Questions

Rewrite each sentence using the correct phrasal verb. Choices: **catch up (to), head out (to), hurry up, run off (with), take off, walk up (to).**

1. As I was leaving for the museum I remembered to get the discount coupon.

_____

2. Quickly go get dressed or you'll miss the school bus.

_____

3. The spider tried to go as fast as the roach but it couldn't.

_____

4. I wanted to leave in a hurry when my mom told me she was unhappy with my grades, but we were in the car.

_____

5. The hostess approached the guests and asked them how they liked the dinner.

_____

6. The homeless man took my sandwich and left quickly.

_____

7. Don't be so slow!

_____

8. The girl left quickly when she saw the ice cream truck.

_____

9. My new shoes prevented me from going as fast as Matt.

_____

10. She left for her boyfriend's house in her new dress.

_____

11. I didn't like the lecture so I left quickly.

_____

12. Joey approached Andy and gave him a hug.

_____

CHAPTER 3

AT THE TOP OF MY CLASS (STUDYING)

Be Up On   Know all about something

Is followed by a noun phrase or pronoun

You may hear it used like this: I failed my test because I **wasn't up on** all the presidents.

It's time to meet some of our characters. Read these conversations aloud.

Arnold (67, the customer): "Excuse me, what are your *specials* tonight?"

Kelli (26, the waitress): "I'm new, so I'm **not up on** that yet. But I think we have *Snail* Soup and Super Snail *Sushi.*"

A while later . . .

Michaela (64, Arnold's wife): "Herb, Arnold started to feel sick after dinner. Do you know if he is *allergic to* raw foods?"

Herb (62, Arnold's brother):   "No, I'm **not up on** Arnold's stomach. But I do know that he has very big feet."

Let's perform the skits. Take roles, add your ideas, and practice the phrasal verbs.

Skit 1   Kelli has returned home after her first day of working at the Snail *Pail* Restaurant. She is studying a large piece of yellow paper and a small blue one. Gina (30, her sister) wonders what she's doing. Kelli tells her that tomorrow she needs to **be up on** the Snail Pail menu and specials because she didn't know them today. Gina tells her not to worry. She will test her. She asks if Kelli **is up on** the breakfast specials. Kelli thinks that Snail Scones are popular but can't remember anything else. Gina then asks if she's **up on** the lunch specials. Kelli isn't but thinks the word "snail" is in there somewhere.

Skit 2   Later that week, Arnold and Herb are having dinner at the Snail Pail Restaurant. Herb asks Kelli, their waitress again, what the dessert specials are. She describes the color and flavor of Snail Pie and Snail Ice Cream. They each choose one. While the men are waiting for their treats, Herb asks Arnold some questions about the Snail Pail. How many times has Arnold eaten here (sixteen)? What's his favorite dish (Crème de Snail)? When was the restaurant built? Arnold tells Herb he **is not up on** the restaurant's history, but he will ask Kelli when she returns.

Write sentences using the phrasal verb and bonus words in italics.

1. Why isn't Kelli up on the menu and specials?

_____

2. Is Arnold up on the restaurant's history? Do you think Kelli is?

_____

3. Is your teacher up on the customs in your country?

_____

4. Would you be patient with a waitress if she wasn't up on the menu?

_____

Go Over   Review/discuss

Is followed by a noun phrase or pronoun

You may hear it used like this: She suggested I **go over** my notes before the test.

It's time to meet some of our characters. Read these conversations aloud.

Mrs. Lee (47, the mom): "Before I leave for my trip, Toby, I'd like to **go over** some things with you."

Toby (28, the babysitter): "Well, I don't think we really need to **go over** anything, Mrs. Lee. I clearly remember that you want me to keep the kids clean and give them some pickles while you are away."

A while later . . .

Jimmy (8, a naughty child): "I don't want to have a bath now!"

Toby: "I'm sorry but your mom and I **went over** everything very carefully. You and your brother need to be clean when she returns tonight. Don't worry, you can throw a pickle at her when she opens the door."

Let's perform the skits. Take roles, add your ideas, and practice the phrasal verbs.

Skit 1   Jimmy and Billy (6, Jimmy's younger brother) are downstairs after their bath. They are both in their *PJs*. Toby is *draining* the bathtub and has told the boys to play quietly. However, they don't like having a babysitter, so they always do something naughty. Jimmy tells Billy he has a good plan. They will *lure* Toby into the bathroom and give him a bath. Billy is not sure what he should do, so he asks Jimmy to **go over** the plan with him. Jimmy says that Billy will wash Toby's hair and Jimmy will clean Toby's fingers. They are still **going over** the details when Toby walks up to them.

Skit 2   Mrs. Lee has returned from her trip to Little *Llama* Hot Springs. She feels very relaxed. When she opens the front door, the children throw dill pickles at her. She opens her mouth to enjoy the snacks. Toby is sitting on the couch and looks very clean. Mrs. Lee asks Toby to **go over** what happened while she was away. Toby gives a short summary of what happened and mentions how the kids gave him a bath too. He says he didn't mind because he needed one. Mrs. Lee then wants to **go over** with Toby the dates he can babysit again.

Write sentences using the phrasal verb and bonus words in italics.

1. Does Toby need to go over Mrs. Lee's instructions?

_____

2. What is Toby doing when the boys go over the details of their plan?

_____

3. Did you go over Chapters 1 and 2 of this book before starting Chapter 3?

_____

4. Has your family gone over a plan in case there is a fire in your house?

_____

Hand In/Turn In   Give a finished assignment to the teacher

"Hand in" and "turn in" mean the same thing; can take an object between the verb and the preposition

You may hear it used like this: OK, class. Stop working and **turn in** your tests now.

It's time to meet some of our characters. Read these conversations aloud.

Mr. Cooke (41, a *Home Ec* teacher): "OK, class, please **hand in** your homework assignment now. I
    hope everyone remembered to bring me their family's favorite recipe."
Alec (11, a student): "I did, Mr. Cooke! I did! My recipe is called Garbage Cookies. It has carrot *peels*
    and pieces of spaghetti in it."

A while later . . .

Mr. Cooke: "Hi, honey. My students **turned in** some really interesting recipes today. Do we have
    any old vegetables and pasta in the house? I'd like to make some cookies."
Mrs. Cooke (38, the teacher's wife): "No, I don't think so. I used those *leftovers* in the pie we gave
    your mother yesterday."

Let's perform the skits. Take roles, add your ideas, and practice the phrasal verbs.

Skit 1   Alec and Lucy (9, his sister) are playing "teacher and student." Lucy, the teacher, has asked
Alec, the student, to **hand in** his grammar assignment. Alec has not finished his homework so he
tells Lucy that his pet goldfish ate his homework. Lucy does not believe him. Alec asks her why not.
She reminds Alec that last time they played, he didn't **turn his math homework in**. Alec says that
Gil the goldfish was very hungry this morning so he had to feed him something. He promises Lucy
that he will sit far from the goldfish whenever he does his homework. She says OK and gives him a
new assignment to **hand in** tomorrow.

Skit 2   Alec has just come home from school. He tells Cynthia (39, his mom) that he has an
interesting assignment to **turn in** tomorrow and needs her help. Mrs. Peck, his art teacher, wants
him to **hand in** a drawing of his mother's wrist. Alec wants to know what time she can be a model.
Cynthia tells him she will be ready after Alec does his chores. As Alec is going upstairs, Cynthia asks
him if he **turned in** his cookie recipe to Mr. Cooke. Alec tells her that his teacher was very happy to
see the family's delicious recipe.

Write sentences using the phrasal verb and bonus words in italics.

1. Did Alec turn in a delicious recipe?

_____

2. What kind of drawing does Alec have to hand in?

_____

3. Do you always hand in your assignments on time?

_____

4. What does your teacher say if you forget to turn something in?

_____

Look Up   Search for information in a reference book or other source

Can take an object between the verb and the preposition

> You may hear it used like this: I forgot my friend's phone number so I **looked it up.**

It's time to meet some of our characters. Read these conversations aloud.

Lena (43, Ben's friend): "Ben, have you ever **looked up** your name on the Internet?"

Ben *Baldwin* (48, a shop owner): "Yes, I **looked it up** just last week. Did you know there is another Mr. Baldwin who sells colorful *hairpieces*? I can't believe two of us are in the same business!"

A while later...

Mrs. Robinson (39, a customer): "Excuse me, how much is that hairpiece in the window? There's no price tag."

Ben Baldwin: "The green one? Let me see. I need to **look that up.** I'll be back in a minute. While you wait, why don't you look at the latest issue of Hairy Magazine?"

Let's perform the skits. Take roles, add your ideas, and practice the phrasal verbs.

Skit 1   Teresa (16, Ben Baldwin's daughter) is writing an essay on hair loss in America. She needs help finding useful information about when colorful hairpieces were first used. Her dad suggests she **look that up** in an encyclopedia. Teresa then asks where she can **look up** information on recent sales. He says that according to *Shiny* Head Weekly, *neon* hairpieces are very popular right now. He recommends that she **look up** other interesting facts in that publication.

Skit 2   Mrs. Robinson is wrapping her new green hairpiece. She plans to give it to her father for Christmas. Ricardo (20, Mrs. Robinson's son) asks his mom what she's wrapping. Then he says that he feels like cooking a stir-fry for dinner tonight. He **looked up** "vegetable stir-fry" in the index of some cookbooks, but he didn't find any recipes. Mrs. Robinson reminds him that he probably needs to **look up** each vegetable individually. She asks him what vegetables are in the fridge. He tells her they have only beets and asparagus. She says that sounds like a delicious combination and suggests a cookbook to use.

Write sentences using the phrasal verb and bonus words in italics.

1. Why did Ben Baldwin have to look up the price of the green hairpiece?

_____

2. In what publication will Teresa look up information on recent sales?

_____

3. Have you ever looked up your name on the Internet? What did you find?

_____

4. How often do you look words up in the dictionary?

_____

Read Up On   Read a lot on a subject

Is followed by a noun phrase or pronoun

You may hear it used like this: They **read up on** Alaska before they took a cruise there.

It's time to meet some of our characters. Read these conversations aloud.

Dirk (50, the father): "Rita, have you been **reading up on** things for the family to do on Grammar Island?"

Rita (36, the mother): "Yeah. I've been going over those *brochures* you gave me. Preposition Park sounds really *neat* for the kids. We might also want to visit The Cave of Commas."

A while later . . .

Bobby (14, the son): "In, out, up, and through. I **read up on** prepositions and so did you!"

Anna (17, the daughter): "Bobby, stop singing that silly song! You've already sung it twenty-three times! Let's find Mom and Dad so we can visit The Cave of Commas."

Let's perform the skits. Take roles, add your ideas, and practice the phrasal verbs.

Skit 1   Dirk is asking Bobby what he and Anna did in Preposition Park while Dirk and Rita were visiting Verb Land. Bobby says a very tall man asked him and Anna to pick a brochure out of a big hat. Bobby's brochure was about "Up" and Anna's was about "On." They **read up on** their prepositions for about fifteen minutes and then the man tested them. Dirk asks what kind of test it was. (They had to use their prepositions in three sentences.) Bobby gives his dad an example. Dirk then asks what else they did. (Anna ate a hot dog, and Bobby sang silly songs.) Bobby sings one of the songs for his dad.

Skit 2   Anna is back at school and the students are explaining what they did on summer vacation. Mrs. Kim (38, Anna's teacher) tells Anna it's her turn. Anna tells the class that when her mom **read up on** Grammar Island, it seemed like the perfect place to visit. Mrs. Kim seems very interested in the island and asks her about the restaurants there. She also asks if Anna is up on the island's speed limit. Anna answers these questions and then asks Mrs. Kim what she did on vacation. Mrs. Kim says she went to work with her husband. Mr. Kim is a *pirate*, so she saw lots of *tropical* islands.

Write sentences using the phrasal verb and bonus words in italics.

1. What did Rita learn about Grammar Island when she read up on it?

_____

2. Did Anna and Bobby enjoy reading up on prepositions in Preposition Park?

_____

3. Do you like reading up on a new place you will be visiting or would you rather just go there?

_____

4. If you want to learn about something, do you read up on it or do you ask someone about it?

_____

Sit In On   Attend as a visitor

Is followed by a noun phrase or pronoun

> You may hear it used like this: When she **sat in on** his cooking class, she ate a lot.

It's time to meet some of our characters. Read these conversations aloud.

Nobuhiro (19, a student): "Hi, professor. Can my friend Rocky **sit in on** your class today?"

Mrs. Stone (51, a college professor): "Sure, as long as he doesn't know more about *geology* than I do."

A while later . . .

Mrs. Stone: "So, Rocky, what did you think of my discussion of diamonds?"

Rocky (22, Nobuhiro's friend): "Actually, it wasn't worth **sitting in on**. I learned more yesterday at my job in a jewelry store."

Let's perform the skits. Take roles, add your ideas, and practice the phrasal verbs.

Skit 1   Rocky works at *A Ton of* Jewels, where he washes the windows. He is bored doing that, so he asks Maggie (37, his boss) if he can **sit in on** the managers' meeting. Maggie agrees. Rocky asks her when and where the meeting is. (It's at midnight at the university's geology museum.) He asks for directions. He also wants to know what they will talk about in the meeting. Maggie is not sure if they will discuss sales of nose rings or toe rings. Both kinds of rings have been *selling like hotcakes*.

Skit 2   Nobuhiro is having lunch with Rocky, who is wearing a new toe ring with diamonds on it. Nobuhiro asks him about it. Rocky says that when he **sat in on** the managers' meeting the other day, his boss gave him the Best Toes award. Nobuhiro looks at Rocky's toes and agrees with Maggie that they are nice. They are long and thin like French fries. Nobuhiro thinks he'll order some fries with lunch. Rocky then explains that his new job is to sit in the window and model the toe ring. Nobuhiro asks if any other people **sat in on** the meeting. Rocky's co-worker April was there. She won Best Nose.

Write sentences using the phrasal verb and bonus words in italics.

1. What class did Rocky sit in on? Did he like it?

_____

2. What happened when Rocky sat in on the managers' meeting?

_____

3. What school subject would you like to know more about? Would you like to sit in on a class about it?

_____

4. Do future students sit in on your English class?

_____

Chapter Review Questions

Rewrite each sentence using the correct phrasal verb. Choices: **be up on, go over, hand in/turn in, look up, read up on, sit in on.**

1. I wanted to review the directions with my husband before we got on the highway.

_____

2. Tanya went with her friend to his conversation class.

_____

3. The teacher counted how many essays she had and saw that three students hadn't given them to her.

_____

4. The scientist has been an expert on shells for the last seventeen years.

_____

5. He searched for the information in his book but it wasn't there.

_____

6. The tour guide suggested they read various brochures about the university after the tour.

_____

7. Graham wanted to learn about elephants so he searched for information in the nature magazine.

_____

8. I was late giving my essay to the substitute teacher.

_____

9. Marci studied a lot of books about chemistry.

_____

10. We discussed the shopping list before I went to the store.

_____

11. The triplets attended the lecture but they had to share the two remaining seats.

_____

12. He didn't know about the rules of sumo wrestling but he learned them when he watched a tournament.

_____

CHAPTER 4

IN THE PRIME OF LIFE
(YOUTH)

©fag2002

Break Out (In)   Get *pimples* or have another skin problem

If not followed by "in," does not take an object; if used with "in," is followed by a noun phrase or pronoun

You may hear it used like this: She **broke out** right before she got her picture taken.

It's time to meet some of our characters. Read these conversations aloud.

François (25, Vinny's friend): "Vinny, thanks for giving me all that chocolate pie yesterday. It was really *yummy* but I think it made me **break out**."

Vinny (24, a baker): "Why don't you hide your face with this lemon pie?" (He throws a pie in his friend's face.)

A while later...

Goran (25, Vinny's friend): "Vinny, what happened to your hand? It has spots all over it."

Vinny: "Oh! I must have **broken out** from those pies I baked for François."

Let's perform the skits. Take roles, add your ideas, and practice the phrasal verbs.

Skit 1   Later that day, Vinny's hand starts to hurt, so he goes to the doctor. Doctor Skinner (54) asks him why he thinks he **broke out in** a *rash*. Vinny explains about giving the pies to François. Vinny then throws a pecan pie in the doctor's face. "Yummy," the doctor says. The doctor says it is very unusual to **break out** because of pie. Vinny agrees. Doctor Skinner thinks for a few seconds and then asks if Vinny used any ingredients that he might be allergic to. Vinny admits that he used a lot of chili peppers in the pies.

Skit 2   When Doctor Skinner gets home, he decides to read up on skin allergies. He spends the next two hours in his home office looking up various allergies. At 7:30 p.m., Mrs. Skinner (53) asks him what he's doing. He tells her about how one of his patients **broke out in** spots because of pie. His wife asks where the boy **broke out** and if the boy will be OK. Then she offers the doctor some dessert. He says, "No, thank you" because he's not hungry. He then tells her that the patient brought him some pie and he has some left behind his ear. He'll eat it later.

Write sentences using the phrasal verb and bonus words in italics.

1. What did Vinny break out in?

2. Why does Doctor Skinner think Vinny broke out?

3. Are you embarrassed when you break out?

4. Do you break out in a sweat if you are nervous?

Carry On   Whine/cry to get attention

Does not take an object

You may hear it used like this: Stop **carrying on** and be quiet!

It's time to meet some of our characters. Read these conversations aloud.

Jasmine (5, a whiny girl): "Mommy, I don't want to clean my room. That's your job."

Yukiko (29, Jasmine's mother): "Well, Jasmine, that's true. You usually **carry on** so much that I clean it for you. This time, though, I hope I don't find any old pizza under the bed."

A while later . . .

Jasmine: "Daddy, I want a big fudge sundae and I want it now!"

Arnie (34, Jasmine's father): "No, it's too early in the morning for ice cream. You can **carry on** all you want, but I'm putting in my *earplugs* now."

Let's perform the skits. Take roles, add your ideas, and practice the phrasal verbs.

Skit 1   Arnie is talking with Andrew (31, his brother) about how Jasmine is often naughty and **carries on** a lot. He needs his brother's help. Andrew asks Arnie in what situations his niece **carries on**. (It happens almost every time Jasmine is unhappy.) Andrew asks if she **carries on** in the car. In the grocery store? In the park? Arnie says she has *had a tantrum* almost everywhere. Andrew suggests that instead of using earplugs, Arnie should see what happens if he **carries on** when Jasmine does. She might see how unpleasant it is.

Skit 2   The following weekend, Andrew and Jasmine are at the zoo. He tells her it's time to see the giraffes, but she suddenly takes off towards the lions. Andrew *yells* at her to hurry up and come back because he is going to let her have some ice cream. He is surprised when she starts to **carry on**. Andrew **carries on** a bit also. He wants to see what Jasmine will do. After about a minute, Jasmine stops whining. Andrew asks her what's wrong. Nothing's wrong. She just wanted to see if Andrew would **carry on** too. She thinks it's funny when her dad does it.

Write sentences using the phrasal verb and bonus words in italics.

1. What does Andrew suggest when Arnie tells him that Jasmine carries on a lot?

_____

2. Did Andrew's suggestion prevent Jasmine from carrying on?

_____

3. What should a parent do if a child carries on loudly at the grocery store?

_____

4. At what age do you think a child should be able to resist carrying on in public?

_____

Look Up To   Admire

Is followed by a noun phrase or pronoun

You may hear it used like this: My son **looks up to** his smart teacher.

It's time to meet some of our characters. Read these conversations aloud.

Nicolas (72, Jenny's grandpa): "Hello! Anyone home? I've finished climbing the mountain. Can I have a sandwich now?"

Justine (40, Nicolas' daughter): "Sure. Here's one that Jenny made especially for you. She **looks up to** anyone who can climb a mountain *barefoot*."

A while later . . .

Jenny (8, Justine's daughter): "Wow, Grandpa, you ate that sandwich fast. You should enter an eating contest."

Nicolas: "Good idea! I heard about a contest where you have to eat fifty mustard sandwiches. If I won, the whole world would **look up to** me!"

Let's perform the skits. Take roles, add your ideas, and practice the phrasal verbs.

Skit 1   Jenny goes with Grandpa Nicolas to the sandwich-eating contest. Nicolas has not eaten anything for two days so he is *starving*. Jenny meets another girl at the contest, Monique (9). Jenny introduces herself and then proudly tells Monique about how her grandpa can climb mountains barefoot. And, he eats really fast. She asks Monique who she's with and what he can do. Monique answers that she **looks up to** her Uncle Henry, a bus driver. He can eat ten sandwiches in one minute. He can also fix his bus when it breaks down.

Skit 2   The eating contest is over. Nicolas finished second. Jenny tries to *console* her grandpa. She praises his looks, his intelligence, and all his other good qualities. Nicolas is still sad but thanks her for saying such nice things. He then says he's worried she will not **look up to** him anymore. She says that she will always **look up to** him, even though his hair is really messy. Nicolas smiles and suggests they go buy a comb. Jenny agrees and adds, "It better be a big comb!"

Write sentences using the phrasal verb and bonus words in italics.

1. Why does Jenny look up to her grandpa?

_____

2. Does Jenny still look up to her grandpa after the contest?

_____

3. Which famous person do you look up to the most?

_____

4. If you were famous, do you think people would look up to you?

_____

Put Up With   Unhappily allow

Is followed by a noun phrase or pronoun

> You may hear it used like this: Shhh! I can't **put up with** your shouting anymore.

It's time to meet some of our characters. Read these conversations aloud.

Mrs. Singh (28, a schoolteacher): "OK, kids. Before we go on our *field trip* to the cheese factory, I want to remind you that I will not **put up with** any noise when the tour guide is talking."

Wesley (16, a student): "Yes, Mrs. Singh. Oh, Mrs. Singh, I heard that the tour guide eats five pounds of cheese daily. Is that true?"

A while later . . .

Mr. Daly (40, the tour guide): "Welcome to *The Big Cheese* Factory. I'll be your tour guide. A warning: I only do this job for the free cheese. I don't like **putting up with** big groups of noisy kids."

Mrs. Singh: "I see. So it's true! You <u>do</u> eat cheese all day."

Let's perform the skits. Take roles, add your ideas, and practice the phrasal verbs.

Skit 1   Mr. Daly brought some cheese home. He asks Mrs. Daly (40, his wife) if she can make some *quesadillas,* his favorite food. She agrees and asks him about his day. How many tour groups did he have to **put up with** (thirteen)? What kind of cheese did he eat today (cheddar)? Did he have to **put up with** any brats (no, not today)? Mr. Daly tells her about Mrs. Singh's class and this nice boy Wesley. (They talked about cheese.) Mrs. Daly then says that she spent the whole day looking at the *Chunky* Cheese Catalog she got in the mail. She couldn't decide which cheese plate to buy. Mr. Daly gives some suggestions.

Skit 2   Wesley is home after the field trip and decides to cook a surprise for Marcy (45, his mom). Marcy works at a day care center and has to **put up with** a lot of yelling and lots of dirty diapers. When Marcy comes home, she is happily surprised. As she is eating, Wesley tells her about visiting the cheese factory and meeting Mr. Daly. Mr. Daly really likes cheese but doesn't like noisy kids. Marcy doesn't like noisy kids either. She says she had to **put up with** one child who sang "Mary Had a Little Lamb" all day long.

Write sentences using the phrasal verb and bonus words in italics.

1. What won't Mrs. Singh put up with on the field trip?

_____

2. What did Marcy have to put up with today?

_____

3. Do you have to put up with a lot of traffic on the way to school/work?

_____

4. If someone is noisy in a movie theater, do you put up with it or do you complain?

_____

Take After   Have the same characteristic as someone in your family

Is followed by a noun phrase or pronoun

You may hear it used like this: Her son **takes after** her; both have green eyes.

It's time to meet some of our characters. Read these conversations aloud.

Pepe (10, Adam's friend): "Adam, who does your twin brother Zack **take after**? Your mom or your dad?"

Adam (9, Zack's twin brother): "He likes to sleep a lot, so I think he **takes after** the cat."

A while later . . .

Adam: "Dad, I've been trying to wake Zack up, but *banging* these pots together isn't working."

Stan (38, father of the twins): "I guess he **takes after** my Aunt Hilda. She's a very *heavy sleeper*. Once I even threw water on her, but she didn't wake up."

Let's perform the skits. Take roles, add your ideas, and practice the phrasal verbs.

Skit 1   Adam and Zack are in the grocery store with Beth (37, their mom). The boys are waiting by the shopping cart while she looks at a magazine. They look bored so Dean (16, a grocery store clerk) starts chatting with them. When Beth returns a minute later, Dean looks at the boys and the mom. He says to Beth that he can see that the twin boys **take after** their father because they do not look like their mom. Beth disagrees and shows Dean how she and both boys have the same fat earlobes. She admits that the boys do **take after** their father in one way: all three of them love looking up words in the dictionary.

Skit 2   Stan and Beth are visiting his Aunt Hilda (67) for dinner. They haven't been to her house lately, so Beth has to drive around until she finds it. When they arrive, they hear really loud noises coming from inside. Hilda is *snoring* in her armchair. Beth says she is glad Stan doesn't **take after** his aunt. Stan says that he may not snore like her, but they both have red hair. Beth agrees that red hair *runs in the family* because the twins have it too. Hilda continues snoring with her mouth open. Beth adds that Stan's tongue seems similar to Hilda's. Stan starts moving closer to his aunt to see if he does **take after** her.

Write sentences using the phrasal verb and bonus words in italics.

1. Who does Zack take after? Why?

_____

2. Does Stan take after Hilda?

_____

3. Do your parents take after your grandparents?

_____

4. In what way do you take after your dad?

_____

Tell Off   Scold

Can take an object between the verb and the preposition

You may hear it used like this:	Her dad **told her off** when she yelled in his ear.

It's time to meet some of our characters. Read these conversations aloud.

Suzanne (46, Carmen's friend): "Carmen, I've noticed that your 7-year-old has been drawing on the wall with *crayons*. Why don't you **tell Max off**?"

Carmen (45, Max's mother): "Actually, we *don't mind*. Max is such a good artist that we've sold one of his drawings for $500. They're taking the wall away this afternoon."

A while later . . .

Mr. Miller (38, a TV interviewer): "So, young Max, you seem to draw circles very well. How did you get to be so good?"

Max (7, the wall artist): "I've had a lot of practice. My parents never **tell me off** for drawing on things like the silk curtains. They always encourage me."

Let's perform the skits. Take roles, add your ideas, and practice the phrasal verbs.

Skit 1   Max has finished giving his interview. He wants to go to the playground, so Carmen takes him there. Max sees Norman (7, his friend), who is with Kathy (40, Norman's mother). Max suggests he and Norman have a sand fight, but Norman says he can't. His mother always **tells him off** when he does that. "OK," says Max. "Why don't we play Mother and Son? I will do bad things and you can keep **telling me off**." Max and Norman enjoy playing this game for three minutes, but they stop when Kathy **tells both of them off**.

Skit 2   Carmen and Greg (44, Max's father) are relaxing after Max is asleep. Greg asks her if Max had fun at the playground. Carmen says he *had a blast* playing the tell-off game with Norman. Greg asks what that is, and Carmen explains. She then tells Greg about Kathy, who was very strict. Kathy kept **telling Norman off** although he wasn't being bad. Greg wants to know if Kathy **told Max off**. Carmen says yes. She then tells Greg what Max said to Kathy when she scolded him. Greg laughs when he hears what Max said to Kathy.

Write sentences using the phrasal verb and bonus words in italics.

1. Why don't Carmen and Greg tell Max off when he draws on the wall?

_____

2. Did Max enjoy telling Norman off at the playground?

_____

3. In what situations should parents tell children off in public?

_____

4. Do you tell people off if they do something bad or do you keep quiet?

_____

Chapter Review Questions

Rewrite each sentence using the correct phrasal verb. Choices: **break out (in), carry on, look up to, put up with, take after, tell off.**

1. The boy made a lot of unpleasant noise when his mother wouldn't buy him the toy.

_____

2. I don't like it when the kids scream, but I don't say anything.

_____

3. The policeman told the girl she was bad when she crossed the street without looking.

_____

4. The 13-year-old bought some acne medicine when she got a pimple on her nose.

_____

5. I hope my children are just like me.

_____

6. The teacher asked her students to write a report about someone they admire.

_____

7. I think my dad is so smart.

_____

8. The boy yelled at the dog that it was bad but it didn't understand.

_____

9. He whines when he doesn't want to do what his father asks.

_____

10. She usually gets a rash if she uses that particular cream.

_____

11. Carlos and his mom are both tall.

_____

12. They don't want to listen to that bad music.

_____

CHAPTER 5

AROUND THE HOUSE
(AT HOME)

©cag 2002

Clean Off   Clear everything (or things you don't want) from on top of something

Can take an object between the verb and the preposition

You may hear it used like this: He needs to **clean off** his desk because it's too *messy.*

It's time to meet some of our characters. Read these conversations aloud.

Richard (46, the father): "Please **clean all your stuff off** the dining room table. We are having *company* this evening."

Raquel (15, the daughter): "Oh, are Mr. and Mrs. *Super Neat* having dinner here tonight?"

A while later . . .

Mrs. Super Neat (42, one of the dinner guests): "Raquel, could you **clean off** my chair before I sit down? I don't like sitting on crumbs."

Raquel: "I don't see any crumbs. *Then again,* I don't usually notice when things are messy."

Let's perform the skits. Take roles, add your ideas, and practice the phrasal verbs.

Skit 1   Mr. Super Neat (50) and his wife have finished eating dinner at Raquel's house. Raquel invites Mrs. Super Neat to see her bedroom. When Raquel opens the door, Mrs. Super Neat is very shocked and tells Raquel off for being so messy. Mrs. Super Neat wants to sit on the bed but it is covered with clothes and shoes. Raquel starts to **clean off** the bed for her, but Mrs. Super Neat tells her not to **clean it off**. Mrs. Super Neat wants to go home. She yells, "Thanks for dinner!" as she and her husband head out to the car. Richard says to Raquel, "Yeah! They're gone! We can be messy again."

Skit 2   Mr. and Mrs. Super Neat have just arrived at the park for a picnic. A lot of families are enjoying the sunshine. Mrs. Super Neat asks her husband to **clean off** the picnic table because there are a lot of leaves and pieces of food on it. Mr. Super Neat happily **cleans it off** and tells his wife that he is glad they don't have any children. If they did, they'd have to put up with a lot of mess. Mrs. Super Neat disagrees. Their baby would probably take after them and would be very neat. They continue discussing the good and bad points of having children.

Write sentences using the phrasal verb and bonus words in italics.

1. Why does Raquel have to clean off the dining room table?

_____

2. What does Mrs. Super Neat say when Raquel starts cleaning off her bed?

_____

3. Do you often clean off your desk or do you leave a lot of old papers on it?

_____

4. Do you think that restaurant workers enjoy cleaning off messy tables?

_____

Clean Out   Clear everything (or things you don't want) from inside something

Can take an object between the verb and the preposition

You may hear it used like this: You're fired! Please **clean out** your desk before noon.

It's time to meet some of our characters. Read these conversations aloud.

Mrs. Rogers (52, a *real estate agent*): "So, Mrs. Holmes, did you **clean out** the garage as I suggested?"

Mrs. Holmes (42, the homeowner): "Yes, we removed the boxes of old books and almost all of our *junk*. We just need to find our pet hamster. He escaped from his cage yesterday and is in the garage somewhere."

A while later...

Mr. Holmes (44, Mrs. Holmes' husband): "Hurry up and help me take these boxes of books out of the living room. We need to **clean the living room out** before Mrs. Rogers and the buyer arrive."

Mrs. Holmes: "You're right! We shouldn't have moved our junk from the garage into the living room. Now we have to move it all somewhere else."

Let's perform the skits. Take roles, add your ideas, and practice the phrasal verbs.

Skit 1   Mrs. Rogers and Miss Jansen (29, the buyer) have arrived at the Holmes house to go over the selling price and other details. Miss Jansen makes small talk with Mrs. Rogers while they wait for the sellers to be ready. Mr. Holmes is looking for his hamster, and his wife is packing her clothes. Mrs. Holmes has a ton of clothes in her *walk-in closet*. She comes back into the living room in a few minutes. Miss Jansen asks why she is wearing six shirts, three skirts, one pair of pants, and two pairs of shoes. Mrs. Holmes says that she was just **cleaning out** the closet. Mr. Holmes comes in and says he found the hamster in the garage. It was in a box of old shoes.

Skit 2   Mr. Holmes has decided to bring his hamster to the office because he likes to talk to it. A couple weeks later Mr. Barnes (57, his boss) comes into his *cubicle* and asks him what smells so bad. Mr. Holmes says he doesn't know. Mr. Barnes then sees the hamster cage on the floor. He warns Mr. Holmes that if he doesn't immediately **clean out** the hamster's smelly cage he'll be fired. Mr. Holmes tells his boss why he loves his stinky pet so much. Mr. Barnes must then decide whether to fire Mr. Holmes or explain that hamster cages need to be **cleaned out** regularly.

Write sentences using the phrasal verb and bonus words in italics.

1. Why did Mr. and Mrs. Holmes have to clean out the living room?

_____

2. Does Mr. Holmes know how to clean out his hamster's cage?

_____

3. Do you like cleaning out your closet?

_____

4. How often should a pet store clean out the animal cages?

_____

Clean Up/Straighten Up   Make an area neater by picking things up

"Clean up" and "straighten up" mean the same thing; can take an object between the verb and the preposition

Clean Up After   Clean up someone else's mess

Is followed by a noun phrase or pronoun

You may hear them used like this:	I'm tired of **cleaning up after** you.
	Please **straighten things up**.

It's time to meet some of our characters. Read these conversations aloud.

Damian (26, Andrea's housekeeper): "Your work friends will be arriving in an hour. Do you want me to **straighten up** the house before they come or after they leave?"

Andrea (27, a secretary): "Hmmm. Before, please. There are too many newspapers on the table, and my husband left his socks all over the floor. As a reward for **cleaning up**, you can sit in on our chat. We're going to be *gossiping* about our bosses."

A while later . . .

Damian: "My goodness! You ladies sure left a lot of trash on the floor."

Andrea: "Sorry. You don't mind **cleaning up after** us, do you? It's just that we are tired of **straightening up** since we do that a lot at work."

Let's perform the skits. Take roles, add your ideas, and practice the phrasal verbs.

Skit 1   Andrea is at work. After lunch, Mr. Rooney (43, her boss) asks her to **straighten up** the conference room because he just had a lunch meeting there. There are paper cups and plates all over the floor. And maybe some pieces of food. Andrea asks Mr. Rooney if he enjoyed the ham sandwiches she ordered for the meeting (yes). She then asks him if his favorite words are *oink oink*. He says they are, because he likes to pretend to be a *pig*. Andrea says that he does a very good job. However, she and the other secretaries will no longer **clean up after** the little pigs in the office. He says . . .

Skit 2   Andrea and Anke (28, a secretary who went to Andrea's house earlier) are *carpooling* on Monday evening. Anke asks Andrea if she told Mr. Rooney to **clean up after** himself. Andrea happily tells her about her discussion with Mr. Rooney. Anke then asks her to describe him. Anke says she thinks she saw Mr. Rooney in the conference room with a big trash bag. He was saying, "Oink oink." Anke asked him what he was doing. He said that he was **straightening up**. Anke then noticed that he was eating something. Mr. Rooney said that he wanted to **clean up** all the pieces of sandwich on the floor because he was hungry.

Write sentences using the phrasal verb and bonus words in italics.

1. Why does Andrea want Damian to straighten up?

2. Does Mr. Rooney clean up after himself at the office?

3. Do you clean up after your family members or do they clean up after you?

4. If you left a mess on the table at home, how long would it take you to clean it up?

Run Out (Of)   No longer have a supply of something

If not followed by "of," does not take an object; if used with "of," is followed by a noun phrase or pronoun

> You may hear it used like this: He **ran out of** stamps so he couldn't mail the letter.

It's time to meet some of our characters. Read these conversations aloud.

Arnaud (45, a man having a barbecue): "Hey, Yves. I think we just **ran out of** napkins. Can't have a barbecue without napkins."

Yves (48, Arnaud's brother): "I guess I could go to the store. Or maybe everyone could *wipe* their hands on their shirts as I've been doing."

A while later . . .

Luciano (37, a guest at the barbecue): "*How come* you've got all those *grease stains* on your pants?"

Yves: "Well, I was using my shirt as a napkin since we **ran out**. But then I **ran out of** space on my shirt so I used my pants."

Let's perform the skits. Take roles, add your ideas, and practice the phrasal verbs.

Skit 1   The barbecue is over. Arnaud and Yves start discussing what a fun party it was. Arnaud tells Yves that it was a great idea to **run out of** napkins. Yves agrees and hopes the guests will get their shirts cleaned where he works: the cheapest cleaner in town. Yves adds that he was going to give a business card to everyone, but he **ran out of** them halfway through the party. Arnaud tells him not to worry. He thinks most of the guests know where Yves works. Arnaud asks Yves if the cleaner has enough detergent to wash a hundred shirts. Yves wouldn't want to **run out**.

Skit 2   Yves is at work. Luciano, who went to the barbecue, comes in with a large *load* of dirty shirts. Luciano tells Yves that everyone who went to the barbecue wants their shirts cleaned for free. Yves asks why. Luciano says that everyone thinks that Yves deliberately **ran out of** napkins so the guests would get their shirts dirty and have them cleaned where Yves works. Yves says that the guests didn't have to use their shirts as napkins. They could have wiped their hands in their hair. Luciano **runs out of** patience and says . . .

Write sentences using the phrasal verb and bonus words in italics.

1. What did Yves suggest when the brothers ran out of napkins at the barbecue?

_____

2. Why doesn't Yves want to run out of detergent?

_____

3. When you run out of clean clothes, do you go shopping or do you do laundry?

_____

4. Has your neighbor ever asked to borrow a cup of sugar because he/she ran out?

_____

Throw Away/Throw Out   Put something you don't need in the trash

"Throw away" and "throw out" mean the same thing; can take an object between the verb and the preposition

You may hear it used like this: She **threw away** the empty cereal box.

It's time to meet some of our characters. Read these conversations aloud.

Stephanie (21, a college student): "Have you seen my collection of *rags*? I want to iron them."
Gabriela (20, Stephanie's roommate): "Oh, those old things? I **threw them away**. Sorry, but the garbage man already came."

A while later . . .

Stephanie: "I can't believe my roommate **threw out** my rags. I wanted to sell them at the *swap meet*."
Barbara (22, Stephanie's friend): "If you give me $10, you can sell these old socks at the swap meet. They have lots of holes in them."

Let's perform the skits. Take roles, add your ideas, and practice the phrasal verbs.

Skit 1   *Business is slow* at the swap meet. Stephanie decides to stop selling the socks and look at the other items for sale. Much to her surprise, she sees Gabriela at another table selling the rags she thought had been **thrown out**—$3 each! Stephanie walks up to the table, and Gabriela turns red. Stephanie asks her why she lied about **throwing away** the rags. Gabriela says she needed money to pay their rent. Stephanie asks how she gets people to buy the wrinkled rags. With a $3 rag, each customer gets to see Gabriela dance for three minutes. She shows Stephanie her dance.

Skit 2   Michel (25, Barbara's husband) is waiting for Barbara to come home. When she arrives, he asks her where his socks are. Barbara reminds him that last week they talked about cleaning out his drawers and **throwing away** some old clothes. He remembers, but he didn't want her to *get rid of* his favorite old socks with all the holes. Barbara says she may have **thrown some of them out**. She'll check. She hurries into the bedroom and calls Stephanie. Barbara tells Stephanie that she wants the socks back and explains why. Stephanie's advice is to go to the swap meet tomorrow. It opens at 9 a.m.

Write sentences using the phrasal verb and bonus words in italics.

1. What did Gabriela say she threw away?

_____

2. What did Michel agree to throw out?

_____

3. Have you ever thrown away something valuable by accident?

_____

4. Do you usually throw out old clothes or do you give them to charity?

_____

Wash Up   Clean your hands/body or the dishes/pans

Usually does not take an object; if you want to be more specific, can take an object between the verb and the preposition

> You may hear it used like this: Dinner's ready. Please **wash up**.

It's time to meet some of our characters. Read these conversations aloud.

Mr. *Nutty* (62, a man who likes nuts): "I need to **wash up** before I *pick weeds* in the garden. I don't want to get the plants all sticky."

Mrs. Nutty (60, Mr. Nutty's wife): "Why didn't you use a spoon to eat your jar of peanut butter?"

A while later . . .

Mr. Nutty: "Gosh, those almond pancakes were outstanding! I'm so full!"

Mrs. Nutty: "I guess you don't need to **wash up** tonight. It seems you have *licked* both sides of your plate."

Let's perform the skits. Take roles, add your ideas, and practice the phrasal verbs.

Skit 1   Mr. and Mrs. Nutty recently opened a china shop. Nora Nutty (40, their daughter) is in town to help them get the store ready for Monday's customers. She ate a lot of peanuts on the airplane so she doesn't need a snack when she arrives. Nora notices that everything for the store has already been **washed up**—the cups, bowls, and plates. She asks her mom about it. Mrs. Nutty tells Nora that they didn't need to **wash anything up** after dinner because her dad licked all the dishes clean. Nora is surprised that her parents use the dishes before they sell them. Mrs. Nutty tells her that the store is very successful.

Skit 2   Nora Nutty is back home and is making spaghetti for dinner. Chris (20, her son) has been playing in the yard with his pet *worms*. She tells him that the spaghetti is almost ready and he needs to **wash up** before he can eat. He comes inside and washes his dirty hands and face. While she is putting the sauce on the spaghetti, Nora asks Chris what game he and the worms were playing (hide and seek). Chris then asks his mom if he can put two of his pets on the plate so they can see what is happening. Nora agrees but says the worms will have to **wash up** too.

Write sentences using the phrasal verb and bonus words in italics.

1. Why doesn't Mr. Nutty need to wash up tonight?

_____

2. Why do the worms have to wash up?

_____

3. Do children enjoy washing up before eating?

_____

4. Do you usually wash up after dinner or do you leave dirty dishes in the sink?

_____

Chapter Review Questions

Rewrite each sentence using the correct phrasal verb. Choices: **clean off, clean out, clean up/ straighten up/clean up after, run out (of), throw away/throw out, wash up.**

1. She got rid of what she didn't need.

_____

2. The waiter removed the food from the chair before I sat down.

_____

3. The dishwasher is broken so you will have to clean the plates tonight.

_____

4. The wife didn't want to remove her husband's dirty clothes from the floor.

_____

5. I don't have any more garbage bags.

_____

6. Please take away everything you don't want from your sock drawer.

_____

7. This plant is dead so you need to put it in the trash.

_____

8. He used the last match so he needs to buy more.

_____

9. Your desk has too many things in the drawers so I suggest you remove what you don't want.

_____

10. The woman removed the plates from the table.

_____

11. She needs to remove all the dirt from her hands.

_____

12. Before the guest arrives, I need to pick up the baby's toys. They are all over the floor.

_____

CHAPTER 6

ON SALE
(CLOTHING)

©caf2002

Break In
Wear something new (usually shoes) a lot so that it becomes more comfortable; train a new employee

Can take an object between the verb and the preposition

You may hear it used like this: I need to **break in** these shoes before I run the race.

It's time to meet some of our characters. Read these conversations aloud.

Raul (36, an *amateur* sailor): "Constantine, would you like to go sailing with me this weekend? I'm making a *raft* and it will be ready on Saturday."

Constantine (35, Raul's friend): "Sure. I've been waiting for an opportunity to **break in** my new *flippers*. Don't forget to bring yours in case we fall in the ocean."

A while later . . .

Constantine: "*Ow*, ow, ow! I thought my new flippers would be easy to **break in**."

Ashley (29, Constantine's wife): "Wow! Those are some pretty big blisters. You probably shouldn't have worn the flippers backwards, honey."

Let's perform the skits. Take roles, add your ideas, and practice the phrasal verbs.

Skit 1   Raul is helping Constantine buy some shoes for work. Constantine needs shoes that are comfortable right away so he won't have to **break them in**. He tells Raul about his blisters from last week and how his feet still hurt. Gene (18, a shoe store employee) asks Raul if he needs help. Raul asks Gene which shoes are the cheapest. This is Gene's first day, so he isn't up on the shoe prices. Mr. Horn (42, Gene's boss) apologizes, saying that he hasn't had time to **break in** the new employee. Mr. Horn then shows Constantine some $10 slippers with a cute umbrella design. Raul says they look comfortable and will be easy to **break in**.

Skit 2   Constantine has arrived at his new job as a TV weatherman. Mr. Morimoto (45, his boss) looks at him and asks Ms. Mason (34, the personnel manager) to visit his office. When Ms. Mason arrives, Mr. Morimoto says that he doesn't want to **break in** another bad weatherman. The previous one quit after only two days. Ms. Mason asks what's wrong with Constantine. Mr. Morimoto points to Constantine's feet. Constantine explains why he is wearing slippers instead of **breaking in** new dress shoes. He then shows them the weather-related umbrella design. They agree that Constantine should sit behind a desk while giving the weather report so that viewers won't see his shoes.

Write sentences using the phrasal verb and bonus words in italics.

1. What does Constantine plan to break in this weekend?

_____

2. Why didn't Constantine want to break in new dress shoes?

_____

3. Do you like breaking in new boots?

_____

4. How long do you think it takes to break in a new employee at a clothing store?

_____

Dress Up (In)   Wear fancy clothes/wear a *costume*

If not followed by "in," does not take an object; if used with "in," is followed by a noun phrase or pronoun

Dress Down (In)   Wear casual clothes

If not followed by "in," does not take an object; if used with "in," is followed by a noun phrase or pronoun

> You may hear them used like this: She **dresses up** for dates but **dresses down** on weekends.

It's time to meet some of our characters. Read these conversations aloud.

Araceli (16, a girl going to a party): "I'm looking forward to **dressing up** for Mimi's *black tie* dinner. What are you going to wear?"

Patrick (17, Araceli's friend): "I was thinking I'd **dress up in** my new bow tie and dress shoes, but I can't decide if I should wear a shirt too."

A while later . . .

Mimi (18, the hostess): "Would someone please give Patrick a shirt? This is not a casual party."

Patrick: "Hey, I didn't **dress down**. I wore a black bow tie, and your invitation said 'Black Tie.'"

Let's perform the skits. Take roles, add your ideas, and practice the phrasal verbs.

Skit 1   Araceli is helping Patrick decide what to wear for Halloween, which is in three days. Patrick wants to wear an easy costume. He thinks maybe he could **dress up** as a baby and then carry on at each house. Araceli says that's a bad idea because he won't get much candy that way. Patrick agrees, because he likes candy. His next idea is to be a businessman on a casual Friday. He can **dress down in** jeans, a shirt, and tennis shoes. Araceli asks if he will bring a briefcase to carry all his candy. Patrick says he'd rather bring a lunch box.

Skit 2   On Halloween morning, Patrick calls Araceli *in a panic*. He just looked in the mirror and discovered he broke out while he was asleep. He would be embarrassed to show his face. Araceli tells him he can change his costume. He can **dress up** as a ghost. Patrick thanks her and they agree to meet at his house at 7 p.m. to *go trick-or-treating*. He asks Norma (37, his mom) if he can use one of her sheets so he can **dress up** for Halloween. Norma gives him a sheet with flowers on it. At 7 o'clock, Araceli arrives. Patrick is already in his costume. Araceli looks very surprised and tells him that he needs to cut holes in the sheet so he can see.

Write sentences using the phrasal verb and bonus words in italics.

1. What did Patrick dress up in for the black tie dinner?

_____

2. Why does Patrick dress up in a sheet?

_____

3. Have you ever dressed up for Halloween?

_____

4. Do you prefer to dress up or dress down for school/work?

_____

Hang Up   Put clothing on a hanger
Can take an object between the verb and the preposition

> You may hear it used like this: **Hang up** your dress so it doesn't get wrinkled.

It's time to meet some of our characters. Read these conversations aloud.

Margarita (22, a young businesswoman): "Colin, are you almost done in the bathroom? I need to get ready for work and I **hung my dress up** in there last night."

Colin (27, Margarita's husband): "Is there anything else you can wear? The clothes you **hung up** in here are all wet because I just had a shower."

A while later . . .

Margarita: "Alicia, don't you hate living in such a *teeny* apartment? We have to **hang our clothes up** on the *shower rod* because we have no other space. What do you do with your clothes?"

Alicia (24, Margarita's neighbor): "It would be nice to have a closet, but we don't. You should do what I do. Don't **hang up** your clothes."

Let's perform the skits. Take roles, add your ideas, and practice the phrasal verbs.

Skit 1 Colin and Margarita have rented a new apartment. It is much bigger than their old one. The day after they move in, Margarita returns from work to find lots of clothes all over the floor. She tells Colin that she is not going to clean up after him so he should **hang up** his clothes in the closet. She then goes to **hang up** her coat in the closet but there is no more space. Colin says he was so excited to have a closet that he bought a lot of new clothes and **hung them up** in the closet. He put the extra clothes on the floor. Margarita says she'll have to **hang up** her coat somewhere else.

Skit 2 Alicia sees Margarita in the market. Alicia's clothes look very *rumpled*. Margarita remembers that Alicia doesn't **hang up** any of her clothes, so Margarita offers to buy her an iron. Alicia accepts. Alicia then asks Margarita about her new apartment. Margarita describes how many rooms there are and what color the wallpaper is. Alicia asks if Margarita misses her old apartment. Surprisingly, Margarita does. Margarita tells her about Colin's *shopping spree* and how there is no room in their closet for her clothes. She tells Alicia she is still **hanging her clothes up** in the bathroom.

Write sentences using the phrasal verb and bonus words in italics.

1. Where do Colin and Margarita have to hang up their clothes in their small apartment?

____

2. Where does Alicia hang up her clothes?

____

3. Do you always hang your clothes up?

____

4. Where would you hang up your coat if you ran out of space in the closet?

____

Put On   Put clothing or other items on your body

Can take an object between the verb and the preposition

> You may hear it used like this: Please **put on** your gloves because it's cold outside.

It's time to meet some of our characters. Read these conversations aloud.

Samantha (7, a young girl): "Daddy, can I borrow your beret? My snowman needs to **put on** a hat."

Bruce (30, Samantha's father): "Sure. Does the snowman want to **put on** some *long johns* too? It's pretty cold outside."

A while later . . .

Candace (30, Bruce's wife): "Bruce, I was going to **put my long johns on** but I just noticed that they are outside next to the snowman. Do you know how they got there?"

Bruce: "Samantha wanted to borrow them for the snowman to **put on**, but I guess she discovered that she didn't give the snowman any legs."

Let's perform the skits. Take roles, add your ideas, and practice the phrasal verbs.

Skit 1   Bruce is helping Samantha get ready for school. She **puts on** a blue dress and yellow sandals while her dad puts the leftover *Sloppy Joe sandwich* in her lunch bag. Bruce tells her she looks really pretty but asks her to **put on** warmer clothes because it's cold outside. Samantha says that it's school picture day today and she wanted to dress up a bit. They *compromise* and she **puts a jacket on**. As Bruce is driving Samantha to school, she takes a quick bite of her lunch. *Oops!* She spills sauce on her dress. Samantha tells her dad she knew she should have worn her bib. She decides to **put on** the bib.

Skit 2   It's Samantha's turn to get her picture taken. She is still wearing the bib to hide the stain from this morning. Mr. Takahashi (47, the photographer) asks her if she wants to leave the bib on for the picture. She says there is a stain underneath. He suggests that she **put on** a scarf instead of the bib. Samantha asks him to show her the scarf. The only scarf he has is bright green and doesn't match. She thinks for a few seconds and decides that the bib looks better. She tells Mr. Takahashi she'll keep the bib on. She then smiles for the camera.

Write sentences using the phrasal verb and bonus words in italics.

1. What does Candace want to put on?

_____

2. Why does Samantha want to put on a bib?

_____

3. Do you always put on your coat when it's raining or do you like to get wet?

_____

4. Did your teacher put on matching clothes today?

_____

Take Off   Remove clothing or other items you are wearing

Can take an object between the verb and the preposition

> You may hear it used like this: She **took off** her raincoat when it stopped *pouring.*

It's time to meet some of our characters. Read these conversations aloud.

Miss Park (46, a tour guide at an aquarium): "Welcome to the *grand opening* of the new aquarium. Everyone please **take off** your shoes because the fish are sleeping."

Johnny (8, a boy visiting the aquarium): "We came here to see the fish swim, not snore. Do I have to **take my roller skates off?**"

A while later . . .

Miss Park: "Sir, I'm going to have to ask you to **take off** your roller skates too."

Grandpa Strauss (56, Johnny's grandpa): "OK, ma'am, but I was hoping to look at the fish really quickly. Johnny has to be at his piano lesson in an hour."

Let's perform the skits. Take roles, add your ideas, and practice the phrasal verbs.

Skit 1 Johnny and his grandpa are enjoying the aquarium but don't have much time to look at the fish. They try to run so they can see everything but they can't. It is too dangerous because they **took off** their shoes and are wearing just their slippery socks. They decide to **take their socks off** too. They both start running towards the octopus tank. Mr. Wright (36, a security guard) tells them to slow down. Grandpa Strauss apologizes to the guard for going too fast. He explains why they are in a hurry. Grandpa then looks at his watch and realizes it's time to leave. He tells Johnny that they should go wash up. Their feet are *filthy.*

Skit 2 Johnny is at his grandma and grandpa's house after his lesson. Sandra (54, his grandma) asks him what he did today. Johnny tells her all about the aquarium and how they didn't have time to see the big octopus. His grandma then notices he is wearing very unusual shoes. Sandra asks why. Johnny says that they all had to **take off** their shoes at the aquarium because it was *nap time* for the fish. He then explains that when he and Grandpa had to leave, he couldn't find his shoes so he borrowed someone else's. The hot pink sandals were the only ones that fit him.

Write sentences using the phrasal verb and bonus words in italics.

1. Why do the people visiting the aquarium have to take off their shoes?

_____

2. When Johnny and his grandpa take off their socks, what happens?

_____

3. How often do you take off your glasses and clean them?

_____

4. Do you take off your shoes when you go inside?

_____

Try On   Put on clothing to see if it fits

Can take an object between the verb and the preposition

You may hear it used like this: You should **try on** these shoes before buying them.

It's time to meet some of our characters. Read these conversations aloud.

Martina (23, a woman about to get married): "Mom, I'm tired of **trying on** these high heels. My feet are starting to hurt."

Natasha (50, Martina's mother): "Well, we've spent three hours in this shoe store and nothing seems to fit you. Maybe you should just wear white tennis shoes at your wedding."

A while later . . .

Deborah (23, Martina's *maid of honor*): "Martina, I **tried on** the bridesmaid's dress you want me to wear, but it's not very *flattering*. I think the other bridesmaid, Sylvie, will agree."

Martina: "Why don't you **try my dress on**? If it fits, you and Sylvie can wear the same kind, only yellow."

Let's perform the skits. Take roles, add your ideas, and practice the phrasal verbs.

Skit 1   At the wedding *reception*, Martina tells Guillermo (27, her new husband) that she's glad she wore tennis shoes at the ceremony. Guillermo says he's glad too because she would have tripped in high heels. Mrs. Hernandez (60, Guillermo's mother) then joins them. She says it was a beautiful ceremony but wants to know why Martina wore tennis shoes. Martina tells her how she **tried on** so many high heels but none of them fit her very narrow feet. Mrs. Hernandez understands because she has very wide feet. She remembers how she wore men's shoes at her own wedding.

Skit 2   Martina and Guillermo have gone on their honeymoon. Deborah and Sylvie (22, the other bridesmaid) are relaxing. Sylvie is visiting from another state and wasn't able to **try dresses on** with Deborah. She asks Deborah if she enjoyed shopping for dresses with Martina. Deborah says that she loves her best friend Martina but thinks she *has bad taste* in dresses. She explains how she had to **try on** so many ugly yellow dresses. Even Martina's wedding dress was ugly. Deborah asks Sylvie if she will wear the bridesmaid's dress again. Sylvie says, "Certainly not!" but then adds that she loves the yellow tennis shoes Martina asked them to wear.

Write sentences using the phrasal verb and bonus words in italics.

1. Why is Martina trying on so many pairs of shoes?

_____

2. What kind of dresses does Deborah have to try on? Are they pretty?

_____

3. Do you have to try a lot of clothes on before you find something that fits?

_____

4. Would you try on something you thought was ugly if it was inexpensive?

_____

Chapter Review Questions

Rewrite each sentence using the correct phrasal verb. Choices: **break in, dress up (in)/dress down (in), hang up, put on, take off, try on.**

1. Although the dry cleaner always puts my clothes on hangers, they are always wrinkled.

_____

2. She removed her bracelet because it was time for bed.

_____

3. They wear casual clothes at work.

_____

4. I need to wear these shoes for a while even though they are uncomfortable now.

_____

5. My mom checked to see if the dress she wanted to buy was the right size.

_____

6. She forgot to wear her glasses, so she couldn't take the driving test.

_____

7. Her father is always a size extra-large, so he never has to see if shirts fit.

_____

8. The boy had to wear a new shirt because he spilled soda on the one he was wearing.

_____

9. The boss wears a suit and tie every day.

_____

10. She wore her new boots until they were more comfortable.

_____

11. The kids removed their slippers and went to bed.

_____

12. My wife put my clothes in the closet for me because I was too lazy.

_____

CHAPTER 7

IN SICKNESS AND IN HEALTH
(THE BODY)

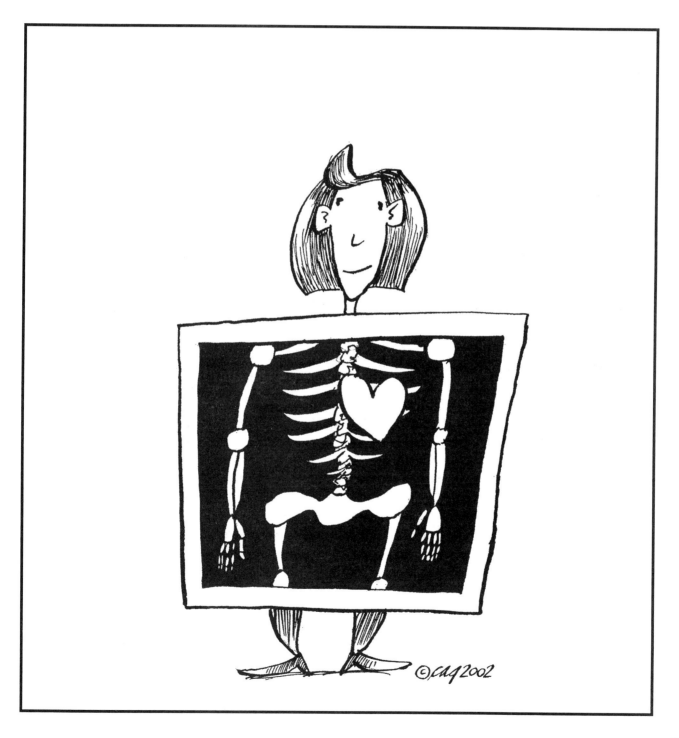

Come Down With   Become sick with an illness

Is followed by a noun phrase or pronoun

You may hear it used like this: I feel like I'm **coming down** with a cold.

It's time to meet some of our characters. Read these conversations aloud.

Rhonda (37, a woman watching a fisherman): "How long have you been fishing and have you caught anything?"

Sanjay (39, the fisherman): "I've been here about two hours but haven't caught much yet. Maybe the fish have **come down with** *sleeping sickness*."

A while later . . .

Sanjay: "Amruta, can you check if I feel warm? I don't feel very well."

Amruta (37, Sanjay's wife): "No, your forehead feels fine. You're just hoping to **come down with** something because you have to give a talk on *infectious diseases* tomorrow."

Let's perform the skits. Take roles, add your ideas, and practice the phrasal verbs.

Skit 1   At 11 p.m. on Sunday night, Sanjay starts to feel really sick and breaks out in a sweat. He goes to the hospital. Doctor Kirby (46) asks Sanjay to tell him how he feels. Sanjay describes his symptoms (hot, sweaty, and nervous). He then tells the doctor that he has been reading up on infectious diseases. He works in a laboratory and has to give a talk on them tomorrow. Sanjay is afraid he is **coming down with** a serious disease. The doctor tells the patient he has no fever and seems fine. Doctor Kirby tells him it's just *stage fright*.

Skit 2   It's 6 a.m. on Monday and Sanjay is nervous about his 8 a.m. presentation. He feels better after having some coffee and donuts. Amruta asks what the doctor said at the hospital. Sanjay explains. Amruta says she knew he wasn't **coming down with** anything. She gives him a hug as he goes out the door. When Sanjay arrives at work at 7:30 a.m., only Miss Moya (37, a secretary at his office) is there. Sanjay asks where everyone is. Miss Moya tells him that a lot of people have **come down with** *food poisoning*. Many of them ate donuts from Dora's Donuts.

Write sentences using the phrasal verb and bonus words in italics.

1. Did Sanjay come down with something or was it his imagination?

_____

2. What did Sanjay's co-workers come down with?

_____

3. When you come down with a cold, do you see a doctor or do you wait to see if you get better?

_____

4. How do you know if you have come down with the flu?

_____

Come To   Wake up after being hit on the head

Does not take an object

> You may hear it used like this: When she **came to**, she didn't know where she was.

It's time to meet some of our characters. Read these conversations aloud.

Brooke (28, a lady who saw a car accident): "Somebody call a doctor! There's been a car accident. Wait a minute, the driver has just **come to**. Sir, are you OK?"

Alain (28, the man hurt in the car accident): "Uhhhhhh. Where am I? Oh, is that you, Brooke? I haven't seen you since high school. Why wouldn't you go to the *prom* with me?"

A while later . . .

Alain: "Hey, Bernadette, why did you hit me on the head with your shoe? I was just in a car accident and **came to** in the middle of the street. Now I have a really big headache."

Bernadette (27, Alain's wife): "Sorry, but I was jealous that you were *reminiscing* about Brooke."

Let's perform the skits. Take roles, add your ideas, and practice the phrasal verbs.

Skit 1   The day after the car accident, Alain and Bernadette go to his 10th *high school reunion*. After the dinner, Alain sees Troy (28, an old friend) and asks him what he does. (Troy is a rich banker.) Troy asks Alain the same question. Alain is embarrassed that he is just a cashier. Troy then asks Alain what happened to his head. Alain explains about his car accident yesterday. He says he **came to** in the middle of the street and saw his old girlfriend Brooke there. Troy then tells Alain that he and Brooke have been married for eight years. Alain faints and Troy asks Brooke to help Alain **come to**. She offers to throw cold water on him.

Skit 2   Alain has **come to**. He is lying on the floor surrounded by his old classmates. Eddie (28, another friend from high school) helps him up. Alain and Eddie start chatting about *the good old days*. Eddie reminisces about how he and Alain used to play football together and how Alain always used to trip. Alain remembers that it was rather embarrassing to hit his head and then **come to** in front of the cheerleaders. Eddie tells Alain that he always liked him because of his clumsiness.

Write sentences using the phrasal verb and bonus words in italics.

1. When Alain comes to after the accident, what does he ask Brooke?

_____

2. Where is Alain when he comes to and Eddie helps him up?

_____

3. What would you do if you came to in a strange place?

_____

4. How does a boxer feel when he comes to and realizes he lost the match?

_____

Give Out   Become physically exhausted

The subject of the sentence is always a part of the body; does not take an object

---

You may hear it used like this: His knees **gave out** during the race and he fell down.

It's time to meet some of our characters. Read these conversations aloud.

Noreen (17, a girl taking a walk): "I think we're lost. I don't see the farmers' market, and we've been walking for two hours now."

Desirée (15, Noreen's sister): "You're right. My legs are about to **give out**. I think I can *crawl* toward that taxi over there. Can you?"

A while later . . .

Desirée: "Sir, can you lift me into the taxi? My arms are about to **give out** from crawling for the past five minutes. We've been trying to find the farmers' market for the last two hours and we were too tired to walk."

Clint (28, a taxi driver): "Sure, I can lift you up, but the market is just one block away."

Let's perform the skits. Take roles, add your ideas, and practice the phrasal verbs.

Skit 1   Noreen and Desirée took the taxi home. The sisters were too tired to buy zucchini at the farmers' market. When they arrive home, André (49, their father) asks them why they look so *beat*. Noreen tells him that they got lost looking for the market. They walked up and down hills until their bodies almost **gave out**. Desirée tells him she feels lucky they found a taxi. André tells them that they should rest now because tomorrow he wants them to start training for the *marathon* they agreed to run next month. The young ladies agree that they need to get stronger so their legs won't **give out** during the race.

Skit 2   Noreen and Desirée are running together in the marathon. They are almost at the finish line when Noreen starts feeling really tired. She tells her sister she might not be able to finish the race. Desirée encourages her to keep going. Desirée says that if Noreen's legs **give out** and they quit, their dad won't give them any dessert when they get home. They agree that they can't wait to eat their *banana splits*. They decide to crawl instead of run for a while. To pass the time, Desirée asks Noreen what toppings she's planning to put on her banana split. Noreen answers that she wants her whipped cream to be a foot high.

Write sentences using the phrasal verb and bonus words in italics.

1. When Noreen and Desirée's legs give out while they're looking for the market, what do they do?

_____

2. Do you think the girls' arms give out when they crawl during the marathon?

_____

3. How many pitches do you think a pitcher can throw before his arm gives out?

_____

4. Would your legs give out if you had to run a marathon?

_____

Knock Out   Hit someone so that he/she loses consciousness

Can take an object between the verb and the preposition

> You may hear it used like this: The boxer **knocked out** his opponent after only five minutes.

It's time to meet some of our characters. Read these conversations aloud.

Arlene (68, a professional boxing granny): "Hi, Emily. Are you ready to start our boxing match?"
Emily (67, another professional boxing granny): "Yes I am. Sorry if I **knock you out.**"

A while later . . .

Marcus (35, TV announcer one): "For a minute there it looked like Emily was going to **knock Arlene out**, but Arlene *ducked* just in time."
Barry (38, TV announcer two): "Yes, these grannies are really entertaining the crowd. *Aw*, look. Now they're hugging."

Let's perform the skits. Take roles, add your ideas, and practice the phrasal verbs.

Skit 1   Arlene and Emily's boxing match ended in a tie because nobody was **knocked out** after ten *rounds*. Marcus and Barry interview the boxers after the match to see what happened. Marcus asks Emily why she couldn't **knock Arlene out**. Emily says that her boxing gloves weren't broken in enough, so they were too tight. She adds that Arlene was more athletic than she thought. Barry then asks Arlene some questions about the match. After the interviews, the two grannies hang up their gloves and go eat a big steak dinner.

Skit 2   Marvin (35, Arlene's son) comes home from work and gets ready to meet his mom at the ice skating rink at 8 p.m. He is eager to hear about what happened at the boxing match. At the rink, Marvin asks Arlene how the match went. Did she **knock out** Emily? Did she get **knocked out**? Arlene explains what happened. Marvin then asks her about the TV interview. Arlene tells him what questions Marcus and Barry asked them. She then says her arms gave out from hugging Emily so much.

Write sentences using the phrasal verb and bonus words in italics.

1. Did anyone get knocked out after ten rounds?

_____

2. Why did the grannies hug each other instead of knocking each other out?

_____

3. Has anyone ever knocked you out?

_____

4. Would you knock out a robber if he tried to steal something from you?

_____

Throw Up   Be sick/vomit

Can take an object between the verb and the preposition but usually does not take an object

You may hear it used like this: While she was pregnant she felt sick and **threw up** a lot.

It's time to meet some of our characters. Read these conversations aloud.

Ingrid (41, Sandy's mom): "Oh no, the *parrot* **threw up** his snack again. And I just put new paper in his cage."

Sandy (19, a college student): "Oh dear. Can you help me clean up the mess before my *blind date* arrives?"

A while later . . .

Emilio (21, Sandy's blind date): "Good evening, Sandy. You're more beautiful than I imagined."

Sandy: "Oh, thank you! Hey, I can't go to the movies right now. My parrot, Pepper, has been **throwing up** and I'm worried about him. Let's go to the *vet's* office for our date. OK?"

Let's perform the skits. Take roles, add your ideas, and practice the phrasal verbs.

Skit 1   Sandy, Pepper, and Emilio have arrived at the vet's office. Doctor Meyer (50) asks what the problem is. Sandy explains how Pepper has **thrown his snack up** three times this week. The doctor asks what Pepper has been eating. Sandy says that the bird's favorite snack is apple pieces. Emilio adds that as he came into the house for the first time, he heard the bird saying, "Pepper! Pepper!" Sandy says that the bird always asks for some pepper on his food. Doctor Meyer thinks the bird is just saying his name. No more pepper for Pepper.

Skit 2   After the bird is back home, Emilio and Sandy decide to continue their date. They go to a diner and get to know each other. Emilio asks Sandy what kind of job she wants to have after she graduates. She says she used to think she'd be a pilot but she gets sick on airplanes. She then explains that when she was little, her parents took her to a lot of different countries but she always **threw up** on the plane. One time her dad had to change his shirt while in his airplane seat because she was sick on the shirt. Her dad didn't mind when two ladies behind them *peeked* at him through the seats.

Write sentences using the phrasal verb and bonus words in italics.

1. Why has Pepper been throwing up?

_____

2. What happened a long time ago when Sandy threw up on her father's shirt?

_____

3. Do you ever throw up when you are sick?

_____

4. If your pet threw up, would you take it to the vet?

_____

Work Out   Exercise

Does not take an object

You may hear it used like this: He **worked out** every day for a month and lost weight.

It's time to meet some of our characters. Read these conversations aloud.

Ramona (16, a good bowler): "Dad, I can't wash the car now because I have to **work out** before my bowling tournament."

Joshua (40, Ramona's dad): "Are you going to the bowling alley to practice lifting the bowling balls again, or are you going to the gym this time?"

A while later . . .

Ramona: "Ms. Olson, I really look up to you. You are such a great bowler. How can I improve my bowling game?"

Ms. Olson (54, a professional bowler and Ramona's *mentor*): "Well, you have to **work out** harder at the bowling alley. You need to lift balls heavier than eight pounds. Those are for little kids."

Let's perform the skits. Take roles, add your ideas, and practice the phrasal verbs.

Skit 1   Ramona is competing at a local bowling tournament. Joshua and Ms. Olson are talking as they watch her. Joshua thanks Ms. Olson for helping his daughter, and he asks her what bowling advice she has given Ramona. Ms. Olson tells him she has suggested that Ramona **work out** harder. Joshua says that Ramona **works out** three times a week. How much more should she **work out**? Ms. Olson tells him that Ramona isn't really **working out** as much as her dad thinks. She and Ramona sometimes meet to play *Ping-Pong*. Joshua asks for more details about these meetings.

Skit 2   Ramona was one of the top bowlers in the tournament but she didn't win. She tells her dad that she needs to go **work out** at the gym so that she can *get in better shape*. Joshua says that's a good idea. He then asks her why she sometimes goes to play Ping-Pong with Ms. Olson instead of **working out** and practicing her bowling. She says she likes going to Ms. Olson's house to play table tennis because Ms. Olson's son sometimes plays, and he is cute. Ramona adds that she's really good at Ping-Pong, and she does get to **work out** by running from side to side. Joshua says that maybe she should quit bowling and play Ping-Pong instead.

Write sentences using the phrasal verb and bonus words in italics.

1. What advice does Ms. Olson give Ramona about working out?

_____

2. Does Ramona get to work out when she plays Ping-Pong?

_____

3. Do you prefer to work out at a gym or in your home?

_____

4. Are you in shape or do you need to work out more?

_____

Chapter Review Questions

Rewrite each sentence using the correct phrasal verb. Choices: **come down with, come to, give out, knock out, throw up, work out.**

1. My legs were so tired I thought I was going to fall down.

_____

2. She felt like being sick when she was pregnant.

_____

3. A car ran over him, and when he woke up he was in the middle of the street.

_____

4. They like lifting weights at the gym.

_____

5. I hope I don't become sick with the flu this year.

_____

6. She was hit on the head with a baseball and lost consciousness.

_____

7. He likes doing all of his exercises in the morning before work.

_____

8. The boxer fell on the floor when the other man hit him.

_____

9. She was sick with a cold last week.

_____

10. My legs couldn't support me after I swam across the big lake.

_____

11. After surgery, she woke up in the hospital.

_____

12. The cat vomited on the carpet so we took him to the vet.

_____

CHAPTER 8

AT FIRST SIGHT
(THE SENSES)

Come Across As/Come Off As   Give an impression

"Come across as" and "come off as" mean the same thing; are followed by an adjective or noun phrase

You may hear it used like this: She **comes off as** shy but she talks a lot with her family.

It's time to meet some of our characters. Read these conversations aloud.

Mr. Banks (50, a *loan officer*): "Ma'am, I'm afraid we can't give you the loan for the unusual sweeping business you want to start. You do **come across as** weird, though."
Penny (42, a woman dressed as a *witch*): "Oh, thank you. I'm glad you think so."

A while later . . .

Penny: "I didn't get the loan. I **came off as** too strange."
Nick Ell (45, Penny's husband): "Oh, I'm sorry to hear that. Maybe you should leave your broom at home next time."

Let's perform the skits. Take roles, add your ideas, and practice the phrasal verbs.

Skit 1   Marco (37, Mr. Banks' neighbor) is sweeping leaves in front of his house. He asks Mr. Banks if he knows anyone who could help him sweep his large driveway. Mr. Banks says he might know someone good, although she **comes off as** weird. He then tells Marco about the strange lady, Penny, who came to the bank for a loan. She dressed up as a witch but **came across as** a good sweeper. She had a broom with her and swept the bank's floor very well. Marco asks why she needed a loan. Mr. Banks tells him about the business she wanted to start. She needed money to buy more brooms and to hire other ladies who like dressing up as witches.

Skit 2   Marco would like to hire Penny to sweep his driveway once a week. They are meeting at 8 p.m. at his house. Before leaving for the job interview, Penny puts on a big black hat and practices her witch's laugh. She then asks her husband how she looks and sounds. Nick Ell thinks she will **come off as** a harder worker if she brings two brooms, so Penny carries a red one and a blue one. When Penny knocks on Marco's door, Olivia (11, Marco's daughter) looks through the *peephole* and screams. Marco tells her it's OK. The lady **comes across as** scary but she's not a real witch. She dresses up that way to get more business.

Write sentences using the phrasal verb and bonus words in italics.

1. Why does Penny come off as strange to Mr. Banks?

_____

2. Does Penny come across as scary to Olivia?

_____

3. Do you come across as shy or outgoing?

_____

4. Which person in your class comes off as the silliest?

_____

Give Off   Produce a smell

Is followed by a noun phrase

You may hear it used like this: What's **giving off** that weird smell?

It's time to meet some of our characters. Read these conversations aloud.

Renée (25, the saleswoman): "Why don't you try this perfume? It's called Tea Breeze, and I'm sure your wife will love it."

Mr. Chen (40, the customer): "She does like tea, but I'd prefer a perfume that **gives off** more of a coffee smell. May I try Spray *Au Lait*?"

A while later . . .

Mr. Chen: "Happy Valentine's Day, honey. Here's some new perfume I chose especially for you."

Mrs. Chen (38, Mr. Chen's wife): "Oh, thank you. It **gives off** just the right combination of *coffee grounds* and *sour* milk."

Let's perform the skits. Take roles, add your ideas, and practice the phrasal verbs.

Skit 1   Mrs. Chen is the top salesperson at the used-car lot where she works. Mr. Carson (41, her boss) asks her what her secret is. He suggests her friendly personality and nice clothes as possible reasons. Mrs. Chen says it's something else. She tells him about the perfume her husband gave her and then sprays it on herself. Mr. Carson smiles and says it **gives off** a smell that reminds him of relaxing at a European café. Mrs. Chen agrees that it **gives off** a very nice smell. She says it must be making the customers feel very relaxed. Mr. Carson says he's going to buy some Spray Au Lait for all the employees to spray on themselves. Sales are really going to increase!

Skit 2   Mr. Carson is buying twenty bottles of Spray Au Lait from Renée. She says that this perfume is very popular because as soon as she sprays it on someone, it **gives off** an *aroma* that makes people want to spend money. Mr. Carson tells Renée that he already knows this. He mentions Mrs. Chen and how many used cars she has sold recently. As Mr. Carson is about to buy the twenty bottles of Spray Au Lait, Renée sprays some Tea Breeze on his wrist. He smiles and says it **gives off** a smell that reminds him of sitting in a noodle shop in China. Renée smiles and says that this perfume **gives off** a smell that makes people want to fly on airplanes.

Write sentences using the phrasal verb and bonus words in italics.

1. What kind of smell does Spray Au Lait give off?

_____

2. Does Tea Breeze give off a good smell?

_____

3. Do you prefer perfumes that give off a smell of flowers or ones that smell like the ocean?

_____

4. Do you like the smell that sour milk gives off?

_____

Listen Up   Listen closely or carefully (usually said loudly to a crowd)

Does not take an object

> You may hear it used like this: **Listen up.** I'm only going to tell you once.

It's time to meet some of our characters. Read these conversations aloud.

Antonio (24, an ESL student): "OK, **listen up.** Before Mrs. Turner gets to class, we need to get everything ready for her surprise birthday party. Vincenzo, did you wrap her present?"

Vincenzo (22, Antonio's classmate): "I tried to, but the frog was too fast. It's still hopping around the classroom."

A while later . . .

Mrs. Turner (30, the ESL teacher): "Hi, class. Please be quiet and **listen up.** We have a test today on phrasal verbs."

Vincenzo: "Wait a minute, Mrs. Turner. We have a test for you too! We want to see if you can catch up to your birthday present."

Let's perform the skits. Take roles, add your ideas, and practice the phrasal verbs.

Skit 1 Mrs. Turner and the students have been chasing her birthday frog for fifteen minutes. She is getting really tired and her legs are about to give out. She tells everyone to stop running and **listen up.** Mrs. Turner thanks the students for giving her such a nice birthday surprise. Then she says it's time for the test on phrasal verbs. She asks Antonio to use "cut off" in a sentence. He does. Then he must ask Vincenzo to use "tell off" in a sentence. Vincenzo says he's going to find the frog and tell it off for making everyone so tired. He says to the frog, "**Listen up,** Mr. Frog. I'm coming to get you!"

Skit 2 Mrs. Turner is on her way home and needs to fill up at a gas station. The frog is in the backseat. When she gets out of the car, the frog *leaps* up and escapes. Mrs. Turner doesn't notice that the frog is *missing* until she is about to leave. When she sees the empty backseat, she asks everyone at the station to **listen up.** Has anyone seen her pet frog? Doug (16, a boy gassing up his motorcycle) hears her and points to the frog at his feet. The frog is eating some bugs that Doug collected and is keeping in his pocket. The frog catches a bug with its tongue. It then leaps into Mrs. Turner's hand and kisses her.

Write sentences using the phrasal verb and bonus words in italics.

1. Why does Mrs. Turner tell the class to listen up?

_____

2. Why does everyone at the gas station have to listen up?

_____

3. Do you listen up when your teacher tries to get your attention?

_____

4. When you were a kid, did you always listen up when you were told to?

_____

Look Around   Look at your surroundings; *browse* in a shop

Does not take an object

> You may hear it used like this: Let's **look around** before the mall closes.

It's time to meet some of our characters. Read these conversations aloud.

Julio (27, a customer): "Excuse me, I need to find a good one-year-anniversary present for my wife, Hattie. I've been **looking around** but everything nice is too expensive."

Inge (25, a saleswoman): "Well, let's see, one year of marriage is the paper anniversary. How about this paper hat? It's only $1.99."

A while later . . .

Julio: "Karin, have you seen the present I bought for Hattie? I need to wrap it before she gets home."

Karin (52, Julio's mother-in-law): "I don't think so, but I'll help you **look around**. Oh, *by the way*, I saw the cat playing with a bright green paper hat. I threw it away so the cat wouldn't eat it."

Let's perform the skits. Take roles, add your ideas, and practice the phrasal verbs.

Skit 1   It's 9 p.m. and Julio is trying to fix the paper hat that was in the trash. He spent a lot of time **looking around** for a present and doesn't want to spend any more. Just then, Hattie (25, his wife) gets home. He quickly puts the broken hat away. Hattie asks him to clean off the table because she has a surprise gift for him. Julio tries to guess what it is. A big basket of flowers? A new tank for his pet turtle? Hattie smiles and tells Julio to **look around** and see what their apartment needs. He says he can't see anything because their lights are not working. Using a flashlight, Hattie shows him her present. He says, "Ooooh! A big box of light bulbs!"

Skit 2   Julio is apologizing to Hattie that he can't give her his anniversary present right now. He explains how he **looked around** all day for the perfect present but that the cat broke it by accident. Hattie says it's OK, she can wait for a new one. She'd still like to see the gift. Julio says he'll be back in a minute. He then takes out the flat hat and she tries it on. *Thrilled*, she tells him she's been **looking around** for a casual hat. And green is her favorite color.

Write sentences using the phrasal verb and bonus words in italics.

1. How long did Julio look around for a present? Does Hattie like it?

_____

2. What did Julio see when he looked around their apartment?

_____

3. When choosing a gift, do you look around for a while or do you buy something quickly?

_____

4. Look around your classroom. Who's wearing the nicest shoes?

_____

Put Off   Make someone want to leave/repel

Can take an object between the verb and the preposition

You may hear it used like this: Her bad attitude **puts me off**.

It's time to meet some of our characters. Read these conversations aloud.

Stefano (25, Eve's neighbor): "Hi and welcome to the apartment complex. Here are some cookies I made last week."

Eve (46, a new tenant): "Hello. Goodbye. It **puts me off** when new neighbors knock on my door and try to feed me sweets."

A while later . . .

Stefano: "Joy, I saw our new neighbor today but we didn't talk long. She said I **put her off**."

Joy (24, Stefano's wife): "Why? She doesn't like men with hairy knees?"

Let's perform the skits. Take roles, add your ideas, and practice the phrasal verbs.

Skit 1   The neighbors are having a *block party* on a sunny afternoon. Joy wants to invite Eve, but Stefano tells her that Eve doesn't like knocks on the door. Stefano thinks Eve might come outside to meet everyone if she hears all the noise, so he suggests that they be really noisy. Joy and Stefano start yelling and throwing *deviled eggs* at each other. Some of them hit Eve's window. "Oops," Stefano says, telling Joy that Eve will probably be even more **put off** by the neighbors. Joy is surprised to see Eve stick her head out the window and say, "Thanks! I really like deviled eggs!"

Skit 2   The evening of the block party, Eve goes to work at her job in a fabric shop. Tonight, however, she is not selling very much. She asks Mick (34, her co-worker) how sales are going for him. He tells her *so-so*. Mick then tells her not to be mad but he thinks she's **putting off** the customers. She says that customers usually like it when she tells them what fabric to buy. Mick says he doesn't think that is what's **putting them off**. Eve is surprised and asks what it could be. Mick thinks that it's her unusual hair decorations. They almost smell like deviled eggs.

Write sentences using the phrasal verb and bonus words in italics.

1. Is Eve put off by hairy knees or is it something else?

_____

2. In what way is Eve putting off the customers in the fabric shop?

_____

3. If someone you knew put you off by acting badly, would you tell the person about it?

_____

4. Do some Americans put you off? How?

_____

Watch Out (For)   Be vigilant of/careful about

If not followed by "for," does not take an object; if used with "for," is followed by a noun phrase or pronoun

> You may hear it used like this: **Watch out!** That bus almost ran you over.

It's time to meet some of our characters. Read these conversations aloud.

Brenda (20, a college student): "**Watch out for** that flying bat! It's going to land on your head."
Luke (25, Brenda's boyfriend): "What bat? That's just a leaf."

A while later . . .

Luke: "Mom, my girlfriend is afraid of everything. She tells me to **watch out for** things like leaves
    and paper cups."
Iris (50, Luke's mom): "Well, you'd better **watch out** that you don't fall in love with her. If you do,
    you'll be **watching out for** things your whole life."

Let's perform the skits. Take roles, add your ideas, and practice the phrasal verbs.

Skit 1   Brenda and Luke are in the library. Luke is in a comfortable chair reading a magazine while
Brenda browses in the *automotive* section. All of a sudden, she runs towards Luke shouting, "**Watch
out! Watch out!**" Mr. Booker (47, the librarian) tells her to be quiet. Luke doesn't stop reading
because Brenda always says that. Frustrated, Brenda yells again and continues running. When she
reaches Luke, she pulls him out of his chair and yells, "**Watch out for** that really big snake!" Luke
falls down and says, "Too late. It bit me."

Skit 2   Mr. Booker is driving Luke and Brenda to the hospital. Luke is lying in the backseat while
Brenda is giving Mr. Booker directions. Mr. Booker is driving really fast because he's worried about
Luke. He knows that some snakebites can be *fatal*. Brenda yells, "**Watch out for** that pedestrian!"
Mr. Booker *swerves* to the left. Brenda tells Mr. Booker that this isn't a racecar. Mr. Booker knows
that, but did Brenda know that racecar spelled backwards is racecar? Wow, she didn't know that.
She tells Mr. Booker that he's really smart. Then, Luke tells Brenda that in case he dies, he wants her
to know he has fallen in love with her.

Write sentences using the phrasal verb and bonus words in italics.

1. What kind of books is Brenda looking at when she first tells Luke to watch out for the snake?

_____

2. What does Mr. Booker do when Brenda tells him to watch out for the pedestrian?

_____

3. Do you have to watch out for snakes in your country?

_____

4. If you saw a bat near someone's head, would you say, "Watch out!" or do you like bats?

_____

Chapter Review Questions

Rewrite each sentence using the correct phrasal verb. Choices: **come across as/come off as, give off, listen up, look around, put off, watch out (for).**

1. She looked in various places but she couldn't find her checkbook.

_____

2. Be careful! There's a big piece of glass on the carpet.

_____

3. OK everyone, listen carefully and don't speak.

_____

4. That man seems very friendly.

_____

5. I like the aroma of your perfume.

_____

6. He wants to leave when women wear too much perfume.

_____

7. I get the impression that she's very smart.

_____

8. The old man doesn't like it when old women color their hair purple.

_____

9. Everyone please pay attention because the president is about to give a speech.

_____

10. Be sure to notice the lion that's coming toward you.

_____

11. They searched for the perfect gift in a lot of shops.

_____

12. That candle smells great.

_____

CHAPTER 9

ON THE TIP OF MY TONGUE (COMMUNICATING)

Bring Up   Mention (usually something unexpected or new)

Can take an object between the verb and the preposition

You may hear it used like this: She **brought up** the idea of going to the movie.

It's time to meet some of our characters. Read these conversations aloud.

Sara (14, a girl on her first date): "Thanks for taking me to the beach. I had a really good time."
John (16, Sara's date): "You're welcome. I didn't want to **bring it up** earlier, but why did you put sunscreen on your sunglasses?"

A while later . . .

John: "Sara, my mom **brought up** the idea of taking me to the *drive-in* next weekend but I'd rather go with you. Are you free?"
Sara: "Sure. I've been wanting to see 'Attack of the ESL Teachers.'"

Let's perform the skits. Take roles, add your ideas, and practice the phrasal verbs.

Skit 1   Dudley (39, Sara's father) is asking Sara if she enjoyed going to the drive-in with John. She tells him the *plot* of the film, a really exciting adventure movie. Dudley then asks her if she likes John. She says he's a nice guy but he needs to clean out his car. There was so much stuff in the front seat that she could barely sit down. Dudley asks her what John said when Sara mentioned the mess. Sara says she didn't **bring it up** because she didn't want to be rude. However, she is planning to get him a *gift certificate* for his birthday. She recently saw an advertisement for Car Maids, a car-cleaning service.

Skit 2   Daisy (31, an employee of Car Maids) knocks on John's door and introduces herself. John is surprised when Daisy tells him that her visit is a surprise birthday present from someone named Sara. Daisy asks if he has any questions. He says he'd like her to go over what she will clean. Daisy looks inside his car and sees a big mess. She tells him she plans to clean off the front seat and clean up all the mess. When Daisy is done, she knocks on the door again. John notices that she seems to want something. He asks her if she wants a cold drink. She points to her hand and tells John that she didn't want to **bring it up** before, but he owes her a big *tip*. John says she should **bring it up** with Sara.

Write sentences using the phrasal verb and bonus words in italics.

1. What idea did John's mother bring up? Did he like the idea?

_____

2. Is John surprised that Daisy brings up that she wants a tip? What does he say?

_____

3. If people forgot to tip you for carrying their heavy bags, would you bring it up?

_____

4. If someone brought up that your English was improving, what would you say?

_____

Drive At/Get At   Usually used by someone who doesn't understand what another is trying to say

"Drive at" and "get at" mean the same thing; usually do not take an object

You may hear it used like this: I don't understand what you are **driving at**.

It's time to meet some of our characters. Read these conversations aloud.

Leon (30, a man who is not very *handy*): "The *thingamajig* in the kitchen is broken. You know, that thing where the water comes out."

Claire (29, Leon's wife): "*What on earth* are you **driving at**? Do you mean the faucet is broken? Let's call Vin the plumber."

A while later . . .

Leon: "Vin, thanks for coming so quickly. Now, what were you **getting at** when you told me I should wear a bathing suit this evening?"

Vin (45, a plumber who is at Leon's house): "Well, I can't fix your leaky faucet until tomorrow, so it will probably get pretty wet in your house. Perhaps you'll be more comfortable in a bathing suit."

Let's perform the skits. Take roles, add your ideas, and practice the phrasal verbs.

Skit 1   That evening, Leon and Claire are sitting in their living room. Leon starts daydreaming aloud. He says it would be nice to see the ocean every day, to swim in the sea, and to watch out for sharks. Claire asks him what he's **driving at**. Isn't he happy watching TV with her every evening? Leon says he's not satisfied with that anymore. He wants to quit work and buy a houseboat. Claire says that it seems they already live in a houseboat. Leon asks her what she's **getting at**. She tells him to notice all the water that is leaking into the living room. Leon says he's glad he's wearing his bathing suit and suggests that Claire put hers on too.

Skit 2   It's midnight, and Leon and Claire are trying to get all the water out of their living room. They have been filling buckets with water and throwing it out the window for the past two hours. Claire says she's really cold in her bathing suit. Leon calls Vin and asks him if he can fix the leak now. Vin tells Leon he doesn't really know what he is **driving at** because Leo is talking too fast. Vin just knows it's an emergency and goes to Leon's house quickly. When Vin arrives, Claire asks him where his tools are. Vin says he accidentally brought his bowl of fish instead of the tools because he was in a rush and it was dark. Claire says the fish can have a swim in the living room while Vin goes home to get his tools.

Write sentences using the phrasal verb and bonus words in italics.

1. Why doesn't Claire know what Leon is getting at when something in their house is broken?

_____

2. What is Leon driving at when he says he wants to watch out for sharks?

_____

3. Do people always know what you're getting at when you speak English?

_____

4. What should you say if you don't know what someone is driving at?

_____

Get Across   Make someone understand what you are trying to say

Can take an object between the verb and the preposition but is usually followed by a noun phrase

You may hear it used like this: Nobody understood what she was trying to **get across**.

It's time to meet some of our characters. Read these conversations aloud.

Roberta (17, a Chilean student on a *home stay* in Alaska): "Being in a foreign country is so frustrating. I can't **get across** what I want to say."

Julia (16, Roberta's roommate, also from Chile): "Well, maybe you should open your mouth instead of waving your arms!"

A while later . . .

Julia: "I've been trying to **get across** to our English teacher that she should talk more slowly, but she doesn't seem to understand me."

Roberta: "Why don't you use English, not Spanish, when you ask her to slow down?"

Let's perform the skits. Take roles, add your ideas, and practice the phrasal verbs.

Skit 1   Roberta and Julia have been on their home stay for three weeks now. Each day, their communication skills are improving and they can now **get across** most of what they want to say. The roommates are at a restaurant and confidently order their food. While waiting for it, they talk about what they like best about Alaska (delicious seafood and beautiful scenery). When the food arrives, Roberta looks at her plate in surprise. She tells Julia that she thought she **got across** that she wanted the *lox*. Roberta then asks Ryan (28, the waiter) why he brought her the wrong food. Ryan says he thought Roberta said rocks, not lox.

Skit 2   Pilar (42, Julia's mother) is visiting Julia in Alaska. She is flying first class. Pilar has never been to America and doesn't know much English. On the airplane, she reads up on Alaska in her Spanish guidebook. She learns that many moose and bears live there. When it's time to eat, Kathy (25, a flight attendant) tells Pilar what's on the menu (chicken or beef for the main dish, and a cookie or chocolate mousse for dessert). The only word that Pilar understands is "moose." However, she doesn't understand that "moose" and "mousse" are *homonyms*. Kathy spends a couple minutes trying to **get across** that it's chocolate mousse, not chocolate moose.

Write sentences using the phrasal verb and bonus words in italics.

1. What should Roberta do differently to get across what she wants to say?

_____

2. What did Julia fail to get across in the restaurant?

_____

3. Are you good at getting across what you want to say in English?

_____

4. If you were visiting Iceland, how would you get across your meaning if you didn't speak Icelandic?

_____

Run By   Get someone's opinion of something; check something with someone

Always takes an object between the verb and the preposition, and is then followed by a noun phrase or pronoun

> You may hear it used like this: He has to **run it by** his wife. They might be busy then.

It's time to meet some of our characters. Read these conversations aloud.

Céline (34, a saleswoman at a plant shop): "Sir, I'm sure your wife will love getting this plant for her birthday. Would you like to buy her the yellow one or the red one?"

Brian (46, the customer): "I'm not sure what her favorite color is. I'll have to **run it by** her."

A while later . . .

Brian: "I've **run the color choices by** my wife and she would like the red plant. Yellow is her least-favorite color."

Céline: "I'm sorry but while you were gone, someone bought all the red plants. Perhaps you could buy your wife this red bush instead. I think it gives off a bad smell, but some people think it smells good."

Let's perform the skits. Take roles, add your ideas, and practice the phrasal verbs.

Skit 1   Patsy (40, Brian's wife) loves the small red bush and thinks it smells great. When looking for a place to plant it, she decides to redo the whole front yard, where there are a lot of weeds. Patsy calls Mr. Benton (32, a *landscaper*). When Mr. Benton arrives, he tells Patsy that he thinks the front yard is very nice already, but he can help her get new plants if she wants them. They discuss for a minute what she likes. He then asks her if she wants to **run all of her choices by** her husband. She says that she can't because Brian came down with something yesterday and is sleeping. She adds that if she did **run it by** him, he would probably say that $3,000 is too expensive.

Skit 2   A few days later, Brian feels better. He looks out the window and is shocked to see new plants in the front yard. He asks Patsy what happened to the old plants, and she explains. When Patsy leaves for an appointment, Brian calls Mr. Benton and tells him that he wants the landscaper to take out the new plants and put back the old ones. Mr. Benton asks if Brian has **run that by** his wife. She seemed to *have a strong opinion about* the plants. Brian says that he's not going to **run it by** her. He's sure it will be OK with her, especially if Mr. Benton puts back all the weeds. Patsy really enjoyed those weeds.

Write sentences using the phrasal verb and bonus words in italics.

1. Why does Mr. Benton suggest that Patsy run things by Brian when she buys new plants?

_____

2. Do you think Patsy will be mad that Brian didn't run things by her?

_____

3. If you wanted to buy an expensive gift for your mom, would you run it by someone in your family?

_____

4. If someone ran something by you and you didn't like the idea, what would you say?

_____

Speak Up   Talk more loudly; not be shy about expressing an opinion

Does not take an object

You may hear it used like this: When talking in front of the class, be sure to **speak up**.

It's time to meet some of our characters. Read these conversations aloud.

Charlie (18, an unfashionable man): "Please **speak up**. I can't hear you if you whisper."

Molly (14, Charlie's sister): "OK, but don't get mad. You're wearing one green shoe and one blue one. And neither of them matches your black pants."

A while later . . .

Charlie: "Thanks for telling me, Molly. I know I'm not very fashionable, but no one has ever brought that up before."

Molly: "Well, I **spoke up** because I didn't want your girlfriend to laugh at you."

Let's perform the skits. Take roles, add your ideas, and practice the phrasal verbs.

Skit 1   While on a date with Beverly (18, Charlie's girlfriend), Charlie trips and breaks a tooth. He puts ice on it. Beverly takes him to the dentist's office, where Nicola (30, the *obnoxious* receptionist) is talking very loudly on the phone to a friend. Nicola asks Charlie if he has an appointment. He says, "A oo a oo a." Nicola loudly asks him to **speak up**. Beverly explains what happened. Nicola is still chatting loudly to her friend, so she doesn't hear what Beverly says. Nicola says to her friend on the phone that she wishes everyone would **speak up** when talking to her. Beverly **speaks up** and says to Nicola that she would hear others better if she didn't talk so loudly.

Skit 2   Charlie needed some surgery to fix his tooth. Afterwards, Beverly drives him to a pharmacy. While waiting, she reads a magazine and Charlie sleeps. After waiting more than thirty minutes, Beverly decides to **speak up**. She asks Ms. Pilsner (37, the pharmacist) if Charlie's medicine is ready yet. Ms. Pilsner shakes her head and quietly *mumbles* something. Beverly asks her to **speak up** a little and explain the delay. Strangely, Ms. Pilsner writes Beverly a note. It says that the other pharmacist *went on a break* and will help Beverly soon. Then Ms. Pilsner opens her mouth. Beverly sees that she has no teeth, so it is difficult for her to talk.

Write sentences using the phrasal verb and bonus words in italics.

1. Why can't Charlie speak up at the dentist's office?

_____

2. Why does Beverly want to speak up at the pharmacy?

_____

3. Do you speak up about your opinions or are you generally shy?

_____

4. Do you generally talk loudly or do people often ask you to speak up?

_____

Talk Into   Convince someone to do something

Always takes an object between the verb and the preposition, and is then followed by a noun phrase, pronoun, or verb phrase

Talk Out Of   Convince someone not to do something

Always takes an object between the verb and the preposition, and is then followed by a noun phrase, pronoun, or verb phrase

You may hear them used like this: She didn't want to do it but her brother **talked her into** it. They **talked him out of** jumping off the bridge.

It's time to meet some of our characters. Read these conversations aloud.

Jacob (37, a man who likes *hiking*): "There are three good reasons for you to go on a hike with me: you can see lots of trees, get a lot of exercise, and eat granola bars."

Kay (32, Jacob's wife, who doesn't like hiking): "OK, you've **talked me into** it. But I sure hope we don't see any bears."

A while later . . .

Mr. Walker (39, a *park ranger* who helps Jacob after he walked up to a bear): "Ma'am, it looks like your husband will be OK. The bear just scared him. Why did you let him approach the momma bear and her *cub*?"

Kay: "I tried to **talk him out of** it, but he really wanted to feel the cub's soft fur."

Let's perform the skits. Take roles, add your ideas, and practice the phrasal verbs.

Skit 1   Jacob is telling Brandon (37, his friend) about the bears. When Jacob went near the cub, the momma bear growled really loudly. Jacob was so frightened that he fainted. When he came to, a park ranger helped him up and asked him if he was OK. Jacob told the ranger he was fine and wanted to continue hiking. Brandon asks Jacob if the ranger tried to **talk him out of** walking more. Jacob says that both Mr. Walker and Kay tried, but Jacob wanted to finish collecting firewood. Brandon asks if it was hard to walk with all that wood in his arms. Jacob tells him no because Kay carried it.

Skit 2   Kay is telling Jesse (34, her co-worker) that Jacob **talked her into** going hiking last Saturday. Jesse asks her if she had a good time. She says she didn't enjoy it at first but when Jacob asked her to carry firewood, she started liking it. She then mentions what happened when Jacob saw the bear. Jesse then asks her what she and Jacob are planning to do next weekend. She's not sure, but she says she won't let herself be **talked into** going anywhere near bears.

Write sentences using the phrasal verb and bonus words in italics.

1. How did Jacob talk Kay into going hiking with him?

_____

2. What did the park ranger try to talk Jacob out of doing?

_____

3. Is it hard or easy for someone to talk you into exercising?

_____

4. Would you try to talk someone out of giving you a surprise party if you suspected one was planned?

_____

Chapter Review Questions

Rewrite each sentence using the correct phrasal verb. Choices: **bring up, drive at/get at, get across, run by, speak up, talk into/talk out of.**

1. I'm not sure what you're trying to say because you are not talking too clearly.

_____

2. His dad tried to convince him not to eat all the fudge.

_____

3. Don't be shy about talking.

_____

4. When Grandma mentioned that my room was messy, I offered to clean it up.

_____

5. He needs to ask his wife's opinion of that.

_____

6. I tried to explain it to the doctor, but he didn't understand what I was trying to say.

_____

7. I had to convince my husband to go shopping with me.

_____

8. What are you trying to say?

_____

9. She wasn't able to make them understand what she meant.

_____

10. At dinner, he mentioned that he wanted to study abroad.

_____

11. Mom needs to check with Dad.

_____

12. Could you please talk more loudly?

_____

CHAPTER 10
ON MY MIND (THINKING)

Come Up With   Think of (often something original) using mental effort
Is followed by a noun phrase or pronoun

> You may hear it used like this: He tried to **come up with** a good idea but couldn't.

It's time to meet some of our characters. Read these conversations aloud.

Brent Bird (50, a man who drives an expensive car): "Patti, I'd like to get a *personalized license plate* but I can't **come up with** anything good to put on it. Do you have any ideas?"
Patti (45, Brent's wife): "How about 2 LEGS? You do like birds, and birds have two legs."

A while later . . .

Brent Bird: "Hello. I'd like to get a personalized license plate that says 2 LEGS."
Dee M. Vee (29, a woman who works at the Department of Motor Vehicles [DMV]): "I'm sorry but that's already taken. You need to **come up with** something else and stand in line again."

Let's perform the skits. Take roles, add your ideas, and practice the phrasal verbs.

Skit 1   It's 8 p.m. and Patti is worried about Brent. He left for the DMV at 2 p.m. and hasn't returned yet. She is about to call the police when Brent comes home. Patti asks him why he is so late. He tells her he had to wait at the DMV for more than five hours. He explains that he had to **come up with** something else for the license plate because 2 LEGS was taken. Patti asks what the new license plate will say. Brent tells her that he had a lot of time to think about it and he **came up with** something really good: TOOLEGS. Patti says, "Oh no! You've spelled it wrong! It should be TWOLEGS!"

Skit 2   Ignacio (47, Brent's neighbor) has just noticed Brent's new license plate and wonders what it means. He asks Brent how he **came up with** such an interesting license plate. Brent tells Ignacio about his recent visit to the DMV. Brent adds that he is embarrassed about the big spelling mistake he made. Ignacio tells him not to worry because everybody makes mistakes. Ignacio sees a lot of errors because he's a grammar teacher. Ignacio then says he has just **come up with** a great idea: Ignacio can give Brent a spelling lesson. Brent agrees to spell the words that Ignacio says. Ignacio starts by saying "Four Legs." Ignacio is surprised when Brent spells "For Legs."

Write sentences using the phrasal verb and bonus words in italics.

1. What special license plate did Brent Bird come up with first?

_____

2. What was wrong with the second license plate that Brent came up with?

_____

3. Can you come up with a fun license plate that would be appropriate for your teacher?

_____

4. What's the best idea you have ever come up with?

_____

Figure Out   Find a way to understand

Can take an object between the verb and the preposition

You may hear it used like this: I can't **figure out** this math problem. Help!

It's time to meet some of our characters. Read these conversations aloud.

Rika (37, a housewife): "Honey, that's a lovely drawing, but I can't **figure out** what it's supposed to be."

Louisa (8, Rika's daughter): "You can't? It's a picture of you in the morning! These are your pajamas with the sheep on them, and this is your messy hair."

A while later . . .

Rika: "Good morning, dear. You were *talking in your sleep* again, but I couldn't **figure out** what you were saying this time."

Eduardo (41, Rika's husband): "Well, I dreamed I was *counting sheep.* Maybe I was counting them out loud."

Let's perform the skits. Take roles, add your ideas, and practice the phrasal verbs.

Skit 1   It's Monday morning and almost time for Louisa to go to school. She is trying to put on her new shoes. She tells her dad that she can't **figure out** how to open the big buckles on her shoes. Eduardo sees that she is *having a hard time* and tells her he will **figure them out** in a minute. First he has to **figure out** how to put on his own tie. Rika usually does that for him, but she has already left to run errands. While he is struggling with his tie, Louisa asks him what he's doing. He explains. After about five minutes, Eduardo is ready to help Louisa. It takes him a while to **figure it out** but he finally helps her put on her shoes. Louisa thanks him and then says goodbye.

Skit 2   Eduardo is at work and everybody seems to be laughing. He asks Shelly (28, his co-worker) what's so funny. She tells him he might want to look in the mirror. Eduardo asks her to just tell him. Shelly points to his tie and says he shouldn't have tied it in a bow. While she helps him put his tie on properly, Eduardo thanks her and tells her he had a *stressful* morning. She asks him what happened. He tells her about how he had to put on his tie by himself and then had to **figure out** how to open his daughter's shoe buckle. He jokes that his daughter takes after him because both need help **figuring out** how things work.

Write sentences using the phrasal verb and bonus words in italics.

1. Could Rika figure out what Eduardo was saying in his sleep?

_____

2. Did Eduardo figure out how to put on his tie?

_____

3. Are you good at figuring out how to fix things?

_____

4. Is it hard to figure out what people are saying when you watch a TV program in English?

_____

Look Into   Explore an idea; research

Is followed by a noun phrase, pronoun, or verb phrase

You may hear it used like this: After **looking into** some colleges, she chose one near home.

It's time to meet some of our characters. Read these conversations aloud.

Hillary (17, a high school student): "Dad, I need to find a place to practice my *comedy act*."

Allen (41, Hillary's father): "Have you **looked into** performing at the *retirement home*? I'm sure the residents would enjoy a visit from *Hilarious* Hillary."

A while later . . .

Fran (89, a resident of the retirement home): "Have you ever **looked into** becoming a professional comedian? I think you're really funny."

Hillary: "Oh, thank you. No, I haven't **looked into** it because I can't write my own jokes. My dad writes them for me."

Let's perform the skits. Take roles, add your ideas, and practice the phrasal verbs.

Skit 1   The next week, Hillary visits Fran again. Hillary has decided to **look into** becoming a professional comedian and wants Fran's opinion. Is it important for a professional to write her own jokes? Fran doesn't think so. In fact, Fran has written some jokes for Hillary. Hillary likes them, so she asks Fran to travel around the country with her as her assistant. Fran says she'll **look into** leaving the retirement home, but she's not sure her family will think it's a good idea. They pay a lot of money for her to stay there. Then again, she adds, maybe her family will like the idea. Her great-grandson, Sean, often calls her Funny Fran.

Skit 2   Sean (14, Fran's great-grandson) is visiting Fran at the retirement home. After he asks her how she is, she says she wants to run something by him. Fran then tells him about how she is **looking into** travelling around the country with Hilarious Hillary. Does he think it is a good idea? Sean says that to help her decide, he will ask her some questions about the plan. Has Hillary **looked into** possible places to perform? Fran doesn't think so. Has Hillary figured out what they will charge? Fran says she'll have to **look into** it. Sean then asks if Fran is happy at the home. Yes, she is. Fran adds that the other residents are probably less happy, because they have to put up with her bad jokes.

Write sentences using the phrasal verb and bonus words in italics.

1. What does Hilarious Hillary have to look into before she can become a professional?

---

2. Does Fran want to look into leaving the retirement home?

---

3. Did you look into your English school before you chose it?

---

4. What kinds of things do you need to look into when choosing a home for a relative?

Make Up   Think of/invent something original (often a story or a lie)

Can take an object between the verb and the preposition

> You may hear it used like this: He's good at **making up** stories.

It's time to meet some of our characters. Read these conversations aloud.

Hank (42, Melinda's father): "So, Melinda, I hear you're having another *sleepover* tonight."

Melinda (12, a girl hosting a *slumber party* on Halloween): "Yes, but please promise you will not **make up** a scary story like you did last year. We couldn't sleep because we thought the man with three heads was going to come in the house."

A while later . . .

Janet (39, Melinda's mother): "Hank, Melinda's friends will be arriving any minute. Are the midnight snacks ready?"

Hank: "Yes. The *gingerbread men* I baked are done. Melinda didn't want me to **make up** any scary stories about three-headed men, so instead I **made up** a recipe for some scary three-headed cookies."

Let's perform the skits. Take roles, add your ideas, and practice the phrasal verbs.

Skit 1   Melinda is having her sleepover. At 2 a.m., she suggests that everyone go to sleep. Paula (12, a girl at the sleepover) says she'd rather **make up** a story. Melinda and the others agree to listen. They secretly hope it will be a scary story. Paula starts **making up** a story about a man who wears his clothes backwards. Melinda and the others begin *yawning*, and Melinda tells Paula that her story is boring. Melinda then says she'll go wake up her dad. He's much better at **making up** stories than Paula.

Skit 2   It's the afternoon after the slumber party. Hank has just had a nap because he told stories to the girls until 3 a.m. Janet asks him to mow the lawn. She says that the grass is as tall as she is. Hank jokes that five feet tall isn't so high. Hank then goes outside to mow the lawn. When he comes back inside, Hank asks Janet what she would like for dinner. Janet isn't sure. Hank says he can probably **make up** a good recipe using the leftover three-headed gingerbread cookies.

Write sentences using the phrasal verb and bonus words in italics.

1. What kind of recipe does Hank make up?

_____

2. What does Melinda do when Paula starts making up a story?

_____

3. Have you ever made up a convincing lie?

_____

4. Do you like making up new dishes or do you prefer to follow a recipe?

_____

Sleep On Consider for a day or two

Is followed by a noun phrase or pronoun

You may hear it used like this: I'm not sure I want to do that. I need to **sleep on** it.

It's time to meet some of our characters. Read these conversations aloud.

Ian (38, a man planning a vacation): "So, where do you want to go for our vacation? We could go to Burger Land or Hot Dog Heaven."

Lynn (32, Ian's wife): "Burger Land sounds fun, but I need to **sleep on** it. I have to decide if I want to eat hamburgers all day or hot dogs."

A while later . . .

Ian: "So, honey, have you decided where we should go?"

Lynn: "I **slept on** it and decided that I'd rather spend a week in Salad City. I heard that Dressing River is *spectacular.*"

Let's perform the skits. Take roles, add your ideas, and practice the phrasal verbs.

Skit 1 Ian and Lynn have been enjoying Salad City. One day, Ian visits Broccoli Falls by himself while Lynn goes to Lettuce Lake. At the falls, some large pieces of broccoli hit Ian on the head and knock him out. When he comes to, Donna (20, another tourist, who is also a lawyer) helps him up. Donna tells Ian he may want to *sue* Salad City. Ian asks why. Donna says that Salad City should have a sign that *warns* tourists not to stand under the falls. Ian says he'll have to **sleep on** it. He's not sure he wants to do that, but maybe he'll feel differently in a couple days. Ian then says he has to meet his wife at Lettuce Lake. Would Donna like to come? Donna agrees because she loves romaine lettuce.

Skit 2 Ian and Donna walk to Lettuce Lake. When they find Lynn, Ian introduces the women to each other. Ian asks Lynn what she has been doing at the lake (enjoying a book called "A Tale of Two Tomatoes"). Then, Lynn asks if Ian liked Broccoli Falls. Donna tells Lynn what happened there and that she recommends Ian sue Salad City. Ian says he's going to **sleep on** the idea. Lynn says he doesn't really need to **sleep on** it because Salad City has already given her a free month's stay. She explains that she was standing next to Dressing River when she accidentally fell in. They gave her the free vacation so she wouldn't sue.

Write sentences using the phrasal verb and bonus words in italics.

1. What made Lynn decide to go to Salad City after she slept on it for a while?

_____

2. Why doesn't Ian have to sleep on the idea of suing Salad City?

_____

3. When you decided to take an ESL class, did you sleep on it for a while?

_____

4. If someone rich and smart asked you to get married, would you sleep on it?

_____

Think Through   Think about very carefully

Can take an object between the verb and the preposition (often "it")

> You may hear it used like this: Be sure to **think it through** before you go to that college.

It's time to meet some of our characters. Read these conversations aloud.

Claudia (45, the mom): "Arturo, have you decided what kind of lessons you want to take this summer? Tennis or drum?"

Arturo (16, the son): "Well, Mom, I've had a while to **think this through**. I'd prefer drum lessons so I can wake up the neighbors when I practice late at night."

A while later . . .

Claudia: "Tara, please stop hitting those two pots together. It's too noisy."

Tara (14, Arturo's sister): "But, Mom, Arturo and I want to start a band. We've **thought it through** and have come up with a great name: The Headache Band."

Let's perform the skits. Take roles, add your ideas, and practice the phrasal verbs.

Skit 1   Claudia and Gabriel (46, her husband) are listening to Tara and Arturo play their instruments. Both adults now have a headache. Gabriel tells Tara that she bangs her pots with style. Claudia adds that Arturo has good rhythm. Gabriel asks the kids if they still want to start a band. Tara says that she and Arturo have really **thought it through**. They plan to perform at their school's *talent show* next week. Then they will perform for all the neighbors who haven't already heard them in the middle of the night. Arturo adds that they will be ready when the audience gets a headache. Can he have some money so he can buy a big bottle of *aspirin*?

Skit 2   Mr. Green (36, a record company employee) was at the school's talent show. He really liked The Headache Band as well as Loud Larry, who shouted into his microphone very well. Mr. Green wants to ask them to record an album for his record company. He calls Ms. Brown (55, his boss) and runs his idea by her. Ms. Brown says she might like to do that. However, the last band she worked with didn't sell any records, so she has to **think it through**. Mr. Green can give a presentation about it tomorrow at the office. When Mr. Green gets home, he practices his presentation. He will say that since The Headache Band didn't have a singer and Loud Larry didn't use any instruments, they can combine the bands into one and call it Larry and The Headaches.

Write sentences using the phrasal verb and bonus words in italics.

1. After thinking it through, why did Arturo decide to take drum lessons?

_____

2. Why does Ms. Brown need to think things through?

_____

3. How long would you think it through before asking someone to marry you?

_____

4. When you have to buy a birthday gift, do you think it through or do you buy something quickly?

_____

Chapter Review Questions

Rewrite each sentence using the correct phrasal verb. Choices: **come up with, figure out, look into, make up, sleep on, think through.**

1. She can't find a way to understand her math homework.

_____

2. He created a good recipe.

_____

3. They considered it very carefully.

_____

4. I was able to think of a good name for my dog.

_____

5. She needs to research it a little more.

_____

6. I'll think about it and let you know tomorrow.

_____

7. Before she accepted his marriage proposal she thought about it carefully.

_____

8. He doesn't know how to open the wine bottle, although he keeps trying.

_____

9. He'll let you know after he considers it for a day or two.

_____

10. Toby's mother researched the baseball camp before she let him go.

_____

11. Dickens was good at creating interesting characters for his books.

_____

12. She thought of ten reasons why she didn't want to do her chores.

_____

CHAPTER 11
IN LOVE (DATING)

Ask Out   Invite someone to go on a date

Always takes an object between the verb and the preposition

| You may hear it used like this: He **asked me out** yesterday and I accepted. |

It's time to meet some of our characters. Read these conversations aloud.

Mick (20, a college student): "Yasuko, I want to **ask my friend Erin out** but I'm not sure where we should go. Do you have any ideas?"

Yasuko (19, a girl in Mick's class): "Well, I usually take my dates to the swimming pool to see how many *laps* they can do."

A while later . . .

Yasuko: "So, did you **ask Erin out?**"

Mick: "Yes. We went to the pool, but she laughed at my *skinny* legs."

Let's perform the skits. Take roles, add your ideas, and practice the phrasal verbs.

Skit 1   Yasuko is flying home at the end of the semester. She is chatting with Timothy (21, another passenger) and asks him what he does (Olympic swimmer). She asks him why he has *shaved* his legs. He tells her that shaved legs help him go faster in the pool. Yasuko then decides to **ask him out**. Would he like to show her how many laps he can do in a pool? Timothy thanks her for **asking him out**, but he has already worked out in the pool today. Yasuko then asks if he can teach her how to shave her legs because she always cuts herself. When Timothy asks her if she uses shaving cream, she says no. Yasuko then **asks Timothy out** again. Would he like to help her buy some shaving cream at the drug store?

Skit 2   As soon as Timothy and Yasuko land, they go to a drug store. When Timothy gets home from his date, he tells Cheryl (25, his sister) about Yasuko. Cheryl tells Timothy she's surprised that Yasuko **asked him out** because his clothes are torn. Timothy says that Yasuko **asked him out** because she was interested in his personality, not his clothes. Also, she liked his legs. Cheryl then asks if he plans to see Yasuko again. Timothy says they might go to the pool sometime, although Yasuko admitted that she doesn't know how to swim.

Write sentences using the phrasal verb and bonus words in italics.

1. When Yasuko asks men out, what does she invite them to do?

_____

2. Why is Cheryl surprised that Yasuko asked Timothy out?

_____

3. Is it easy for you to ask someone out or are you shy?

_____

4. Do you get asked out often?

_____

Fall For   Fall in love with

Is followed by a noun phrase or pronoun

You may hear it used like this: He **fell for** her the first time he saw her.

It's time to meet some of our characters. Read these conversations aloud.

Jorge (32, a single man): "Brad, how did you meet Carol?"

Brad (30, a man dating Carol, 27): "Oh, I saw her at a wedding and **fell for** her immediately. She wasn't the bride, of course."

A while later . . .

Brad (introduces Carol, who has very long nails): "Stacey, I'd like you to meet Carol. She was a bridesmaid at a wedding I went to recently. I **fell for** her pretty nails."

Stacey (25, Brad's sister, who talks to Carol): "Nice to meet you, Carol. Wow, how do you eat with those three-inch yellow nails?"

Let's perform the skits. Take roles, add your ideas, and practice the phrasal verbs.

Skit 1   Carol is meeting Stacey at a nail salon. Stacey is going to get a *manicure* just like Carol's. While they *get their nails done*, Stacey asks Carol why she **fell for** Brad. Stacey wants to know because Brad is usually shy and doesn't talk to ladies very often. Carol says that she was having trouble eating because of her long nails, and Brad offered to help her. Carol says she **fell for** Brad because he was helpful and because he had such nice toenails. Stacey asks Carol how she could see his toenails. Carol says he was wearing sandals even though it was snowing.

Skit 2   When Stacey returns from the nail salon, Brad sees her long yellow fingernails. He asks her why she got them. She says she hopes a nice guy will **fall for** her, just like Brad **fell for** Carol. Brad tells her not to worry about meeting someone. She will **fall for** the right man when the time is right. Stacey then says she's ready for lunch. With her new nails, it will be difficult for her to eat. Can Brad help her? Brad says he'll be happy to help her now, but he won't always be available. Brad suggests that she learn how to eat without using her fingers.

Write sentences using the phrasal verb and bonus words in italics.

1. Why did Brad fall for Carol?

_____

2. Does Brad think someone will fall for Stacey now that she has long nails?

_____

3. Which movie star do you wish would fall for you?

_____

4. Did you like the last person who fell for you?

_____

Fix Up (With)/Set Up (With)   Arrange a date for someone else

"Fix up (with)" and "set up (with)" mean the same thing; if not followed by "with," always take an object between the verb and the preposition; if used with "with," always take an object between the verb and the prepositon, and are then followed by a noun phrase or pronoun

---

You may hear it used like this: Maggie **set him up with** her friend's daughter.

It's time to meet some of our characters. Read these conversations aloud.

Jaime (47, the dad): "Maria, I hope you don't mind, but I've **fixed you up with** a young man named Ronald. He'll be having *Thanksgiving* dinner with us tonight."

Maria (22, the daughter): "OK, but will there be enough turkey for everyone? I was planning to eat a lot."

A while later . . .

Maria: "Wow, I'm glad the evening is over. Ronald came across as really strange, don't you think?"

Conchita (43, Maria's mom): "Yes, he was a little weird. But you know that your dad is very good at **setting you up with** off-the-wall guys."

Let's perform the skits. Take roles, add your ideas, and practice the phrasal verbs.

Skit 1   After Thanksgiving dinner, Jaime sees Maria lying on the couch. She doesn't look very happy, so Jaime asks her what's wrong. Maria doesn't feel like talking because she had too much turkey. Jaime can tell she is unhappy, so he asks her to speak up. She asks him why he always **fixes her up with** *losers*. Jaime is surprised to hear this. He thought that the men he **set her up with** were nice. He asks her why she didn't like Ronald. She tells Jaime she didn't like it that Ronald *poked* her with his finger every five minutes. Jaime says he thought that was funny.

Skit 2   Maria wants Conchita to ask Jaime to stop **fixing her up**. She is tired of it. Conchita thinks that maybe Jaime is planning to arrange a date with another young man. She tells Maria she will try to talk him out of it. Maria then wants to know how Conchita met Jaime. Did she meet him at school? Did he meet her at a dance? Conchita says that Maria may be surprised, but a friend **set them up**. They went on a blind date and fell in love. Maria asks where they went on their first date. Conchita says they went to a donut factory.

Write sentences using the phrasal verb and bonus words in italics.

1. What kind of young man did Jaime set Maria up with for Thanksgiving dinner?

_____

2. Does Maria like it when Jaime fixes her up?

_____

3. Have you ever been fixed up with someone interesting? How about with a loser?

_____

4. If you were a parent, what kind of person would you set your son/daughter up with?

_____

Go Out (With)   Go on a date; be boyfriend/girlfriend

If not followed by "with," does not take an object; if used with "with," is followed by a noun phrase or pronoun

> You may hear it used like this: They **went out** for six months and then got married.

It's time to meet some of our characters. Read these conversations aloud.

Myra (17, a high school student): "Would you like to **go out with** me this evening?"

Aaron (17, Myra's boyfriend): "Great. Let's go to a fun restaurant I heard about. It's called the *Food Fight* Palace."

A while later . . .

Nadia (48, Aaron's mother): "Oh my goodness! What kind of girl are you **going out with**? She threw food all over you!"

Aaron: "Oh, she's a really nice girl. We went to the Food Fight Palace and had a lot of fun throwing mashed potatoes at each other."

Let's perform the skits. Take roles, add your ideas, and practice the phrasal verbs.

Skit 1 Aaron has asked Miguel (18, his friend) if he and Kim (17, Miguel's girlfriend) would like to **go out** on a *double date* with him and Myra. They all agree to go to the Food Fight Palace. Miguel reminds Aaron that he's *vegetarian*, so they order potato salad and peas, along with steak and fried chicken. In the middle of the meal, Myra asks Kim how long Kim and Miguel have been **going out** (one week). Then she asks Kim why she looks so unhappy. Kim says that the chicken leg Aaron just threw at her almost knocked her out. Miguel adds that he has peas in his ears. Kim then asks Miguel if he would like to eat dinner in another restaurant. He accepts and they head out the door.

Skit 2 Kim and Miguel go to a nice, clean restaurant. Kim helps Miguel take the peas out of his ears. Kim says that's the last time she'll **go out with** Myra and Aaron on a double date. Miguel agrees that **going out with** them was a mistake. He knew that Myra and Aaron enjoyed being messy, but he didn't realize how messy. Kim asks Miguel how long Aaron and Myra have been **going out**. Miguel thinks it's been about two months. Kim wants to know where Aaron and Myra met. Miguel thinks they fell for each other at a class on how to remove stains from clothing.

Write sentences using the phrasal verb and bonus words in italics.

1. When Myra and Aaron went out alone, what kind of meal did they have?

_____

2. Did Miguel and Kim enjoy going out with Aaron and Myra?

_____

3. When you go out on a date, where do you like to go?

_____

4. Describe the nicest person you've ever gone out with.

_____

Make Up (With)   Become friendly again after an argument

If not followed by "with," does not take an object; if used with "with," is followed by a noun phrase or pronoun

> You may hear it used like this: We had a fight but then we **made up**.

It's time to meet some of our characters. Read these conversations aloud.

Kirsten (24, the wife): "I don't know if I can forgive you for cutting my *bangs* so short. I look terrible."

Hans (29, the husband): "Honey, I didn't mean to cut them like that. If you **make up with** me now instead of next week, I'll let you *dye* my hair orange. Then we can both have *a bad hair day*."

A while later . . .

Mrs. Carter (52, Hans' boss): "Hans, your orange hair is unacceptable for the office. Please go home and fix it."

Hans: "I'm sorry I can't. My wife was mad at me this morning, so I let her dye my hair this awful color. If I change my hairstyle, I'll have to **make up with** her again."

Let's perform the skits. Take roles, add your ideas, and practice the phrasal verbs.

Skit 1   Kirsten wants Jill (25, her hairdresser) to make her hair look better. Jill asks what happened to her bangs, and Kirsten explains that her husband cut them too short. Kirsten then tells her that she wasn't mad at him for very long. She **made up with** him quickly because he let her dye his hair orange. Jill says how interesting, because she had a new customer this morning. The customer hated his orange hair and wanted her to shave his head. "Wow," Kirsten says, "shave my head too."

Skit 2   Hans and Kirsten agree that they both look bad without hair. Hans promises Kirsten that he will never cut her bangs again. He adds that if he could go back in time, he would **make up with** her by buying her some flowers. Kirsten promises to never bring up their bad hair day again. Hans *changes the subject* and asks her what she wants to do this weekend. She suggests they go buy some wigs. Hans gets mad that she brought up the subject of hair. They start having an argument. How will they **make up**?

Write sentences using the phrasal verb and bonus words in italics.

1. Why does Hans have to make up with Kirsten after he cuts her bangs?

___

2. How does Hans make up with Kirsten? Are both of them happy with the result?

___

3. How would you make up with your boyfriend/girlfriend if you cut his/her hair badly?

___

4. Do you usually make up quickly or do you stay angry for a long time?

___

Take Out (To)   Take on a date

If not followed by "to," always takes an object between the verb and the preposition; if used with "to," always takes an object between the verb and the preposition, and then is followed by a noun phrase or pronoun

You may hear it used like this: My girlfriend **took me out to** a fancy restaurant.

It's time to meet some of our characters. Read these conversations aloud.

Spike (45, husband of Felicity, 43): "I want to **take Felicity out** as a surprise. Do you think she would like to pick peaches at the local orchard? I can bake her a peach pie when we're done."

Penelope (40, Felicity's sister): "I'm sure she'd like that. But remember what happened last time you made a peach pie? She ate so much that she was almost sick."

A while later . . .

Penelope: "So, what did you do yesterday afternoon?"

Felicity: "Well, Spike **took me out to** the peach orchard but he forgot I was *afraid of heights*. So I read a book for three hours while he stood on a tall ladder to pick the fruit."

Let's perform the skits. Take roles, add your ideas, and practice the phrasal verbs.

Skit 1   Patricia (15, Spike and Felicity's daughter) is asking Spike why Felicity is lying on the couch. Spike tells her that he **took Felicity out** yesterday to pick some fresh peaches, and she has a stomachache from eating too much pie. Patricia then tells Spike she needs to bring something for her school's *bake sale* tomorrow. Spike asks her what kind of treat she wants to bring. Patricia says pie or cookies would be good. Spike says they have run out of pie, because Felicity ate it all. But maybe they can go to the orchard to get some cookies. Patricia tells Spike that cookies don't grow on trees. Spike says he knows that. A woman at the orchard was selling some cookies for the people picking the peaches.

Skit 2   The next morning, Felicity is feeling better, and she's helping Patricia get ready for school. Felicity asks Patricia if she would mind staying alone this Saturday for a few hours because Felicity is planning to **take Spike out**. Patricia asks where they are going. Felicity hasn't decided yet. They may pick lemons from the neighbor's tree so she can make a *lemon meringue pie*, or they may pick oranges in a nearby orchard so she can make *orange marmalade*. Either way, she is planning to eat too much of whatever she makes.

Write sentences using the phrasal verb and bonus words in italics.

1. What did Spike forget about Felicity when he took her out to the orchard?

_____

2. What will Felicity make after she takes Spike out on Saturday?

_____

3. Do you prefer to be taken out to dinner or the movies?

_____

4. When you take someone out, where do you like to go?

_____

Chapter Review Questions

Rewrite each sentence using the correct phrasal verb. Choices: **ask out, fall for, fix up (with)/set up (with), go out (with), make up (with), take out (to).**

1. They had a fight but then became friendly again.

_____

2. She took him on a date to the movies.

_____

3. They fell in love on their second date.

_____

4. He asked her if she wanted to go to the museum with him.

_____

5. My friend arranged a date for me.

_____

6. The couple has been dating for three years.

_____

7. Her aunt arranges dates for her, and the men are usually nice.

_____

8. My boyfriend and I are no longer fighting.

_____

9. She went on a date with him only once.

_____

10. I'd like to go with you to the ballpark.

_____

11. I'm too shy to ask the boy to go on a date with me.

_____

12. He fell in love with her immediately.

_____

CHAPTER 12

ON THE ROCKS
(HATING)

© caj 2002

Be Over/Get Over No longer be sad/upset (sometimes about a romance)

"Be over" and "get over" mean the same thing; are followed by a noun phrase or pronoun

You may hear it used like this: She hasn't **gotten over** him yet.

It's time to meet some of our characters. Read these conversations aloud.

Ralph (15, a high school student): "Hey, isn't that your ex-girlfriend Belinda? It looks like she's dating a new guy."

Bernie (16, Ralph's friend): "Yes, that's Belinda, but I **am over** her. Can you believe she ended our relationship because I like to wear a fake mustache?"

A while later . . .

Belinda (15, Bernie's ex-girlfriend): "Do you see that guy with the silly mustache? I used to go out with him."

Matthew (16, Belinda's new boyfriend): "Well, I'm glad you **got over** him and are now dating me. Do you like this fake beard I've been wearing?"

Let's perform the skits. Take roles, add your ideas, and practice the phrasal verbs.

Skit 1 Ralph and Belinda are working together on an experiment in chemistry class. They don't *have anything in common* so they start chatting about Bernie. Ralph asks her what she and Bernie used to do together. Belinda looks sad as she says they used to work out at the gym. Ralph asks her if she **is really over** Bernie. She admits that she thought she had **gotten over** him, but talking about him makes her want to go out with him again. She asks him for Bernie's phone number because she thinks he changed it. Ralph asks how she knew that. She admits that she has been *making crank calls* to his number but an old man always answers. Ralph must decide whether or not to give her the number.

Skit 2 After chemistry class, Ralph sees Bernie in the cafeteria and tells him about his conversation with Belinda. Ralph says that Belinda looked very sad when she told him she hadn't really **gotten over** Bernie. Bernie seems very interested and asks him what else she said. Ralph tells him about the crank calling. Bernie smiles and admits that they used to make crank calls to people after they went to the gym. Ralph guesses that Bernie **isn't over** her. Ralph thinks that these two crank callers *are made for each other*, so he suggests that Bernie make up with her if he still loves her. Ralph decides to change his own phone number so they don't make crank calls to him.

Write sentences using the phrasal verb and bonus words in italics.

1. Is Belinda really over Bernie?

_____

2. Why does Ralph suspect that Bernie hasn't gotten over Belinda?

_____

3. How long did it take you to get over your first boyfriend/girlfriend?

_____

4. If someone you were over asked you out again, what would you do?

_____

Be Through (With)   Be finished (sometimes with a romance)

If not followed by "with," does not take an object; if used with "with," is followed by a noun phrase or pronoun

You may hear it used like this:	They decided they **were through** and got a divorce.

It's time to meet some of our characters. Read these conversations aloud.

Suzanne (40, a lady who sees a man kissing a woman): "Oh my goodness! **Is Klaus through with** his wife Olga?"

Jessica (39, Suzanne's friend, who recently got divorced): "Hey, that's not Klaus *smooching* the lady! That's his twin brother, Albert. Klaus never wears pajamas in public."

A while later . . .

Jessica: "Hi, Olga. Yesterday, Suzanne and I thought you and Klaus **were through**. But it was just Albert kissing a lady. What a relief!"

Olga (41, Klaus' wife): "How interesting! Was Albert wearing his striped or plaid PJs?"

Let's perform the skits. Take roles, add your ideas, and practice the phrasal verbs.

Skit 1   Jessica and Olga are having lunch together. Jessica is still not over her divorce and is telling Olga about her ex-husband Sandy (41). Jessica explains how she and Sandy went on a *romantic getaway* to Greece six months ago. However, it wasn't very romantic, because on this trip she decided she **was through with** him. Olga asks what happened. Jessica explains that Sandy started playing with the sand like a baby. It was very embarrassing. Olga tells Jessica she's sorry and then asks her if she **is through with** her sandwich. Jessica says yes, and adds that she shouldn't have ordered it. Seeing "sand"-wiches always reminds her of Sandy, who ate one every day for breakfast.

Skit 2   Olga is a waitress and has just noticed Sandy is a customer at the restaurant where she works. Olga asks him how he's been since his divorce from Jessica. He says he's happy to be single. Olga then takes his dinner order. He orders a roast beef sandwich *with everything on it*. When Olga returns with the sandwich, she asks Sandy if he is dating anyone. Sandy answers that no, he **is through with** dating. He has decided to focus on starting a business. Olga asks him what kind. He answers that he wants to open a sandwich shop called The Sand Witch. He just needs to find a waitress willing to dress up as a witch.

Write sentences using the phrasal verb and bonus words in italics.

1. Was Klaus really through with Olga?

_____

2. Why did Jessica decide she was through with Sandy?

_____

3. What does your teacher do when he/she is through with the lesson if there is still time?

_____

4. When you're through with a good book, do you lend it to someone else?

_____

Break Up (With) End a romance

If not followed by "with," does not take an object; if used with "with," is followed by a noun phrase or pronoun

You may hear it used like this: We **broke up** and started dating other people.

It's time to meet some of our characters. Read these conversations aloud.

Karl (32, the boyfriend): "Your high voice has been *getting on my nerves* lately. I think we should **break up.**"

Cecilia (29, the girlfriend, whose voice is unusually high): "What? You can't come up with a better reason after six years together? *Personally, I think* my nail biting is more annoying."

A while later . . .

Cecilia (who is talking in her high voice): "Karl **broke up with** me today. He said my voice gets on his nerves."

Jackie (30, Cecilia's friend): "Well, your voice is somewhat annoying. There must be another reason, because he put up with your voice for six years."

Let's perform the skits. Take roles, add your ideas, and practice the phrasal verbs.

Skit 1 Karl is having *brunch* with Beatrice (30, his sister) and is telling her about **breaking up with** Cecilia. Beatrice says she likes Cecilia and can't understand why Karl wanted to end the relationship. Karl decides to speak like Cecilia so that Beatrice can see how annoying Cecilia's voice is. He starts asking Beatrice various questions using the highest voice he can. Beatrice answers all the questions in the lowest voice she can and then tells him that she *gets the point*. They both laugh in their normal voices.

Skit 2 A few days after Karl **broke up with** Cecilia, she is talking with Jackie. Cecilia wants her friend's opinion. Should Cecilia get voice lessons and learn how to speak more deeply? Jackie says that it might be something to look into. Cecilia asks Jackie if she thinks her voice will put men off if she tries to date again. Jackie says that Cecilia should try to speak more deeply when she first meets someone. A few men may **break up with** her after they hear her real voice, but she should keep trying. Jackie thinks Cecilia has a really nice personality.

Write sentences using the phrasal verb and bonus words in italics.

1. Why does Karl want to break up with Cecilia?

_____

2. What are Karl and Beatrice doing when Karl tells her he broke up with Cecilia?

_____

3. Would you break up with someone if that person got on your nerves?

_____

4. Is a restaurant a good place to break up with someone?

_____

Have It Out (With)　Resolve a problem by having a discussion or fight

If not followed by "with," does not take an object; if used with "with," is followed by a noun phrase or pronoun

You may hear it used like this:　They **had it out** at 3 a.m. and woke up the neighbors.

It's time to meet some of our characters. Read these conversations aloud.

Amber (27, a woman having a party at her house): "Can you believe that my husband Jerry ate all of the appetizers? The dinner party hasn't even started yet!"

Lorenzo (25, a guest who arrived a few minutes early): "You better **have it out with** him before he eats the main course too."

A while later . . .

Amber: "So, Dana, last night Jerry and I had a dinner party, and it *was such a disaster*! He ate twenty deviled eggs!"

Dana (26, Amber's friend): "At least you didn't need to **have it out** at 4 a.m. like the last time. Didn't you once find him eating a whole roast chicken in the middle of the night?"

Let's perform the skits. Take roles, add your ideas, and practice the phrasal verbs.

Skit 1　Amber doesn't like having arguments about food with Jerry (30, her husband). They've **had it out** five times in the last month. She wants to recommend that Jerry start attending an eating support group. She just needs to find the right time to bring it up. One night, Amber mentions a group she has heard about: The Naughty *Nibblers*. She tells Jerry that she thinks he has a problem with eating food when he's not supposed to. Jerry admits that he takes food because he knows she will be mad, and he likes **having it out with** her. She looks especially beautiful when she is a little angry.

Skit 2　Two months later, Amber is showing Dana some photos. Dana notices that a lot of the photos are of Amber pretending to look angry. Others are of Jerry looking in the refrigerator. Dana asks Amber why there are so many pictures of the refrigerator. Amber explains that after the dinner party she made up with Jerry. She and Jerry pretend to **have it out**, and then take photos. He looks in the fridge and pretends to eat, and she takes a picture. Then, she pretends to be mad and **have it out** with him, and he takes a picture. Dana says that now she knows why Jerry is looking thinner. He is no longer eating so much.

Write sentences using the phrasal verb and bonus words in italics.

1. Why does Amber need to have it out with Jerry before he eats the main course?

_____

2. Why do Amber and Jerry pretend to have it out?

_____

3. When you have it out with someone, do you argue loudly?

_____

4. Do you always make up with your best friend after you have it out?

_____

Kick Out/Throw Out   Make someone move out

"Kick out" and "throw out" mean the same thing; can take an object between the verb and the preposition

> You may hear it used like this: She **threw him out** so he had to find a new apartment.

It's time to meet some of our characters. Read these conversations aloud.

Becky (24, Antonia's neighbor, who sees a lot of clothes outside the house): "Hi, Antonia. I didn't
    know you were having a *garage sale* today. Has anyone bought anything yet?"
Antonia (23, a woman dating Tyler): "Actually, these are Tyler's things. I **kicked him out** this
    morning. But maybe I should sell his stuff. He owes me money for the phone bill."

A while later . . .

Tyler (24, Antonia's boyfriend, who is in his friend's car): "Thanks for driving me to my girlfriend's
    house. I hope she no longer wants to **throw me out**. I forgot to feed her fish and it died."
Bruno (25, Tyler's friend): "Is that her house with all the cool things on the front lawn? Wow, a
    garage sale! I love browsing at garage sales."

Let's perform the skits. Take roles, add your ideas, and practice the phrasal verbs.

Skit 1   While Bruno is looking at the items for sale, Tyler and Antonia discuss their future together.
Antonia says she **kicked him out** because he owes her $139.68 for his half of the phone bill, and
he killed her fish. Bruno *apologizes profusely* for not feeding the fish. Just then, Bruno says that he
really likes the wide selection of items for sale. He wants to know how much the yellow leather
jacket and the blue roller skates are. Before Antonia can answer, Tyler tells Bruno that those are his
prized possessions and Bruno can't have them. Antonia must then decide whether or not to sell the
items to Bruno.

Skit 2   Tyler is sitting in a coffee shop looking sad. Becky sees him and asks what's wrong. He tells
her that Antonia **threw him out** yesterday. Becky says she already knows about that. She helped
Antonia put price tags on most of the items for the garage sale. Tyler asks Becky how he can
convince Antonia to make up with him. Becky says she's not sure it's possible. This morning she saw
another guy in Antonia's front yard wearing a leather jacket and roller skates. She thinks that he is
Antonia's new boyfriend. His name is Bruno.

Write sentences using the phrasal verb and bonus words in italics.

1. Why did Antonia kick Tyler out?

_____

2. How does Becky know that Antonia threw Tyler out?

_____

3. If you kicked someone out, would you throw his or her clothes out the window?

_____

4. Has anyone ever thrown you out?

_____

Walk Out On   Abandon/suddenly end a relationship and leave

Is followed by a noun phrase or pronoun

You may hear it used like this: She cried when her husband **walked out on** her.

It's time to meet some of our characters. Read these conversations aloud.

Olivia (27, Guy's wife): "Zelda, can I stay at *your place* tonight? I've decided to **walk out on** Guy. I'm tired of taking care of his cats all day."

Zelda (27, Olivia's friend): "Sure you can. But would you mind taking care of my three dogs this evening? I need to run some errands."

A while later . . .

Guy (30, Olivia's husband): "So, Olivia **walked out on** me this weekend. She was mad that I never cleaned up after the cats."

Jason (32, Guy's brother): "Sorry to hear that. Why do you keep seven cats if you don't like changing *kitty litter*?"

Let's perform the skits. Take roles, add your ideas, and practice the phrasal verbs.

Skit 1   Olivia has been staying at Zelda's house for the past week. One evening, Olivia tells Zelda that she is *having second thoughts*. Maybe she shouldn't have **walked out on** Guy. They have been married for three years and have generally been happy. Zelda asks her if she would *get back together with* Guy if he got rid of the cats. Olivia says she might. Zelda suggests that they go to Guy's house to see if Guy is having fun taking care of the cats. Olivia laughs, saying she can imagine him chasing the cats around the house.

Skit 2   When Olivia and Zelda arrive at Guy's front door, they hear Guy shouting inside. He is saying, "Listen up kitties! You've already caused Olivia to **walk out on** me. Now you're making me crazy!" Olivia laughs but feels bad. Zelda opens the door, and they see cats everywhere. Two cats are on top of the refrigerator. Three are in the sink. Guy is chasing two more. Olivia says hello to Guy. He is really happy to see her and apologizes for never taking care of the cats. Olivia agrees that he is not good at taking care of them. Olivia then apologizes for **walking out on** him. She adds that Zelda loves animals and has offered to take all seven cats. Zelda looks very surprised.

Write sentences using the phrasal verb and bonus words in italics.

1. Where does Olivia want to stay when she walks out on Guy?

_____

2. Is Olivia having second thoughts about walking out on Guy?

_____

3. Whose house would you stay at if you walked out on someone?

_____

4. How long would you cry if someone walked out on you?

_____

Chapter Review Questions

Rewrite each sentence using the correct phrasal verb. Choices: **be over/get over, be through (with), break up (with), have it out (with), kick out/throw out, walk out on.**

1. She ended the relationship with him.

_____

2. He had to find a new apartment because she made him move out.

_____

3. They had an argument in the middle of the night.

_____

4. He left her suddenly.

_____

5. The young lady was no longer sad that the young man was no longer her boyfriend.

_____

6. The couple decided their relationship was over and got a divorce.

_____

7. They resolved their disagreement by yelling.

_____

8. I still love him.

_____

9. He made her leave the house.

_____

10. I suspected we were finished when my girlfriend never answered my phone calls.

_____

11. I don't like ending a romance.

_____

12. When she left unexpectedly, he became sad.

_____

CHAPTER 13
THROUGH THICK AND THIN
(FRIENDS)

Come By/Stop By   Visit someone/go somewhere for a short time

"Come by" and "stop by" mean about the same thing ("come by" suggests you are coming somewhere; "stop by" suggests you are going somewhere); usually do not take an object but when they do, are followed by a noun phrase

You may hear it used like this: He **came by** to see the new puppy.

It's time to meet some of our characters. Read these conversations aloud.

Sybil (65, a grandma who is calling her granddaughter): "Hi, Polly. Can Grandpa and I **stop by** later? We'd like you to meet our new pet grasshopper. Mr. Hopper is really big."
Polly (5, Sybil's granddaughter): "Sure, Grandma. While you're here, I'd like to introduce Mr. Hopper to my new lizard, Lizzy. She loves grasshoppers."

A while later . . .
Polly: "Wow, Grandpa. Mr. Hopper is so much bigger than Lizzy!"
Basil (67, Polly's grandpa): "That's good. We don't want Lizzy to eat Mr. Hopper. We'll **come by** another time with lots of other grasshoppers. They can have fun chasing each other."

Let's perform the skits. Take roles, add your ideas, and practice the phrasal verbs.

Skit 1   Basil is asking Sybil why they don't **stop by** Polly's house more often. He really enjoyed seeing Mr. Hopper chase Lizzy. Sybil reminds him that their car broke down last year and it still hasn't been fixed. Sybil says they don't see Polly more often because her house is ten miles away, which is a long way to walk. Basil says he's still looking into how much it will cost to fix the car. Sybil asks him if he can take the car to the shop tomorrow because she is tired of walking everywhere. Basil says that he was thinking of **stopping by** the shop but he doesn't know how to get the car there. Sybil suggests calling a tow truck.

Skit 2   Basil is talking to Manuel (37, the *mechanic*). Basil tells him it's too expensive to tow the car to the shop. Manuel offers to **come by** Basil's house to look at the car. Manuel and Basil arrange a time for Manuel to **stop by**. When Manuel **stops by** later on, Basil thanks him for coming and tells him the car is in the garage. Manuel says he'll *take a look at* it. A minute later, Manuel screams in terror. Basil runs to see what the problem is. When he sees why Manuel is scared, he laughs. He asks Manuel if he is really afraid of twenty little grasshoppers. Basil explains that he has been letting some of his pet grasshoppers live in the car.

Write sentences using the phrasal verb and bonus words in italics.

1. Why did Sybil and Basil want to come by Polly's house?

_____

2. What happens when Manuel stops by Basil's house?

_____

3. How often do you stop by your best friend's house?

_____

4. When someone you're not expecting comes by, what food or drink do you serve?

_____

Get Along (With)   Have a good relationship

If not followed by "with," does not take an object; if used with "with," is followed by a noun phrase or pronoun

You may hear it used like this: She **gets along well with** her mother-in-law.

It's time to meet some of our characters. Read these conversations aloud.

Kristina (20, a college student): "Mom, I haven't been **getting along with** my roommate, Gladys. She wanted me to bring a toaster for the apartment. When I didn't, she started being mean to me."

Janice (47, Kristina's mom): "Well, maybe you can let her borrow the old toaster that's in the garage. It might be broken, though."

A while later . . .

Kristina: "Hi, Mom. The toaster works, but Gladys and I are still not **getting along**."

Janice: "Sorry to hear that. Have you tried buying her some bread to put in the toaster?"

Let's perform the skits. Take roles, add your ideas, and practice the phrasal verbs.

Skit 1   It's *Spring Break* and Kristina is at home. Alejandro (46, her father) asks her what she's been learning at school. Kristina tells him that she recently sat in on an interesting class: Toaster Repair. Alejandro *frowns*, thinking his daughter is not studying hard. Kristina tells him not to worry because she is getting good grades. Alejandro then asks her if she is **getting along better with** Gladys. Kristina tells him that they **get along well** now. Kristina explains that she bought Gladys a microwave to go with the toaster, so Gladys decided to make up with her.

Skit 2   Gladys is also home for Spring Break. She is telling Mitch (45, her father) that until recently she hadn't been **getting along with** her roommate Kristina. Mitch asks her why they were fighting. Gladys tells him about the toaster. She then mentions that she made up with Kristina when Kristina gave her a new microwave. Mitch asks her to describe it. Gladys says it's a really nice orange microwave. Mitch then suggests that she continue to **get along with** Kristina. Maybe Kristina will give her a refrigerator next.

Write sentences using the phrasal verb and bonus words in italics.

1. When does Kristina tell Alejandro that she hasn't been getting along with Gladys?

_____

2. Why did Kristina and Gladys start getting along again?

_____

3. Do you get along well with your family?

_____

4. If you didn't get along with a roommate, would you have it out or change roommates?

_____

Hang Out (With)   Relax and not do very much

If not followed by "with," does not take an object; if used with "with," is followed by a noun phrase or pronoun

You may hear it used like this: The two friends like to **hang out** together.

It's time to meet some of our characters. Read these conversations aloud.

Scott (13, a boy having a pool party): "Listen up, everybody. It's going to rain, so unless you want to get wet, let's go **hang out** in the house."

Trevor (14, a guest at the pool party): "Well, I'm already wet from swimming in the pool, so I think I'll stay outside."

A while later . . .

Trevor: "So, Scott, what did you all do while I **hung out** in the pool by myself?"

Scott: "Well, we decided to be *nosy* and look at the *report card* in your backpack. I can't believe you failed *Woodshop*! It's not difficult to make a wooden duck."

Let's perform the skits. Take roles, add your ideas, and practice the phrasal verbs.

Skit 1 Gretchen (37, Trevor's mom) is asking Trevor if he liked **hanging out with** his friends. He tells her he did, although they made fun of him for failing Woodshop. Gretchen tells him not to worry that he couldn't *carve* a wooden duck. She says that the next time Trevor **hangs out with** Scott, Trevor should tell him that he's writing a cookbook: "How to Cook and Carve a Duck." Trevor agrees, saying he may not know how to carve a duck in Woodshop, but he can carve one very well at the dinner table.

Skit 2 Trevor has asked Scott if he would like to **hang out** on Saturday. Scott agrees to come by around noon. Trevor plans to tell Scott about the cookbook and teach him how to carve a duck. On Saturday morning, Trevor cooks the duck. When Scott arrives, he asks what's giving off that great smell. Trevor points to the duck and asks him if he would like to learn to carve a real duck. Scott agrees and asks Trevor how he knows so much about cooking. Trevor tells Scott about the cookbook. Trevor then adds that he **hangs out with** world-famous cooks. In fact, tonight, Trevor will be **hanging out with** Tom A. Toe, the world-famous tomato cook.

Write sentences using the phrasal verb and bonus words in italics.

1. What did Scott do while Trevor hung out in the pool?

_____

2. What will Trevor teach Scott to do when they hang out together?

_____

3. Who is your favorite person to hang out with?

_____

4. This weekend, are you planning to hang out with someone in your class?

_____

Keep Up (With)   Stay in contact, even after a lot of time has passed

If not followed by "with," does not take an object; if used with "with," is followed by a noun phrase or pronoun

You may hear it used like this: I didn't **keep up with** my best friend from high school.

It's time to meet some of our characters. Read these conversations aloud.

Yvonne (30, Lewis' sister): "Lewis, didn't you used to know someone named Rufus? It says in the paper that a guy named Rufus Hoffman has just opened a bridal shop. I think it's near your house."

Lewis (32, a single man): "Yeah, I knew Rufus in high school, but we didn't **keep up**. If I can ever *get up the nerve to* ask my girlfriend to marry me, maybe Rufus will give us a discount on a wedding gown."

A while later . . .

Lewis: "Honey, let's go to the new bridal shop on Marriage Lane. I knew the owner in high school, but I didn't **keep up with** him. But we might still be able to get a cheap wedding dress."

Doris (28, Lewis' girlfriend of five years): "What are you getting at? If you're finally asking me to marry you, I will. But I want a beautiful wedding gown, not an ugly one."

Let's perform the skits. Take roles, add your ideas, and practice the phrasal verbs.

Skit 1   Rufus is working at his new shop, and *business is booming*. Lewis and Doris are browsing when Rufus recognizes Lewis. Rufus says hi to Lewis, who introduces Doris. Rufus congratulates them on their engagement. Doris then asks both men why they didn't **keep up with** each other. Lewis answers that he didn't **keep up with** anyone from school. Rufus says he didn't either, but he wishes he had. Rufus then asks Doris if Lewis still gets lost easily. Doris tells Rufus that Lewis is much better at finding places than he used to be. It took him only one hour to find the bridal shop.

Skit 2   Carmella (51, Doris' mother) is helping Doris come up with a list of people to invite to the wedding. Doris says she can't think of anyone to invite. She explains that she and Lewis don't have many friends because they didn't **keep up with** anyone from school. Carmella says that it sounds like the wedding will be very small. Most likely, only a few relatives from each family will attend. Carmella asks Doris if she would like to *elope* instead. Doris says that she would, except that she just bought the most expensive wedding dress in Rufus' bridal shop.

Write sentences using the phrasal verb and bonus words in italics.

1. Why didn't Lewis keep up with Rufus?

_____

2. What does Carmella suggest when Doris says she didn't keep up with anyone from school?

_____

3. Do you like keeping up with old friends?

_____

4. If someone you hadn't kept up with suddenly contacted you, what would you do?

_____

Look Up   Contact someone you haven't seen in a while

Can take an object between the verb and the preposition

> You may hear it used like this: She **looked up** a boyfriend she hadn't seen in ten years.

It's time to meet some of our characters. Read these conversations aloud.

Jean-Paul (32, a man with fair skin): "Do you remember Dave Beach from high school? Although he used to make fun of my pale skin, he was good at taking care of our pet rabbit when we went on vacation. I wonder what he's doing now."

Vivienne (30, Jean-Paul's sister): "I remember him. He was kind of unfriendly and very tanned, but our bunny really liked him. You should **look him up**."

A while later . . .

Jean-Paul: "I've been trying to figure out what to say to Dave when I **look him up**."

Vivienne: "Well, he probably won't be impressed that you sell hairbrushes. You should probably make up a story about being a famous ESL teacher."

Let's perform the skits. Take roles, add your ideas, and practice the phrasal verbs.

Skit 1   Jean-Paul has found Dave's phone number and is looking forward to talking with him. Jean-Paul tells Vivienne that before he actually **looks Dave up**, he wants to practice what he will say with Vivienne. She agrees to pretend to be an unfriendly Dave, who is interested only in getting a good tan. Jean-Paul will practice what he's going to say about being a famous ESL teacher. Jean-Paul starts the role play by saying, "Hi, Dave. This is Jean-Paul, the really pale guy from Sunny High. Remember me? I wanted to **look you up** because. . . . "

Skit 2   *The big day* has arrived. Jean-Paul has practiced what he is going to say, so he is ready. He calls Dave (32) and says, "Hi, Dave. This is Jean-Paul, the really pale guy from Sunny High. Remember me? I wanted to **look you up** because. . . . " When Jean-Paul is finished, Dave says how glad he is that Jean-Paul **looked him up**. Dave then apologizes for being unfriendly during high school. Jean-Paul says he's gotten over it. Dave then asks Jean-Paul if he'd like to visit Dave's business, a pet store called *Beach Bunnies*. Jean-Paul asks how he will recognize Dave. Dave says he'll be the one dressed up as a rabbit.

Write sentences using the phrasal verb and bonus words in italics.

1. How does Jean-Paul prepare for the day when he will look Dave up?

_____

2. What happens when Jean-Paul looks Dave up?

_____

3. Have you ever looked up an old classmate?

_____

4. In five years, do you think you'll look up your ESL teacher?

_____

Run Into   Unexpectedly meet (usually someone you know)

Is followed by a noun phrase or pronoun

You may hear it used like this: She **ran into** her best friend at the mall.

It's time to meet some of our characters. Read these conversations aloud.

Violet (21, a recent college graduate): "Hey, Wanda, I **ran into** Beau last night. He told me he enjoyed taking you out to the zoo last month."

Wanda (22, Violet's friend): "Really? I didn't enjoy our date at all. Beau tried to talk me into petting a really long snake, so I took off."

A while later . . .

Beau (24, Wanda's date last month): "Kirk, I've been hoping to meet a woman who likes snakes. What should I do?"

Kirk (26, Beau's brother): "Why don't you just spend this afternoon at the zoo's reptile house? *You're bound to* **run into** some nice ladies there."

Let's perform the skits. Take roles, add your ideas, and practice the phrasal verbs.

Skit 1   Beau has decided to *take Kirk's advice* and is at the zoo. He has been standing next to the python exhibit for about two hours but he hasn't met anyone to ask out. He is getting hungry. On the way to the snack bar, he **runs into** Neil (28, his friend). Beau tells Neil he is glad he **ran into** him because Beau needs some help finding a woman who likes snakes. Neil asks him why he's looking for a date at the zoo. Beau explains why he's spent the last two hours standing next to the python exhibit. Beau adds that he has been making a *hissing* noise to attract women. Should he be doing something different?

Skit 2   Wanda has just **run into** Beau at the mall. Wanda tells Beau she's surprised to **run into** him because most men don't like shopping. She then asks him how he has been since their date (lonely). Beau then tells her about his recent visit to the zoo. Surprised, Wanda mentions that yesterday she **ran into** a friend, Cassie, who recently went to the zoo as well. Wanda says that Cassie told her about a guy who was *making a fool of himself* in front of the python exhibit. Cassie wanted to talk with him but was too shy.

Write sentences using the phrasal verb and bonus words in italics.

1. When Beau runs into Neil, do you think Neil tells him to do something different?

_____

2. What happens when Beau runs into Wanda at the mall?

_____

3. Have you ever run into a famous person?

_____

4. If you ran into a classmate at a restaurant, would you invite him/her to sit with you?

_____

Chapter Review Questions

Rewrite each sentence using the correct phrasal verb. Choices: **come by/stop by, get along (with), hang out (with), keep up (with), look up, run into.**

1. My friends and I like to relax together on weekends.

_____

2. I didn't expect to see him, but I saw him at the store.

_____

3. She and her sister were not friendly with each other.

_____

4. They didn't write letters to each other.

_____

5. The plumber will visit the house at 3 p.m.

_____

6. He decided to contact his old friend.

_____

7. She saw her grandpa by chance when she was shopping for his Christmas present.

_____

8. I relaxed at home last night.

_____

9. May I go to your house tomorrow evening?

_____

10. I was curious about what she was doing, so I contacted her.

_____

11. She was very good at writing to old friends.

_____

12. I enjoy being with my classmates.

_____

CHAPTER 14

ON GOOD TERMS
(NICE)

Go Along With   Agree to something although you don't really want to

Is followed by a noun phrase or pronoun

> You may hear it used like this: He **went along with** the idea although he didn't like it.

It's time to meet some of our characters. Read these conversations aloud.

Carlito (34, a man who likes watching TV): "Simone, I'm tired of watching this TV. The sound has been broken for months."

Simone (32, Carlito's wife): "OK. If you want to buy a new one I'll **go along with** it, but you don't really need sound to watch the Ice Skating Channel."

A while later . . .

Carlito: "I'd like to buy the biggest TV you have. But please don't mention it to my wife. She doesn't know I plan to spend so much money."

T. J. (25, the TV salesman): "OK, I'll **go along with** it, but if I do, I'll have to *charge you double*."

Let's perform the skits. Take roles, add your ideas, and practice the phrasal verbs.

Skit 1   Simone has been watching the new TV a lot and has discovered the *Sign Language* Channel. One afternoon, she tells Carlito that she has learned a little sign language. Carlito asks her to teach him the signs she's learned. A while later, Simone asks Carlito if they can communicate in sign language one evening a week. He tells her it sounds like a strange idea, but he'll **go along with** it. Later that afternoon, however, after they do sign language for an hour, Carlito tells Simone he's sorry he **went along with** it. It took him fifteen minutes just to ask her what they were having for dinner.

Skit 2   Carlito is calling Toni (55, his mother). He tells her that Simone laughs at him when he watches the Ice Skating Channel. He then mentions that he and Simone have learned some sign language. He tells Toni that since he had to **go along with** Simone's idea, he wants to get Simone to **go along with** an idea of his own. He runs his idea by Toni. If Simone will pretend to skate for him one evening a week, he will stop watching the Ice Skating Channel. Toni thinks it's a good idea but is not sure Simone will **go along with** it. Toni asks him how long it will take him to get across his idea in sign language. Carlito thinks it might take two hours.

Write sentences using the phrasal verb and bonus words in italics.

1. Why does Carlito go along with Simone's idea to use sign language?

_____

2. Does Toni think Simone will go along with Carlito's idea?

_____

3. If your teacher asked you to hop on one leg while saying the alphabet, would you go along with it?

_____

4. Do children always go along with what their parents ask them to do?

_____

Look After   Take care of

Is followed by a noun phrase or pronoun

You may hear it used like this: She **looked after** me when I was sick.

It's time to meet some of our characters. Read these conversations aloud.

Suzette (75, Grace's friend): "Hi, how is your husband? I heard Reggie broke his leg this weekend."
Grace (73, Reggie's wife): "Yeah, he fell down while riding his *unicycle*. Do you want to help me
look after him this afternoon? He's really *grumpy* today."

A while later . . .

Suzette: "Hi, Reggie. I'm here to help Grace **look after** you. Can I get you anything?"
Reggie (79, the *invalid*): "Thanks, but I don't need to be **looked after**. I need my unicycle back."

Let's perform the skits. Take roles, add your ideas, and practice the phrasal verbs.

Skit 1   Reggie tells Grace he's upset because she won't let him sit on his unicycle until his leg gets better. Grace tells Reggie she's upset because he won't let her **look after** him. Grace asks Suzette to help her figure out a way to make Reggie feel better. Suzette says to Grace, "Remember that Reggie and I have been taking unicycle lessons. Maybe I can ride my unicycle in the living room and entertain Reggie." Grace thinks that's a great idea. However, she must talk Suzette out of riding the unicycle on the coffee table. She doesn't want Suzette to hurt herself. If she did, Grace would have two crazy unicyclists to **look after**.

Skit 2   Reggie has been resting at home for the last three weeks. Grace has finally let him use his *crutches* and go to a nearby park. He brings some bread to feed the pigeons. When he gets there, he sees Ginny (85, a neighbor), who is already feeding them. Ginny asks Reggie what happened to his leg, so he explains. Reggie then tells her he appreciates that Grace has been **looking after** him, but he wants his independence. Reggie then asks Ginny why she is letting all the pigeons sit on her head and shoulders. Ginny answers that she forgot to bring her hat and coat, so the pigeons are keeping her warm.

Write sentences using the phrasal verb and bonus words in italics.

1. Why does Grace need to look after Reggie?

_____

2. Does Reggie enjoy being looked after?

_____

3. Have you ever had to look after an invalid?

_____

4. If you had to use crutches, would you want someone to look after you?

_____

Look Out For   Make sure another person is OK

Is followed by a noun phrase or pronoun

You may hear it used like this: Big sisters always **look out for** their little brothers.

It's time to meet some of our characters. Read these conversations aloud.

Kara (40, Elena and Ernie's mom): "Elena, remember that Ernie is starting at your school tomorrow. Please be sure to **look out for** him."

Elena (11, Ernie's big sister): "OK, but can you tell him not to wear his *earmuffs* in the classroom? The other kids will probably make fun of him because it's hot outside."

A while later . . .

Cody (7, the class *bully*): "Who's that girl following you?"

Ernie (6, Elena's brother): "Oh, that's my big sister. She's **looking out for** me, so you should probably stop wearing my earmuffs."

Let's perform the skits. Take roles, add your ideas, and practice the phrasal verbs.

Skit 1   Kara is asking Ernie if he enjoyed his first day of school. Ernie tells her he liked being in class better than playing at *recess*. In class, Elena wasn't **looking out for** him. He appreciates that his sister is making sure he's OK, but she was watching him too closely at recess. Kara says she will tell Elena not to **look out for** him so much. Ernie says he doesn't mind if Elena **looks out for** him for a few more days. He was hoping she would ride the slide with him tomorrow at recess.

Skit 2   A week later, Kara is talking with Elena about Ernie. She asks Elena if Ernie is doing well at school. Elena says that he has *made some friends* and has started a club, The Earmuff Boys. The boys hang out together at recess. Elena says she doesn't think Ernie wants her to **look out for** him anymore. Kara is glad that Ernie is becoming more independent, although Kara knows that Ernie looks up to Elena. Elena says she knows that Ernie thinks his big sister is great. That's why he started copying her by wearing earmuffs in the classroom.

Write sentences using the phrasal verb and bonus words in italics.

1. Why does Elena need to look out for Ernie at school?

_____

2. A week after school starts, does Elena have to look out for Ernie at recess?

_____

3. Did you look out for a younger sibling at school?

_____

4. Did you like it when your parents looked out for you when you were younger?

_____

Put Up   Give someone a place to stay/pay for someone to stay somewhere

Can take an object between the verb and the preposition

> You may hear it used like this: While he was looking for an apartment, we **put him up**.

It's time to meet some of our characters. Read these conversations aloud.

Tiffany (42, the mom): "Grant, our family will be hosting an *exchange student* from Brazil soon. His name is Gustavo. Can we **put him up** in your room?"

Grant (14, the son): "Sure, but he might want to sleep on the couch because I snore loudly."

A while later . . .

Hannah (33, an airline employee): "I'm sorry, sir, but your flight has been cancelled. You can take the first flight tomorrow. Do you know anyone who can **put you up** tonight?"

Gustavo (16, who is on his way to Grant's house): "No, but that's OK. I need to stay awake and practice saying, 'I'd like another cheeseburger please.'"

Let's perform the skits. Take roles, add your ideas, and practice the phrasal verbs.

Skit 1   Gustavo has arrived at Grant's house and looks very tired. Tiffany asks Gustavo if he had a good trip. Gustavo just says, "I'd like another cheeseburger please." Tiffany feeds him a cheeseburger and then lets him go to bed. She knows he will learn more English soon. A few hours later, Gustavo wakes up feeling a lot better. Grant asks him why he was so tired. Was it because of *jet lag*? After looking that up in his dictionary, Gustavo says no. Grant starts asking Gustavo some more questions. Does he like cheeseburgers? Did the airline **put him up** in a hotel when his flight was cancelled? Does Gustavo want to see Grant's pet pig?

Skit 2   Several weeks later, Gustavo's English has improved. People now know what he's getting at. One evening, he and Grant are eating cheeseburgers and Grant mentions that he wants to learn Portuguese. Gustavo says he can ask his mom if his family could **put Grant up** next summer. Grant says that would be great, because he wants to keep up with Gustavo. Gustavo mentions that his brother Jorge talks in his sleep. Would Grant mind sharing a room with Jorge even if he won't get much sleep? Grant says that would be OK. He can practice speaking Portuguese with Jorge at night.

Write sentences using the phrasal verb and bonus words in italics.

1. Did the airline put Gustavo up in a hotel?

_____

2. Where will Gustavo's family put Grant up?

_____

3. Would you put up a friend if you had a very small apartment?

_____

4. If seven relatives were visiting, would you put them all up at your house?

_____

See To   Make sure something gets done

Is followed by a noun phrase or pronoun (usually "it")

You may hear it used like this: I thanked him for **seeing to** it while I was away.

It's time to meet some of our characters. Read these conversations aloud.

Laurie (53, a woman going on vacation): "Bud, I wanted to *ask you a favor*. Could you pick up our newspapers for a few days? Phillipe and I are going on vacation."

Bud (56, a painter who is Laurie and Phillipe's neighbor): "Sure, I'll **see to** it. Would it be OK if I read the papers and cut out some interesting articles?"

A while later . . .

Marta (55, Bud's wife): "I just noticed that Phillipe's fence has a big hole in it. Why don't you **see to** it while he and Laurie are away?"

Bud: "That's a good idea. Do you think Phillipe would mind if I repaired it and then painted the whole fence with black and yellow stripes?"

Let's perform the skits. Take roles, add your ideas, and practice the phrasal verbs.

Skit 1   The morning after Phillipe (54) and Laurie return from their vacation, Phillipe goes to Bud's house to get his newspapers. Bud says he hopes it's OK that he cut out an interesting article on fence repair. Phillipe says he doesn't mind. Bud then tells Phillipe that Marta discovered a big hole in Phillipe's fence. Phillipe looks outside and sees the newly painted fence. Phillipe thanks Bud for **seeing to** it. He thinks the fence looks really nice. Bud asks if Phillipe would like him to paint anything else. Phillipe says his car needs a *new paint job*. Could Bud **see to** it right away?

Skit 2   Phillipe loves his car's new paint job. When driving around town, he runs into Cal (51, his cousin). Cal tells Phillipe that he likes his car's interesting paint job. Did Phillipe come up with the idea of painting purple and green polka dots on it? Phillipe tells him that his neighbor Bud did it for him. Phillipe then notices that Cal's car, parked nearby, looks *rusty*. Phillipe asks Cal if he wants Bud to paint it for him. Cal asks if Bud could **see to** it soon. Cal says that next weekend he's taking a new girlfriend out and thinks she'll be impressed with a car painted with blue and orange diamonds.

Write sentences using the phrasal verb and bonus words in italics.

1. What does Laurie ask Bud to see to while she and Phillipe are away?

_____

2. When Phillipe notices that Cal's car needs a new paint job, does Phillipe promise to see to it quickly?

_____

3. When someone asks you a favor, do you usually see to it?

_____

4. If your teacher asked you to fix his/her car, would you see to it?

_____

Stand Up For/Stick Up For   Defend (usually verbally)

"Stand up for" and "stick up for" mean the same thing; are followed by a noun phrase or pronoun

> You may hear it used like this: She **stood up for** me when the boy was mean to me.

It's time to meet some of our characters. Read these conversations aloud.

Colleen (24, a secretary): "Mom, my co-worker Lisa has been teasing me because I *hum* the *national anthem* while I type. How can I **stand up for** myself without being rude to her?"

Lindsay (44, Colleen's mother): "Maybe you should tell her that the boss hired you because he was looking for a *patriotic* typist."

A while later . . .

Lindsay: "So, did you speak to Lisa about your humming?"

Colleen: "Actually, my boss **stuck up for** me by telling Lisa how much he enjoys my humming. Then he asked me to hum the happy birthday song to him, although it wasn't his birthday."

Let's perform the skits. Take roles, add your ideas, and practice the phrasal verbs.

Skit 1   Colleen is telling Lindsay that Lisa still jokes about her humming. Lindsay says that she needs to learn to **stand up for** herself. Colleen agrees that she is not very *assertive*. Lindsay suggests that she take an assertiveness class at the **Stick Up For** Yourself Academy and shows her the academy's brochure. Colleen says she'll read up on the school. A few minutes later, Colleen tells Lindsay that she's thought it through and will turn in the application tomorrow. Lindsay reminds her to go there early because the brochure says there aren't many parking places. Colleen will have to practice **standing up for** herself if another student steals her parking place.

Skit 2   Colleen is at the **Stick Up For** Yourself Academy. The only other student is Gordy (32, a man who works at a high school). Irving (45, the academy's teacher) asks both students why they are taking the class. Colleen tells Irving about Lisa and the humming. Gordy says he has trouble **sticking up for** himself when the children at the school where he works throw paper airplanes at him. Irving then explains that each student will now practice **standing up for** Irving. First, Colleen will say something mean about Irving, and Gordy will **stick up for** him. Then they will switch. Gordy asks if it's OK to make fun of Irving's very unfashionable glasses and very short pants.

Write sentences using the phrasal verb and bonus words in italics.

1. Why does Colleen need to learn to stick up for herself?

_____

2. Who stood up for Colleen at work?

_____

3. If someone criticized your English, would you stand up for yourself?

_____

4. Did you stick up for a friend when someone was mean to him/her in school?

_____

Chapter Review Questions

Rewrite each sentence using the correct phrasal verb. Choices: **go along with, look after, look out for, put up, see to, stand up for/stick up for.**

1. My older brother made sure I was OK in the playground.

_____

2. She needs to learn to be more assertive.

_____

3. They gave her a place to stay.

_____

4. Although she didn't want her husband to have a pet lizard, she agreed.

_____

5. I'll make sure it gets done.

_____

6. We had to take care of our sick aunt.

_____

7. When the boy made fun of her hairdo, her friend defended her.

_____

8. My mother took care of everything, so the wedding was perfect.

_____

9. She helped him while he was ill.

_____

10. When I went to college, I was sad because my family wasn't there to make sure I was OK.

_____

11. She agreed to the idea although she didn't like it.

_____

12. The airline paid for me to stay at a nice hotel.

_____

CHAPTER 15
UP TO NO GOOD
(CRIMES)

©cag2002

Break In (To)   Enter by force, usually to steal something

If not followed by "to," does not take an object; if used with "to," is followed by a noun phrase or pronoun

You may hear it used like this: The thief **broke into** our house and took some money.

It's time to meet some of our characters. Read these conversations aloud.

Dorothy (42, a woman who is just coming home with her husband): "Oh no! Someone **broke in** while we were out."

Theo (40, Dorothy's husband, who is a teacher): "Well, we're lucky the robber stole the *VCR* instead of the TV, because the VCR was broken."

A while later . . .

Robby (18, the man who took the VCR): "Hi, Aaron. Last night I **broke into** a house and took a VCR for you. Here it is."

Aaron (21, a man taking a class on repairing electronics): "Thank you. I hope it's a broken VCR, because I need to practice fixing VCRs for my class. When I've fixed it, you can return it to the owners."

Let's perform the skits. Take roles, add your ideas, and practice the phrasal verbs.

Skit 1   Dorothy and Theo are at the police station reporting that their house was **broken into**. Tyrone (38, a policeman) tells them that someone has **broken into** several other houses in their neighborhood. In each case, the stolen VCRs were returned a few days later, and each time the broken VCRs were fixed. Theo asks Tyrone what he and Dorothy should do. Tyrone suggests that for the next few nights they wait in the bushes in the front yard so they can catch the suspect. When they see the suspect, they should call *911*. Dorothy says she wants to wait in the bushes with a frying pan instead of a phone.

Skit 2   Later that week, at 4 a.m., Dorothy is waiting in the bushes with a frying pan. Theo didn't wash up after dinner so she has been eating some leftovers in the pan. All of a sudden, she hears a man approaching. Robby is carrying their VCR. Dorothy is about to hit him on the head with the frying pan, but Robby shouts, "Wait!" Dorothy asks him if he **broke into** her house earlier in the week. Robby says he did but explains that the VCR has been fixed. Dorothy asks him if he has been **breaking into** all the neighbors' houses (yes). Robby then explains about Aaron, his friend who needed to practice fixing VCRs for his electronics class. Dorothy says that her husband Theo teaches a class like that.

Write sentences using the phrasal verb and bonus words in italics.

1. Why did Robby break into Dorothy and Theo's house?

_____

2. Is Dorothy and Theo's house the only one that's been broken into lately?

_____

3. Has anyone ever broken into your house? If so, did you call 911?

_____

4. What are thieves usually looking for when they break in?

_____

Break Out (Of Jail/Prison)   Escape (from jail/prison)

If not followed by "of," does not take an object; if used with "of," is followed by a noun phrase or pronoun (usually "jail" or "prison")

> You may hear it used like this: The man **broke out of** prison but was soon captured.

It's time to meet some of our characters. Read these conversations aloud.

Jones (27, a prisoner): "Smith and I are planning to **break out of** jail tonight. Do you want to try to escape also?"

Suzuki (45, another prisoner): "No. If I escape, I won't get *fish sticks* for dinner anymore. That's my favorite food."

A while later . . .

Jones: "So, Smith, we're going to **break out of** here at midnight. Are you ready?"

Smith (25, another prisoner): "No, not yet. First I have to figure out how to get out of my cell."

Let's perform the skits. Take roles, add your ideas, and practice the phrasal verbs.

Skit 1   Casper (29, a prison guard) has just noticed that Jones has **broken out of** his cell. Casper asks prisoners in nearby cells if they know anything about the escape. Suzuki speaks up and says that Jones and Smith were planning to **break out** at midnight. Suzuki says he didn't want to **break out** because he likes the prison food so much. Smith, who is still in his cell, says that he tried to **break out** but he couldn't. Smith then asks Casper for some help. Smith's head *is stuck* between two of the bars and he can't get it out.

Skit 2   Jones is enjoying his freedom. He decides to look up Kathleen (24, an old girlfriend). When Jones stops by her apartment, she is cooking dinner. She is not surprised to see him. She tells him she was just watching the news and saw that he **broke out**. She tells him that the news also talked about a man named Smith who was unable to **break out**. She explains, and Jones laughs. Kathleen then tells Jones she is making what used to be his favorite meal. He frowns and says he doesn't want to eat that. Kathleen asks him why not. He says that the prison served fish sticks every night for dinner and he is tired of eating them.

Write sentences using the phrasal verb and bonus words in italics.

1. Why doesn't Suzuki want to break out of jail?

_____

2. Why couldn't Smith break out?

_____

3. If you were innocent of a crime, would you try to break out of jail?

_____

4. If you saw someone who had just broken out of jail, what would you do?

_____

Get Away   Not be captured (often after you do something bad)
Does not take an object

You may hear it used like this:	The policeman chased the thief but he **got away**.

It's time to meet some of our characters. Read these conversations aloud.

Rosemary (31, a woman who just planted some rosebushes): "Officer, someone just stole all the roses from my front yard. The thief **got away** before I saw who it was."

Mr. Kelly (46, a tall policeman): "Well, hopefully the *thorns* cut the thief's hands."

A while later . . .

Pamela (25, wife of Skip, the rose thief): "Oh, Skip, thank you for the lovely roses. Where did you find such pretty polka-dotted flowers?"

Skip (29, the thief): "Well, the pink roses are from our neighbor's yard. I cut them and **got away** before she noticed me. The red dots are a few spots of my blood because the thorns cut my fingers."

Let's perform the skits. Take roles, add your ideas, and practice the phrasal verbs.

Skit 1   Rosemary is at the *nursery* buying some new rosebushes. She runs into Pamela, who is buying soil. Pamela starts telling Rosemary about the pretty polka-dotted roses that Skip took yesterday. She explains that he was able to **get away** before anyone noticed what he was doing. Rosemary asks Pamela if she can come by later to admire the roses, which sound pretty. Pamela tells her that she and Skip will be home all evening. After Rosemary pays for the new roses, she calls Mr. Kelly and tells him where the rose thief lives. She wants Mr. Kelly to make sure the thief doesn't **get away** this time.

Skit 2   Mr. Kelly is calling Rosemary to tell her he's about to arrest Skip. He says he has a plan to ensure that Skip doesn't **get away**. She thanks him. Mr. Kelly then knocks on Skip's door. Skip smiles when he sees a man dressed up as a chicken. Mr. Kelly says he's giving free fried chicken to all the neighbors and then gives Skip a box of chicken. Skip asks if the chicken suit is comfortable. Mr. Kelly answers that it's more comfortable than prison clothes. Skip asks Mr. Kelly what he's driving at. Mr. Kelly tells Skip he's *under arrest* for stealing Rosemary's roses. Skip tries to **get away** but the six-foot-tall chicken puts handcuffs on him. Skip yells, "How can I eat this chicken if I'm wearing handcuffs?"

Write sentences using the phrasal verb and bonus words in italics.

1. Although Skip got away when he stole the roses, what happened to his fingers?

_____

2. How does Mr. Kelly make sure that Skip does not get away this time?

_____

3. If a robber were trying to get away, would you chase him or call 911?

_____

4. Could you catch a fast runner or would he get away?

_____

Get Away With   Do something bad but not be caught/punished

Is followed by a noun phrase, pronoun, or verb phrase

> You may hear it used like this: He **got away with** eating his niece's ice cream cone.

It's time to meet some of our characters. Read these conversations aloud.

Pablo (12, the brother): "Let's play the prison game again. I'll be the guard and you'll be the prisoner. But this time, don't *tickle* me if I fall asleep outside your cell."

Maureen (9, the sister): "But you never let me **get away with** anything! Remember, I'm in prison because I tickled a policeman while he was *directing traffic*."

A while later . . .

Ronnie (40, the father): "So, Maureen, did you like pretending to be the prisoner today?"

Maureen: "Yes, but Pablo didn't let me **get away with** much. However, when he took a nap outside my cell, I stole some cake that was in his pocket."

Let's perform the skits. Take roles, add your ideas, and practice the phrasal verbs.

Skit 1   Maureen and Pablo are playing the prison game again. A new prisoner (Pablo) and the guard (Maureen) start chatting. Pablo explains that he's in jail because the zoo police caught him feeding the geese last week. He hadn't noticed the "Do not feed the animals" sign. Maureen asks if he has ever fed the animals at the zoo before. Pablo explains that he **got away with** feeding them several times last month. He adds that his goose friends were starting to recognize him. Maureen asks Pablo how he knew the geese recognized him. Pablo says that they recently stopped biting his fingers when he fed them cake.

Skit 2   At breakfast, Maureen is telling Pablo about a dream she had last night. Maureen says she dreamed she was a clerk at a grocery store and Pablo tried to **get away with** stealing a candy bar. In the dream, she stopped him by saying, "I saw you take the candy bar. You're not a very good thief." Then, in the dream, Pablo asked if he could try to **get away with** taking some gum instead. Pablo, at the kitchen table, asks Maureen how the dream ended. Maureen says that the dream got very interesting. She explains that the dream ended with someone who looked like Pablo chewing some gum. However, Pablo had the body of a goose.

Write sentences using the phrasal verb and bonus words in italics.

1. What did Pablo not let Maureen get away with when they first played the prison game?

_____

2. What did Pablo not get away with in Maureen's dream?

_____

3. How do you prevent criminals from getting away with stealing something from a grocery store?

_____

4. Have you ever gotten away with something bad at school, such as putting a frog in the teacher's desk?

_____

Hold Up   Rob (usually when carrying a weapon)

Can take an object between the verb and the preposition, but is usually followed by a noun phrase

You may hear it used like this: He **held up** the convenience store and stole $316.

It's time to meet some of our characters. Read these conversations aloud.

Magnus (41, a lawyer who is representing Clifford, a criminal): "Why did you **hold up** a grocery store?"

Clifford (29, a man who loves vegetables): "Well, I didn't want to, but I was too embarrassed to pay for the eggplants. I don't want anyone to know I like eating vegetables."

A while later . . .

Magnus: "Clifford, will you promise not to **hold up** any more grocery stores?"

Clifford: "Yes, I promise. I'll be too busy cooking my eggplants to **hold anyone else up**."

Let's perform the skits. Take roles, add your ideas, and practice the phrasal verbs.

Skit 1   Clifford *is out on bail*. He is about to apologize to Marcel (51, the grocery store owner) for **holding up** the store. When Clifford arrives at the store, he asks Marcel how much he owes him for the eggplants he took. Marcel tells him that each eggplant costs a dollar, so Clifford owes him $65. Clifford gives him the money and says he's through with **holding up** stores. Marcel asks how many stores Clifford has **held up** and if he has done anything else bad. Clifford tells Marcel that his store is the first grocery store he has **held up**. Clifford adds that last year he got away with talking loudly during a film when he wasn't supposed to.

Skit 2   Clifford is in court. Mr. Han (61, the judge) asks him if he's *pleading guilty or not guilty*. Clifford says he will plead guilty to **holding up** the grocery store, but he promises he won't do it again. He adds that he got rid of the weapon he used in the robbery, a large zucchini. Mr. Han asks him if he threw it out. Clifford admits that he didn't put it in the trash. He ate it. Magnus then tells Mr. Han that Clifford has paid Marcel, the store's owner, for the stolen eggplants. Mr. Han asks Clifford if he has any eggplants left (yes). Mr. Han says that Clifford's punishment will be to cook Mr. and Mrs. Han some *Eggplant Parmesan* tonight.

Write sentences using the phrasal verb and bonus words in italics.

1. Why did Clifford hold up the grocery store?

_____

2. What is Clifford's punishment for holding up Marcel's store?

_____

3. If you worked at a store, would you be afraid of being held up?

_____

4. Do you know anyone who has been held up?

_____

Turn In   Tell the police about what a criminal did

Can take an object between the verb and the preposition

You may hear it used like this: She **turned him in**, and he went to prison.

It's time to meet some of our characters. Read these conversations aloud.

Karla (65, a dog owner): "Boris, are you aware that someone has been stealing dogs in the neighborhood? You should keep *Spot* inside."

Boris (62, Karla's neighbor and Spot's owner): "Yes, it's terrible. Maybe I should offer a reward for whoever **turns in** the suspect. Instead of giving the person money, I'll let Spot give the person a doggy kiss."

A while later . . .

Karla: "Has anyone **turned the suspect in** yet?"

Boris (who is wiping his wet face with a towel): "No, but Spot is ready to give that person a doggy kiss. He practiced his kiss all morning."

Let's perform the skits. Take roles, add your ideas, and practice the phrasal verbs.

Skit 1   Karla and Boris are chatting outside when Lourdes (37, a *dog groomer*) approaches them. Lourdes says she saw some signs in the neighborhood about missing dogs, and she has some information about the dog thief. She says she would like to **turn herself in**. Karla asks what she means. Lourdes says that she has been taking the dogs so that she can practice her dog-grooming skills. Boris is very surprised and says he'll call the police. Lourdes says she knows she needs to go to jail, but she would like to get her reward before Boris **turns her in**. Can Spot give her the doggy kiss now?

Skit 2   Lourdes is in jail. *Miss Demeanor* (28, her lawyer) asks Lourdes why she took the dogs. Lourdes tells her that she recently started a dog-grooming business but she wasn't very good at washing dogs. She never meant to hurt anyone, and she always planned to **turn herself in** when she finished practicing. Miss Demeanor then asks her to describe what happened after she spoke with Boris and Karla. Lourdes explains that while Karla called the police and **turned her in**, Boris got his dog so Spot could give Lourdes a doggy kiss. When Lourdes saw the really dirty dog, however, she decided she didn't want Spot to kiss her. Instead, she washed Spot before the police took her to jail.

Write sentences using the phrasal verb and bonus words in italics.

1. What reward will Boris give the person who turns in the suspect?

_____

2. Why did Lourdes turn herself in?

_____

3. Have you ever turned in a criminal?

_____

4. Would you turn yourself in if you did something bad?

_____

Chapter Review Questions

Rewrite each sentence using the correct phrasal verb. Choices: **break in (to), break out (of jail/ prison), get away, get away with, hold up, turn in.**

1. The police didn't catch the criminal.

_____

2. I knew some information about the robber, so I told the police.

_____

3. Someone came into the house and took the stereo.

_____

4. The man who robbed the bank was never punished.

_____

5. The woman escaped from prison.

_____

6. The robber used a weapon when he stole the money from the store.

_____

7. I saw my neighbor steal the car, so I told the police.

_____

8. The two thieves had a gun when they stole the beer from the restaurant.

_____

9. She saw him commit the crime, but he ran too fast.

_____

10. In the middle of the night, someone took some jewels from the store.

_____

11. She was usually late but never got in trouble.

_____

12. The criminal didn't want to stay in jail, so he tried to escape.

_____

CHAPTER 16

ON BAD TERMS
(MEAN)

Beat Up   Hurt someone physically

Can take an object between the verb and the preposition

You may hear it used like this: The bully **beat my brother up** again.

It's time to meet some of our characters. Read these conversations aloud.

Esteban (55, Casey's father): "So, Casey, who **beat you up?**"
Casey (31, a guy who performs as a clown): "Oh, I started arguing with a *mime* yesterday. We both
    wanted to perform in the same place. The mime won."

A while later . . .

Lester (59, Cy's father): "So, Cy, why is your hand bruised?"
Cy Lence (29, the mime): "Oh, I **beat up** a clown who was trying to perform where I was. You'll be
    interested to know that when we started fighting, we got more tips than usual."

Let's perform the skits. Take roles, add your ideas, and practice the phrasal verbs.

Skit 1   Casey and Cy have run into each other again as they are getting ready to perform. Casey
asks Cy if he can run an idea by him. Casey says last week, when Cy **beat him up,** they got a lot
more money than usual. Cy agrees that it was a very successful day. Casey thinks they should start a
new act together. Casey wants to pretend to have it out with Cy and then **beat him up.** Before they
start, Cy asks how he will know when the pretend fight is over. Cy reminds Casey that he won't be
speaking because he's a mime. Casey says it will be over when Casey knocks Cy out. When Cy looks
worried, Casey tells him he'll just be pretending to **beat him up.**

Skit 2   Casey accidentally hit Cy too hard while he was pretending to **beat him up.** They are now
in the waiting room of the *ER*, and Casey is continuing the act. Cy remains silent because he is a
mime and because he isn't feeling well. Casey asks, "Would anyone like to pretend to **beat me up?**"
Peggy (32, a nurse) speaks up. After they introduce themselves, Casey tells Peggy she can begin. At
first, Casey avoids the fake punches. However, after a minute Peggy accidentally **beats him up** a
little, and his nose starts bleeding. Peggy tells him not to worry because the hospital can put him up
in a room with Cy.

Write sentences using the phrasal verb and bonus words in italics.

1. Why did the mime beat up the clown when they first met?

_____

2. Why did Peggy beat Casey up in the ER?

_____

3. When people get beaten up, do they usually go to the ER?

_____

4. Have you ever been beaten up? Ever beat anyone up?

_____

Hang Up On   Hang up the phone before the conversation is finished

Is followed by a noun phrase or pronoun

You may hear it used like this: I **hung up on** the salesman who called during dinner.

It's time to meet some of our characters. Read these conversations aloud.

Mr. Sellers (37, a phone salesman): "Dear, the neighbors keep **hanging up on** me when I try to sell them my purple and orange shoe polish. What should I do?"

Mrs. Sellers (36, Mr. Sellers' wife): "Well, maybe you should stop calling them so early in the morning."

A while later . . .

Travis (32, Mr. Sellers' neighbor): "Gwen, why did you **hang up on** Mr. Sellers? I thought you were his best customer."

Gwen (29, Travis' wife): "Well, I am, but I don't need any more orange shoe polish right now. I just bought seven containers of polish from him last week."

Let's perform the skits. Take roles, add your ideas, and practice the phrasal verbs.

Skit 1 A week later, Mr. Sellers is telling Mrs. Sellers that he has made a big decision that could affect them both. He announces that after sleeping on it, he has decided to change jobs. He's tired of people **hanging up on** him. Mrs. Sellers asks him what his new job will be. He tells her he doesn't know yet. Mr. and Mrs. Sellers discuss what his new job should be. She suggests a few unusual jobs, but he doesn't like any of her ideas. Finally Mr. Sellers comes up with something. He says he wants to start selling nail polish *door to door*. That way, people can't **hang up on** him.

Skit 2 A week later, Mr. Sellers calls Gwen at 6:30 a.m. She tells him it's too early in the morning and warns him that she is going to **hang up on** him. He asks her not to **hang up on** him because he is no longer selling shoe polish. He explains that he has changed jobs. She asks him what his new job is and why he's calling her. He explains that he is now selling *gallons* of nail polish door to door. He says he was calling her to see if she was planning to be home later this morning. He was thinking of knocking on her door at about 11. Does Gwen **hang up on** him or agree to meet him later that morning?

Write sentences using the phrasal verb and bonus words in italics.

1. Why do Mr. Sellers' customers hang up on him?

_____

2. In your skit, did Gwen hang up on Mr. Sellers when he told her about his new job?

_____

3. Have you ever accidentally hung up on anyone?

_____

4. Do you usually hang up on salespeople if you don't want to buy what they are selling?

_____

Look Down On   Think you are better than someone else

Is followed by a noun phrase or pronoun

You may hear it used like this: The executive **looked down on** the *janitor*.

It's time to meet some of our characters. Read these conversations aloud.

Cassandra (30, a woman at a party): "Oh, who invited Ms. Tripp to the party? She's very *snobbish*."
Leonardo (27, Ms. Tripp's employee): "Well, she does like to **look down on** people, but she's also
    clumsy. The last time I saw her, she tripped on a piece of sushi!"

A while later . . .

Leonardo: "Ms. Tripp, why do you always tell me you're better than I am? I'm a very good worker."
Ms. Tripp (41, Leonardo's boss, a judo teacher): "Well, Leo, you are a good worker. I don't mean to
    look down on you, but I really am better at falling down than you are."

Let's perform the skits. Take roles, add your ideas, and practice the phrasal verbs.

Skit 1   Ms. Tripp is giving Cassandra a free judo lesson. At the beginning of the lesson, Ms. Tripp
explains that Cassandra needs to learn to fall correctly so she doesn't get hurt when an opponent
throws her. Cassandra says she will *give it a shot*, as long as Ms. Tripp doesn't **look down on** her if
she falls awkwardly. Ms. Tripp admits that she does **look down on** people a lot, but she says she'll
try to be nice in future. Ms. Tripp then asks Cassandra to trip on the sushi that's in the middle of the
mat. Cassandra walks across the mat and trips very gracefully. Ms. Tripp tells Cassandra she is quite
good at tripping on sushi and suggests she try tripping on a plate of noodles next.

Skit 2   Leonardo is asking Cassandra if she enjoyed her judo lesson. She tells Leonardo that Ms.
Tripp liked the way she tripped on a plate of noodles. Cassandra tells him that she did it so well that
Ms. Tripp has decided to stop **looking down on** people. Leonardo says he's glad it went well. He
then asks if Cassandra will be going back to the judo studio for a second lesson. Cassandra says that
Ms. Tripp invited her to come back and work there. Her job will be to make sushi for the students to
trip on. Leonardo looks surprised and says he thought she didn't like sushi.

Write sentences using the phrasal verb and bonus words in italics.

1. Why does Ms. Tripp look down on Leonardo?

_____

2. Does Ms. Tripp look down on Cassandra after she trips on the sushi?

_____

3. Were people snobbish to you in school or did you look down on them?

_____

4. If you were a janitor and someone looked down on you, what would you say?

_____

Pick On   Be mean to someone

Is followed by a noun phrase or pronoun

> You may hear it used like this: Her older brother **picks on** her all the time.

It's time to meet some of our characters. Read these conversations aloud.

Quentin (12, a boy without many friends): "Mom, a few kids at school have been **picking on** me. What should I do?"

Victoria (46, Quentin's mother): "Well, you could invite them to your birthday party. Dad can dress up as a monster and scare them when they knock on the door."

A while later . . .

Frankie (13, a bully): "Mom, a boy I've been **picking on** has just invited me to his birthday party. I feel bad that I've been mean to him. What should I give him?"

Eleanor (39, Frankie's mother): "Well, your birthday present could be an apology. Or you could let him poke you in the ribs once for each day you were mean to him."

Let's perform the skits. Take roles, add your ideas, and practice the phrasal verbs.

Skit 1   Quentin is getting ready for his birthday party. Meanwhile, Mack (42, his dad) is putting on his monster costume. Mack asks Quentin who's coming to the party. Quentin tells him that he has invited some boys who like to **pick on** him. Quentin hopes that they will start being nice to him. Mack asks why they **pick on** him. Quentin explains that they make fun of the squid and *mayonnaise* sandwiches he brings for lunch every day. Mack is surprised. Mack then adds that right now, Victoria is making some squid and mayonnaise sandwiches for the party.

Skit 2   It's time for Quentin to open his presents at the party. Most of the boys have given him things like books, but when Quentin opens Frankie's present, he is a little surprised. Frankie's gift is just a card, and in it Frankie wrote that he's sorry for **picking on** him. Quentin accepts the apology and asks Frankie if he liked the squid sandwiches his mom made. Frankie admits that they were *super*. Frankie then tells Quentin he has one more present. He tells Quentin he can poke Frankie in the ribs once for each day Frankie **picked on** him. Quentin says he doesn't think he can count that high.

Write sentences using the phrasal verb and bonus words in italics.

1. Why does Frankie pick on Quentin?

_____

2. What does Frankie let Quentin do because Frankie is sorry he picked on him?

_____

3. When you were younger, did you pick on your classmates or did they pick on you?

_____

4. What's the best thing to say to a bully who is picking on you?

_____

Put Down   Be critical of a person by saying bad things

Can take an object between the verb and the preposition

You may hear it used like this: My boss always **puts me down**, so I want to quit.

It's time to meet some of our characters. Read these conversations aloud.

Giovanni (21, a newly single man): "I just broke up with Megan because she always **put me down**. She especially liked to criticize what I eat."

Stephen (19, Giovanni's friend): "Well, maybe you shouldn't eat cereal three times a day."

A while later . . .

Francesca (20, a clerk at Sausage Mart): "Hi. Why are you buying so many sausages?"

Giovanni: "Well, my ex-girlfriend **put me down** for eating so much healthy cereal, so I thought I'd start eating a lot of fatty sausages instead."

Let's perform the skits. Take roles, add your ideas, and practice the phrasal verbs.

Skit 1   Giovanni is telling Valerie (41, his mother) about Francesca, his new girlfriend. Valerie asks why he's no longer dating Megan. He tells Valerie that Megan often **put him down** for eating cereal three times a day. Valerie asks him what mean things Megan said. He says Megan often told him that his favorite cereal, Rice Rocks, looked like *gravel*. Giovanni then asks if he can invite Francesca to dinner tomorrow. Valerie says she will have to buy more Rice Rocks. She just had some for lunch and is about to run out. Giovanni asks if she can make sausages instead.

Skit 2   Giovanni is introducing Francesca to Valerie. Valerie asks her how she and Giovanni met. Francesca describes how she met him when he bought fifty sausages at Sausage Mart. Valerie then asks Francesca if she would **put someone down** for eating strange food. Francesca tells her she is not like Giovanni's old girlfriend. Francesca says she's very *open-minded*. All three of them smile. Giovanni then invites Francesca to sit at the dining room table, and Valerie starts serving the fabulous dinner she has prepared. She didn't buy any sausages as Giovanni requested. Instead, she made Rice Rocks in the shape of sausages.

Write sentences using the phrasal verb and bonus words in italics.

1. Why did Megan put Giovanni down?

_____

2. Is Francesca the type of person to put people down?

_____

3. What do you do when someone puts you down? Do you stick up for yourself?

_____

4. Do you know someone who often puts people down?

_____

Put Through   Make someone experience something unpleasant

Always takes an object between the verb and the preposition, and is then followed by a noun phrase or pronoun

> You may hear it used like this: He **put her through** a lot during their bitter divorce.

It's time to meet some of our characters. Read these conversations aloud.

Jen (34, a *travel agent* phoning Cindy): "Hi, Cindy. This is Jen, your travel agent. I don't mean to **put you through** any more stress, but I need to change your honeymoon reservations again."

Cindy (25, a woman getting married to Justin next week): "OK, Jen. If Wasp Land is *booked*, we could visit Honeybee Farms instead."

A while later . . .

Georgina (46, Cindy's mother): "So, I hear Jen keeps changing your honeymoon plans."

Cindy: "Yes. But she's not **putting us through** nearly as much stress as Justin's tailor. He keeps changing the color of Justin's tuxedo—from black to green to orange. I think the tailor finally decided to make it red."

Let's perform the skits. Take roles, add your ideas, and practice the phrasal verbs.

Skit 1   Cindy and Justin have just gotten married. Cindy is calling Jen to confirm their honeymoon reservations. Jen asks how the wedding went. Cindy says it was beautiful, although the flowers never arrived and the minister was two hours late. Jen then says that everything for the trip to Honeybee Farms is ready. Jen tells Cindy she's sorry if she **put her through** any stress when making the reservations. Cindy says she was a little stressed, but it's OK. Jen is about to say goodbye when she remembers to ask Cindy if she packed her *insect repellent*. Jen doesn't want Cindy to get stung on her honeymoon.

Skit 2   Cindy and Justin, who are still in their wedding clothes, are on their way to Honeybee Farms. When they arrive at the train's dining car, Justin tells Terrence (22, their waiter, who is wearing a green tuxedo) he is looking for a job and asks him if he enjoys working there. Terrence explains that he does, although the manager **put him through** the tuxedo test before he was hired. Cindy asks what that is. Terrence says he had to prove he could be a waiter all day without spilling anything on his nice clothes. Justin says he wouldn't pass that test because he spilled champagne all over his tuxedo. Cindy suggests that Justin be a *beekeeper* at Honeybee Farms instead. Justin says he would like her idea if he weren't afraid of bees.

Write sentences using the phrasal verb and bonus words in italics.

1. Did Jen put Justin and Cindy through a lot of stress when arranging the honeymoon?

_____

2. What kind of test did Terrence's boss put him through?

_____

3. When you were younger, did you put your parents through a lot of worry?

_____

4. Does your teacher put you through stress by giving you a lot of tests?

_____

Chapter Review Questions

Rewrite each sentence using the correct phrasal verb. Choices: **beat up, hang up on, look down on, pick on, put down, put through.**

1. The rich man doesn't like poor people.

_____

2. She made me very stressed.

_____

3. He put down the phone before she finished talking.

_____

4. The little boy was always mean to the little girl.

_____

5. When the man tried to break into my house, I hit him a lot.

_____

6. She always criticizes her roommate.

_____

7. The doctor made me worry because he didn't tell me the test results for a long time.

_____

8. I didn't like it when other children were mean to me.

_____

9. The children punched each other.

_____

10. Every day, she tells me I'm a bad typist.

_____

11. The salesman called late at night, so I put the phone down while he was speaking.

_____

12. The actress thought she was better than the waiter.

_____

CHAPTER 17
UP AND AT 'EM
(ACTION)

©cag2002

Be Up For/Be Up To   Be willing/physically able to do

"Be up for" and "be up to" mean about the same thing ("up for" suggests willingness; "up to" suggests capability); are followed by a noun phrase, pronoun, or verb phrase

You may hear it used like this: I **am not up for** going hiking with you because I am too tired.

It's time to meet some of our characters. Read these conversations aloud.

Sarah (19, a woman who likes exercise): "Glenn, I was thinking of going on a ten-mile bike ride this afternoon. **Are you up to** going with me?"

Glenn (20, Sarah's boyfriend, who doesn't like exercise): "No, thanks. I'm **not up for** any more exercise. I just spent three hours chasing the cat while trying to give her a bath."

A while later . . .

Sarah: "Hi, I'm home from my bike ride. I'm going jogging now. **Are you up for** a six-mile run?"

Glenn: "No, thanks. I'm tired. The cat and I just finished running up and down the stairs."

Let's perform the skits. Take roles, add your ideas, and practice the phrasal verbs.

Skit 1   Glenn has just seen a newspaper article about a bike race next week. He asks Sarah if she **is up for** riding fifty miles to raise money for the local *pet shelter*. She says she **is probably up to** it since she rides her bike every weekend and her legs never give out. Glenn then suggests she bring their cat Fluffy on the ride. Sarah says that's a great idea, because she and Fluffy get along really well. Glenn says it would be nice not to have to look after Fluffy for a few hours because he doesn't think the cat likes him. Glenn adds that he would rather play with their pet *piranha*, Ron. The fish has seemed a little lonely lately.

Skit 2   Sarah is home from the bike race. Glenn asks her if she and Fluffy enjoyed the ride. Sarah says that Fluffy didn't want to sit in the bicycle's basket at first, but then the cat went along with it. Sarah asks Glenn if he had fun hanging out with Ron (yes). Glenn then mentions he saw an article about a *triathlon* next week. Would Sarah **be up for** participating (yes)? He then asks her if she thinks Ron would **be up for** going to the competition with her. Sarah answers that Ron would definitely **be up for** the swimming part of the race.

Write sentences using the phrasal verb and bonus words in italics.

1. Why isn't Glenn up for riding ten miles with Sarah?

_____

2. Will Ron be up to going with Sarah if she participates in the triathlon?

_____

3. If someone asked you to ride your bike for fifty miles this weekend, would you be up for it?

_____

4. Would you be up to the challenge if your teacher asked you to list twenty verbs beginning with the letter c?

_____

Do Over   Do again

Always takes an object between the verb and the preposition (often "it")

| You may hear it used like this: You need to **do your homework over** because it's wrong. |

It's time to meet some of our characters. Read these conversations aloud.

Luis (40, the dad): "So, Inez, what were you planning to give Mom for *Mother's Day*?"

Inez (15, the daughter): "Well, I've been knitting her a sweater, but I have to **do it over** because I forgot to knit the sleeves."

A while later . . .

Adrian (13, the son): "Dad, here's the Mother's Day card I made for Mom. Do you like it?"

Luis: "Well, you should probably **do it over** since you wrote, 'Happy Birthday' instead of 'Happy Mother's Day.'"

Let's perform the skits. Take roles, add your ideas, and practice the phrasal verbs.

Skit 1   At 6 a.m. on Mother's Day morning, Inez and Adrian are making pancakes and bacon for their mother. Adrian starts frying the pancakes, but then Inez tells him he isn't a very good cook. Adrian says it's too early in the morning for her to be putting him down. Can she wait until later? Inez then says that Adrian should probably **do the pancakes over** because he forgot to add the flour. Adrian agrees and then gets the bag of flour. Instead of putting it in the bowl, however, he decides to be *mischievous*. He pours the flour over Inez's head, and it gets everywhere. Inez jokes that Adrian is lucky she's too sleepy to beat him up. Just then, Luis comes in and asks what's happening. Adrian says they have been redecorating the kitchen because Mom's favorite color is white.

Skit 2   It's now 7 a.m., and Luis is not letting Adrian and Inez get away with making such a big mess. While they clean the flour off everything, Luis says he'll see to the pancakes. When Inez and Adrian finish cleaning up, they start frying the bacon. At 7:30, everything seems ready. Inez checks the tray they will be bringing to Mom in bed, but she notices that something is wrong. She tells Luis he should probably **do the pancakes over**. Didn't he remember that Mom likes to eat square pancakes, not round ones?

Write sentences using the phrasal verb and bonus words in italics.

1. What does Inez have to do over?

_____

2. What happens when Inez suggests that Adrian do the pancakes over?

_____

3. If you realized you made a mistake when making a gift, would you do it over?

_____

4. Does your teacher often ask you to do your homework over?

_____

Get On With   No longer delay doing

Is followed by a noun phrase, pronoun (usually "it"), or verb phrase

You may hear it used like this: Please **get on with** cooking dinner. I'm hungry.

It's time to meet some of our characters. Read these conversations aloud.

Sherry (38, the mom): "I can't believe you haven't finished decorating the Christmas tree! You'd better **get on with** it!"

Zachary (13, the son): "Well, I've been trying, but some of the ornaments are stuck in my hair and I can't get them out."

A while later . . .

Walt (42, the dad): "Zachary, were you planning to *make some cookies for Santa*? If so, you'd better **get on with** it because Christmas Eve is almost over."

Zachary: "Well, I did make some cookie *batter*, but I ate it all instead of baking the cookies."

Let's perform the skits. Take roles, add your ideas, and practice the phrasal verbs.

Skit 1   Santa is having dinner before he delivers presents to all the children. Mrs. Santa notices that he is *procrastinating*, so she tells him to **get on with** it. Santa says he'll be ready in a minute. While Santa puts his boots on, Mrs. Santa goes outside to talk with *Rudolph the Red-Nosed Reindeer*. She asks Rudolph to look out for Santa while they are delivering the presents because he doesn't seem very happy this evening. Rudolph thinks Santa hasn't broken in his boots and is worried about getting blisters.

Skit 2   At 5 a.m. on Christmas morning, Santa arrives at Zachary's house. Santa's feet are really hurting him. Instead of going down the chimney, he rings the doorbell. Zachary answers the door and is very surprised to see him. Santa asks if Zachary has a bandage for his sore feet. Zachary says, "Of course," and invites him to come inside. Zachary starts asking Santa lots of questions about his toy shop. Santa answers some of them, but not very enthusiastically. Zachary then notices that Santa is rubbing his feet and says he'll get the bandage now. Santa says, "Yes, please **get on with** it or I may not be able to give you any Christmas presents."

Write sentences using the phrasal verb and bonus words in italics.

1. What does Zachary have to get on with on Christmas Eve?

_____

2. What is Santa doing when Mrs. Santa tells him to get on with it?

_____

3. How often did your parents have to tell you to get on with your chores?

_____

4. If you were Santa, would Mrs. Santa have to tell you to get on with delivering presents?

_____

Go For   Attempt (often said by someone encouraging another)

Is followed by a noun phrase or pronoun (usually "it")

> You may hear it used like this: You're not sure whether to ask him out? You should **go for** it!

It's time to meet some of our characters. Read these conversations aloud.

Corinne (32, the wife): "I just saw an ad for a contest to see who can sit on a couch for the longest time. You should **go for** it because you're a really good *couch potato*."

Randall (35, the husband): "Do you think I can win? I've been sitting on the couch for *three days straight*, but that may not be long enough to win."

A while later . . .

Gonzálo (42, Randall's neighbor): "I heard that Randall is **going for** the top prize in the town's annual couch potato contest. Do you want to enter too?"

Hazel (39, Gonzálo's wife): "Sure. As you know, I've won the last four years in a row, and each time I won a couch and a gold medal. This time, I'd rather win some potatoes."

Let's perform the skits. Take roles, add your ideas, and practice the phrasal verbs.

Skit 1 Sophie (42, the owner of the sofa shop where the couch potato contest will be held this afternoon) is talking to Mr. Ramirez (55, the town's mayor). Sophie is saying she would like to give some potatoes instead of a sofa to the contest winner. Mr. Ramirez says she should **go for** it. Mr. Ramirez then asks her where she will get the potatoes. Sophie says she'll buy a big bag of French fries and some ketchup at a hamburger shop. Sophie then asks if she should buy fresh or frozen fries. Mr. Ramirez thinks that frozen fries would be delicious.

Skit 2 Randall and Hazel have been sitting on the couch in Sophie's store for four days. They are the only two contestants still **going for** the top prize. Mr. Ramirez announces they have both won and then asks the contestants about their strategy. Hazel says she just *concentrated* and **went for** it. Randall says he just did what he normally does. Sophie then comes into the room with a heavy bag of frozen fries. Hazel and Randall jump up and down in excitement. Randall asks Sophie if she has any ketchup. She apologizes that she ran out. She explains that she needed to write some price tags for the store, and she wanted to use red ink. She couldn't find any pens, so she used her supply of ketchup.

Write sentences using the phrasal verb and bonus words in italics.

1. Why does Randall want to go for the top prize in the contest?

2. What does Mr. Ramirez tell Sophie she should go for?

3. If your dad wanted to buy your mom some diamonds, would you tell him to go for it?

4. Does your teacher tell you to go for it when you mention you want to practice speaking more English?

Go Through With   Do something you didn't think you could

Is followed by a noun phrase, pronoun (often "it"), or verb phrase

You may hear it used like this: I finally **went through with** it and married him.

It's time to meet some of our characters. Read these conversations aloud.

Trixie (42, co-owner of Microphone Madness, where Dale works): "I thought you were going to fire Dale."

Wally (40, the other owner of the store): "Well, I planned to, but I couldn't **go through with** it. Although Dale sings loudly to the customers, he's our best salesman."

A while later . . .

Loretta (54, Dale's wife): "Hi, Dale. I thought you told me you were thinking of leaving Microphone Madness to start a singing career."

Dale (59, a microphone salesman): "Well, I couldn't **go through with** it because I really like working there. Where else can I sing with two microphones at once?"

Let's perform the skits. Take roles, add your ideas, and practice the phrasal verbs.

Skit 1   Dale has just given a concert at Microphone Madness. He held a pink microphone in one hand, and a green one in the other. Trixie asks Wally if they should start offering singing lessons with their microphones. Wally says maybe they should look into it. He then asks Dale if he's up for giving singing lessons. Dale says he'd be happy to do it as long as Wally gives him a *raise*. Wally agrees. Dale then asks if Wally has ever offered singing lessons. Wally answers that a few years ago he was thinking about it but never **went through with** it. Wally explains that Trixie was the only good singer he knew, but she liked to sing the same song over and over again. Wally says that "The Microphone *Blues*" would make the customers too sad to buy any microphones.

Skit 2   Dale has just come home from work and is talking to Loretta. He announces that he finally **went through with** it. Loretta asks him what he means. Dale reminds her that he has been wanting to ask for a raise for three months, and today he finally went for it. Loretta asks what Wally said. Dale says that Wally agreed very easily and explains that he will be giving singing lessons to customers. Loretta asks him what song he's planning to teach. Dale doesn't know. Loretta offers to help him make up a good song. She suggests "The Telephone Blues." Dale loves the idea, saying the first line of the song can be: "Honey, I'm so sad you hung up on me. . . ."

Write sentences using the phrasal verb and bonus words in italics.

1. Why can't Wally go through with firing Dale?

---

2. What did Dale finally go through with?

---

3. Could you go through with turning in a neighbor?

---

4. If a doctor asked you to help with some surgery, could you go through with it?

Keep At   Continue doing

Is followed by a noun phrase or pronoun (often "it")

You may hear it used like this: If you **keep at** it, you will learn English.

It's time to meet some of our characters. Read these conversations aloud.

Corey (14, the son): "Mom, I don't think I'll ever learn how to ride this *skateboard*. I keep falling down."

Rosa (36, the mom): "Well, you just need to **keep at** it. When I was learning how to stand on my head, I practiced a lot, although my face always turned bright red."

A while later . . .

Corey: "Grandpa, how did you get so good at riding your skateboard?"

Abe (68, the grandpa, who lives in Corey's house): "Well, I just **kept at** it until I learned how to do it. Now I skateboard as much as possible. I even skateboard in the house when your mother isn't looking."

Let's perform the skits. Take roles, add your ideas, and practice the phrasal verbs.

Skit 1   Barney (14, Corey's friend) is hanging out at Corey's house. Both of them are trying to ride their skateboards, but they both keep falling down. Barney then notices that Abe has just ridden his skateboard from the living room to the kitchen. Corey says that Grandpa Abe might be able to give them some skateboarding *tips*. Corey introduces Barney to Abe and tells Abe they need help. Corey explains that he and Barney have been trying to ride their skateboards using one foot, but they keep falling down. Abe says they could **keep at** it until they *get their balance*, or they could try using two feet.

Skit 2   Rosa has just arrived home. Corey, Barney, and Abe hide their skateboards. Corey then asks Rosa if she would like something to eat. She tells him she'd like some spaghetti after she stands on her head for a while. When Rosa has finished standing on her head, she goes into the kitchen. She notices that Corey's face is bright red. He tells her he's been trying to open the jar of spaghetti sauce for the last few minutes, but it's too hard to open. Rosa tells him to **keep at** it. While Corey continues to try opening the jar, Rosa looks for Abe. She wants Abe to tell her whose face is redder, hers or Corey's. When Rosa catches Abe riding his skateboard in the house, she says…

Write sentences using the phrasal verb and bonus words in italics.

1. Do you think Corey will keep at it or will he try to skateboard using two feet?

_____

2. What does Rosa tell Corey to keep at when he is in the kitchen?

_____

3. Does your teacher often tell you to keep at it?

_____

4. If you had to do a crossword puzzle in English, would you keep at it until you finished?

_____

Chapter Review Questions

Rewrite each sentence using the correct phrasal verb. Choices: **be up for/be up to, do over, get on with, go for, go through with, keep at.**

1. Her mom always encourages her to try it.

_____

2. You shouldn't procrastinate any longer.

_____

3. He decided to continue doing it.

_____

4. He doesn't feel like cooking dinner for ten relatives.

_____

5. He planned to hold up the grocery store, but then he couldn't do it.

_____

6. Please do your assignment again.

_____

7. Please start doing it.

_____

8. If you practice, you'll improve.

_____

9. I'm not sure I am able to do it.

_____

10. You should try to do it.

_____

11. The teacher told me to do my homework again.

_____

12. I was thinking about walking out on him, but then I wasn't able to.

_____

CHAPTER 18
AT A STANDSTILL
(INACTION)

©cay2002

Get Out Of   Avoid doing

Is followed by a noun phrase, pronoun, or verb phrase

You may hear it used like this: The girl tried to **get out of** cleaning her room by crying.

It's time to meet some of our characters. Read these conversations aloud.

Leanne (9, a girl getting ready for school): "Mom, I don't want to wear this ugly costume for my dance *recital*."

Sayuri (35, Leanne's mother): "I'm sorry, but there's no way to **get out of** it. All the dancers have to dress up as bears for the school's Big Bear Ballet Show."

A while later . . .

Leanne: "Dad, are you sure I can't **get out of** wearing this *ridiculous* outfit? The other kids are going to pick on me."

Nate (40, Leanne's father, who works at The *Yo-Yo* Corporation): "Well, if it will make you feel better, I'll wear my *out-of-date* tie to work. Then we will both look ridiculous."

Let's perform the skits. Take roles, add your ideas, and practice the phrasal verbs.

Skit 1   Ravi (42, Nate's co-worker) is talking to Nate at the office. Ravi asks him about his strange-looking tie. Nate explains that Leanne is having a dance recital and couldn't **get out of** wearing her ugly bear costume. Nate says he wore his ugly tie so they would both look silly. Ravi then says he has a sales meeting with Mr. Carlson (56, their boss) later. He can't find his notes for the meeting, so he hopes he can **get out of** going. Nate says he will meet with Mr. Carlson if Ravi tells him what he should say to Mr. Carlson. Ravi asks Nate to tell Mr. Carlson that sales of orange yo-yos have not been good lately.

Skit 2   Nate is meeting with Mr. Carlson and is telling him that recent sales of orange yo-yos have not been so good. Mr. Carlson then asks where Ravi is. Nate explains that he thinks Ravi made up a story about losing his notes so he could **get out of** meeting with Mr. Carlson. Mr. Carlson asks Nate why he thinks that. Nate says he saw Ravi's notes under his lunch box. Mr. Carlson says he will speak to Ravi later. Mr. Carlson then surprises Nate by telling him he really likes the pictures of yo-yos on his tie. Mr. Carlson asks him where he can buy a tie like that. Nate says he is planning to clean out his closet tonight. He's pretty sure he has another old yo-yo tie he can give Mr. Carlson.

Write sentences using the phrasal verb and bonus words in italics.

1. Why can't Leanne get out of wearing the bear costume?

_____

2. What does Ravi get out of doing?

_____

3. When you were younger, did you try to get out of performing at a recital?

_____

4. If someone asked you to wear a ridiculous outfit, how would you try to get out of it?

_____

Give Up   Stop trying to do

Does not take an object

You may hear it used like this: She tried to yell for help, but after two hours she **gave up**.

It's time to meet some of our characters. Read these conversations aloud.

Lydia (32, James' neighbor): "Hi, James. Happy *Fourth of July*! Do you need some help?"

James (40, a man trying to cook): "Yes, I was about to **give up**. I'm supposed to cook some *grilled cheese sandwiches* for the neighborhood's *Independence Day* party, but I'm having trouble turning the gas grill on."

A while later . . .

Lydia: "Haven't you tried to teach James how to use the gas grill? I had to show him how to do it this morning."

Miranda (38, James' wife): "Yes, I've tried many times, but I've **given up**. Perhaps I'll buy him a toaster oven for next year's party."

Let's perform the skits. Take roles, add your ideas, and practice the phrasal verbs.

Skit 1   The Fourth of July party went well. Almost everyone enjoyed the grilled cheese sandwiches, although some were burned. Lorna (42, Miranda's neighbor) is complaining to Miranda that her sandwich was completely black. Miranda apologizes and tells Lorna that she has tried to teach James how to use the grill but she **gave up**. Lorna says she knows how she feels because Herbert (46, her husband) isn't very handy either. She explains that yesterday she spent a long time trying to show Herbert how to open the trunk of his car. She finally **gave up** after four hours.

Skit 2   James and Herbert have just run into each other outside the *hardware store*. James asks Herbert if he enjoyed the Independence Day party. Herbert says he did, except for the overcooked sandwiches. James apologizes and explains how he has trouble with the gas grill. Herbert then admits he sometimes has trouble with his car. He says that whenever he needs help, Lorna tells him, "Don't **give up**! You can do it!" James says that whenever he tries to use the grill, Miranda tells him, "Keep at it! You can do it!" James then asks if Herbert can help him open his trunk, because it's stuck. Herbert says, "Don't **give up**! You can do it!"

Write sentences using the phrasal verb and bonus words in italics.

1. When James was supposed to make grilled cheese sandwiches, did he give up?

_____

2. Why does Herbert tell James not to give up?

_____

3. Do you ever feel like giving up when you're studying English?

_____

4. If your teacher asked you to guess his or her middle name, how much time would you spend before giving up?

_____

Put Off   Delay doing

Can take an object between the verb and the preposition

You may hear it used like this: He always **puts off** doing laundry until the weekend.

It's time to meet some of our characters. Read these conversations aloud.

Dianne (25, a businesswoman): "I've been thinking of starting a business called **Put It Off** Enterprises. I'll help people who have *waited until the last minute* to buy a gift."

Marcia (28, Dianne's sister): "What a great idea! Can I be your first customer? I need to buy Mom a birthday present, and her birthday's today!"

A while later . . .

Dianne (who is answering the phone): "**Put It Off** Enterprises. May I help you?"

Gunther (42, Dianne's customer): "Yes. I need help buying my wife new glasses because I accidentally sat on her old ones last month. I've been **putting it off** for four weeks, but I can't wait any longer because she can't see anything."

Let's perform the skits. Take roles, add your ideas, and practice the phrasal verbs.

Skit 1   The next morning, Dianne meets Gunther at the *optician's* shop. She asks him what kind of glasses his wife likes (very light ones). Dianne suggests that this time he buy some glasses with heavier *frames*, which won't break as easily. Gunther agrees, telling her he has accidentally sat on several pairs of glasses recently. He then says they'd better get on with it, because he needs to give his wife the new glasses at lunchtime. Dianne asks why he **put it off** for so long. Gunther admits that last month he sat on his own glasses as well. He just got new glasses yesterday, so he was finally able to drive.

Skit 2   Marcia is asking Dianne how her business is going. Dianne says she's enjoying herself and explains how Gunther **put off** buying new glasses for himself and his wife. Marcia says that she has a neighbor named Gunther who always **puts things off**. Marcia explains that last week, Gunther asked her if he could borrow a few pots. Dianne asks why he needed those. Marcia says that Gunther's roof has been leaking for a while and he ran out of pots to catch the water. Dianne asks why Gunther has **put off** getting it fixed. Marcia says that Gunther explained that he likes the sound of the water dripping into the pots. It helps him go to sleep on rainy nights.

Write sentences using the phrasal verb and bonus words in italics.

1. What kind of people will Put It Off Enterprises help?

_____

2. Why can't Gunther put off going to the optician's any longer?

_____

3. Do you put things off until the last minute or do you do things early?

_____

4. Do you ever put off studying?

_____

Sit Around/Stand Around   Sit/stand while not doing very much
Do not take an object

You may hear them used like this: She **sat around** at home while he **stood around** outside.

It's time to meet some of our characters. Read these conversations aloud.

Warren (19, a man waiting in a long line outside a restaurant): "Hi. I've been waiting here for three hours now. I hope the free ice cream tastes good."

René (17, another man waiting): "Me too. Waiting for free ice cream from Grape Paradise is better than **sitting around** at home eating plain grapes."

A while later . . .

Warren: "Hi. I'm so tired from **standing around** for five hours. What did you do while I waited for my free ice cream?"

Esmeralda (18, Warren's girlfriend): "Not much. I just **sat around** and counted how many grapes I could eat. I stopped counting at ninety-nine."

Let's perform the skits. Take roles, add your ideas, and practice the phrasal verbs.

Skit 1   Warren is telling Zoe (49, his mother) that he **stood around** waiting for some free ice cream yesterday. She asks him how it tasted. Warren says it wasn't very good, but he met some interesting people while he was in line. Zoe asks him to tell her about them. Warren says that one man spent thirty minutes trying to bounce a *flat* basketball. Then the man gave up and started dancing. Zoe asks Warren to describe him (about Zoe's age and very tall). Zoe says that the man sounds like someone she used to *have a crush on*. Although his basketballs always ran out of air, he was a very good dancer.

Skit 2   Warren is telling Esmeralda that he's tired of **sitting around** every evening after work. She suggests they go to a magic show, and he agrees. The next evening, they dress up and go to the show. They arrive a little early, so Warren suggests they **sit around** in the *lobby* and look at what everyone else is wearing. Esmeralda notices a man in a purple suit. Warren comments that the man forgot to put on his shoes. Then, it's time for the show to begin. Near the end of the show, Massimo (42, the magician) asks for a volunteer to help him with a trick. Esmeralda offers to help him pull a rabbit out of a hat. When it's time to pull the rabbit out, she is surprised that she pulls out a bunch of grapes instead.

Write sentences using the phrasal verb and bonus words in italics.

1. When Warren stood around waiting for some ice cream, what kind of people did he meet?

_____

2. Where are Warren and Esmeralda sitting around when they notice the man with no shoes?

_____

3. Do you like to sit around and chat on the phone?

_____

4. Would you stand around for a long time to get something free?

_____

Sit Out   Not participate (often used with games)

Can take an object between the verb and the preposition (often "it")

You may hear it used like this: She decided to **sit it out** because she didn't feel like playing.

It's time to meet some of our characters. Read these conversations aloud.

Gérard (17, a boy who likes tennis): "Virginie, do you want to play another game of tennis with me?"

Virginie (16, Gérard's sister): "No, thanks. I think I'll **sit this one out** because I'm having trouble playing in all this snow."

A while later . . .

Gérard: "Auguste, would you like to play tennis with me? Virginie is **sitting it out** because she's cold."

Auguste (14, Gérard's brother): "OK, but I hope you don't mind if I play with my Ping-Pong paddle. I forgot to bring my tennis racket."

Let's perform the skits. Take roles, add your ideas, and practice the phrasal verbs.

Skit 1 Gérard and Auguste are enjoying playing tennis. After a few minutes, Gérard tells Auguste that he too wants to play with a Ping-Pong paddle. Gérard asks Virginie if she could walk home and get him one. She agrees and says she'll bring some Ping-Pong balls too. Auguste then suggests that Virginie get a warm coat so she won't have to **sit out** any more games. Virginie likes the idea and says she'll be back soon. When she returns, she says she's ready to play. Gérard says he'll **sit this game out** so Virginie can play. Auguste then asks Virginie why she's wearing Dad's *windbreaker* instead of her warm ski jacket. Virginie says she couldn't put on her ski jacket because Dad was wearing it while washing the dishes.

Skit 2 Virginie is telling Claude (45, her father) that she *had a ball* playing tennis with her brothers. Claude asks if they argued about whose turn it was. Virginie explains that they behaved well and took turns **sitting it out**. Virginie then mentions they were playing Ping-Pong on the tennis court. Claude starts reminiscing about the good old days, when he played Ping-Pong every weekend with his friends. Virginie says she didn't know he used to play Ping-Pong. Claude explains how he and his friends used to play Ping-Pong with tennis rackets. He remembers that he didn't mind **sitting out** a game or two because it was fun to see how far his friends could hit the Ping-Pong ball.

Write sentences using the phrasal verb and bonus words in italics.

1. Why does Virginie want to sit out the game of tennis with Gérard?

_____

2. Why does Gérard offer to sit out the next game?

_____

3. Do you like to play board games or do you usually sit them out?

_____

4. If your teacher suggested you play a word game in English, would you play or sit it out?

_____

Turn In   Go to bed/sleep
Does not take an object

> You may hear it used like this: They were sleepy, so they **turned in** early.

It's time to meet some of our characters. Read these conversations aloud.

Lionel (24, a man attending a *lion tamers'* convention): "Excuse me, miss. I'm ready to **turn in**. Do I have any messages?"

Britney (19, the front desk clerk at the Pillow Palace Hotel): "Yes, sir. *Housekeeping* wanted me to let you know that the hotel has run out of clean pillows. We're very sorry."

A while later . . .

Lionel (who is calling his wife): "Hi, Katarina. I was going to **turn in** for the night, but there are no clean pillows in the hotel. What can I use instead of a pillow?"

Katarina (22, Lionel's wife): "Hmm. Maybe you can use the stuffed animal you always carry with you. You know, your stuffed lion."

Let's perform the skits. Take roles, add your ideas, and practice the phrasal verbs.

Skit 1   The next morning at the convention, Lionel is really sleepy, so he spends the morning sitting around in an armchair. Wayne (30, another lion tamer) asks him why he's so tired. Lionel explains what happened last night when he wanted to **turn in** early at the Pillow Palace Hotel. Lionel says he tried to use his stuffed lion as a pillow, but it wasn't soft enough. Wayne then tells Lionel he's staying at the *Air Bed* Inn, and he's sleepy too. He says he **turned in** late because he had trouble blowing up his bed. He finally gave up and slept on the floor.

Skit 2   Lionel is driving home from the convention. He calls Katarina on his cell phone and asks her to make sure the bed is ready because he'd like to **turn in** as soon as he gets home. Katarina asks him if he enjoyed the convention. He says he didn't get much sleep, but he learned a lot about brushing *manes*. Katarina asks him if he remembered to ask the other lion tamers about how to brush a lion's teeth. Lionel says he kept putting it off because he was sleepy, and then all of a sudden the convention was over. He's mad at himself for not getting the information. Katarina says that he has a dentist's appointment tomorrow, so maybe he can ask his dentist about it.

Write sentences using the phrasal verb and bonus words in italics.

1. Why does Lionel call Katarina instead of turning in?

2. Why did Wayne turn in late?

3. Do you like to stay up late or do you usually turn in early?

4. What time are you planning to turn in tonight?

Chapter Review Questions

Rewrite each sentence using the correct phrasal verb. Choices: **get out of, give up, put off, sit around/stand around, sit out, turn in.**

1. They like to sit on the couch all day.

_____

2. I usually delay doing my homework.

_____

3. She doesn't want to work, so she's trying to avoid going.

_____

4. He wants to go to sleep early.

_____

5. I tried to learn how to dance but then I stopped trying.

_____

6. She doesn't feel like playing the game this time.

_____

7. I usually go to bed at 11 p.m.

_____

8. He was supposed to mow the lawn before noon, but he waited until the last minute.

_____

9. They usually stand outside the mall on weekends.

_____

10. I was able to avoid taking the test because I was sick.

_____

11. I was too tired to play the game so I didn't participate.

_____

12. She tried to break out of prison but then she stopped trying because it was too difficult.

_____

CHAPTER 19

UP THE CORPORATE LADDER
(WORKING)

Clock In/Punch In/Clock Out/Punch Out   Use a *timeclock* to indicate you are starting/finishing work

"Clock in" and "punch in" mean the same thing; "clock out" and "punch out" mean the same thing; do not take an object

You may hear them used like this: She **clocked in** just as I was **punching out**.

It's time to meet some of our characters. Read these conversations aloud.

Consuelo (41, a worker in a toy factory): "Gaby, why have you been standing next to the timeclock for two hours? Are you trying to get out of working?"

Gaby (33, another worker): "Hi, Consuelo. Well, when I tried to **clock in** this morning, my fingers got stuck in the machine. I'm just waiting for the repairman to arrive."

A while later . . .

Giancarlo (32, the repairman): "Hi, ma'am. I guess no one can **punch out** until I fix this. Have you been having fun watching everyone else work?"

Gaby: "Well, some people might want to stand around instead of working, but I love my job. I sew legs on toy *donkeys*."

Let's perform the skits. Take roles, add your ideas, and practice the phrasal verbs.

Skit 1   Gaby was freed from the timeclock at 1 p.m., five hours after she broke it. She tells Mr. Goodman (50, her boss) that she's not up to doing any work. He says she can **clock out** if she agrees to work extra hard tomorrow. He says he expects her to sew twice as many legs on the toy donkeys as she normally does. Gaby agrees to **punch in** at 5 a.m. tomorrow. Gaby then asks Mr. Goodman if he could **punch out** for her because she doesn't want to go near the machine. He agrees. Then she asks if he could **clock in** for her tomorrow morning. Mr. Goodman says 5 a.m. is too early. He says she can come in at 6 instead.

Skit 2   At 6 a.m. the next day, Gaby and Mr. Goodman arrive at the factory. She thanks him for **clocking in** for her. A while later, Consuelo starts picking on Gaby for getting her hand stuck in the timeclock. Gaby ignores her and starts working. At about 8, Mr. Goodman looks at some of the donkeys Gaby has finished and tells her to **punch out** because she's fired. Gaby is shocked. Mr. Goodman asks her why she sewed eight legs on each donkey. He says these are donkeys, not octopuses. She explains that he told her to sew twice as many legs on the toy donkeys as she normally does. Gaby offers to do them over. Mr. Goodman says he knows of a job opening in the toy octopus department.

Write sentences using the phrasal verb and bonus words in italics.

1. What happened when Gaby clocked in at the toy factory?

_____

2. Why does Mr. Goodman tell Gaby to punch out?

_____

3. Have you had a job where you needed to punch in (instead of writing the time yourself)?

_____

4. Do you prefer to clock out early or late?

_____

Get Off   Leave work (usually at a scheduled time)

Usually does not take an object (sometimes, however, you can say, "get off work")

You may hear it used like this: I usually **get off** work at midnight.

It's time to meet some of our characters. Read these conversations aloud.

Madeleine (20, a waitress): "Vladimir, what are you doing when you **get off** work tonight?"

Vladimir (22, a cook): "Well, I'm going skiing with my brother this weekend, so I thought I'd practice some ski jumping in my living room."

A while later . . .

Misha (25, Vladimir's brother, a shoe salesman): "I can't wait till tomorrow, when we leave for our skiing trip. Do you think you can **get off** early tomorrow?"

Vladimir: "I'm not sure. Someone's renting the restaurant for a big party, so I have to cook two hundred pieces of *French toast* and six hundred pieces of bacon."

Let's perform the skits. Take roles, add your ideas, and practice the phrasal verbs.

Skit 1   The next day, Vladimir calls Misha at 5 p.m. to tell him he can't **get off** work until 7. Misha says he also has to work late. Misha thinks he'll be able to **get off** at 6:30. The shoe store where he works has been very busy because they're having a sale on *flip-flops*. Misha adds that ten businessmen are waiting to try some on right now, so he can't talk long. Vladimir asks Misha to meet him outside the restaurant at 7. Misha agrees and asks if Vladimir can bring some French toast with maple syrup. Vladimir says he's not sure there will be any left, but he will try to bring some in his pockets.

Skit 2   Vladimir has **gotten off** work, and Misha is waiting for him outside the restaurant. Misha asks Vladimir if he brought any French toast. Vladimir takes a *soggy* piece out of his pocket. Misha looks at the bread and says he's not sure he wants to eat it since it's covered in *lint*. Vladimir then tells Misha that they should probably leave because they both **got off** so late. Before they get in the car, they check to see if they have everything they need. When Vladimir notices that he forgot his ski boots, Misha tells him he can borrow a pair of flip-flops that he bought just before he **got off** work.

Write sentences using the phrasal verb and bonus words in italics.

1. Why can't Vladimir get off early tomorrow?

_____

2. What did Misha buy just before he got off work?

_____

3. What do you usually do when you get off work?

_____

4. Do you get off work at the same time every day?

_____

Knock Off   Leave work (usually early)

Does not take an object

You may hear it used like this: I **knocked off** early because I wasn't feeling well.

It's time to meet some of our characters. Read these conversations aloud.

Mr. Workman (52, the boss): "So, Véronique, why do you want to **knock off** so early today? I don't usually let employees leave before their *shift* ends."

Véronique (22, the employee): "Well, sir, I'd like to go home and practice my *juggling*. I'm meeting my boyfriend's parents tonight and I want to make a good impression."

A while later . . .

Tatiana (25, Véronique's roommate): "Véronique, why are you home in the middle of the day?"

Véronique: "Well, the boss let me **knock off** early so I could practice my juggling. Do you know where Timmy the Turtle is? He always likes watching me practice."

Let's perform the skits. Take roles, add your ideas, and practice the phrasal verbs.

Skit 1   It's 5 p.m. and Véronique has been practicing her juggling for the past two hours. She keeps dropping the juggling balls, and Timmy the Turtle has just been sitting around instead of picking them up for her. All of a sudden, the phone rings. Elmer (23, her boyfriend) wants to know if he can stop by at 6. Véronique tells him she thought he was working until 7. Elmer says he was able to **knock off** early because sales at the Juggling *Emporium* were slow. Véronique says it would be great if he came by at 6 because she needs some juggling advice. She says it's really hard to juggle with one hand while hopping on one foot.

Skit 2   Mr. and Mrs. Gibson (54, Elmer's parents) are taking Elmer and Véronique out to dinner. Mrs. Gibson asks Véronique where she met Elmer. Véronique says she fell for him when she saw him performing at the Juggling Emporium three months ago. Elmer adds that on the day they met, he asked his boss if he could **knock off** early because *the woman of his dreams* had just asked him out. Véronique then tells Mrs. Gibson that Elmer's boss wouldn't let him punch out early, so she and Timmy the Turtle watched him sell juggling balls for two hours. Mr. Gibson then asks Véronique if she can juggle. She offers to show Mr. and Mrs. Gibson how she juggles.

Write sentences using the phrasal verb and bonus words in italics.

1. Why does Mr. Workman let Véronique knock off early?

_____

2. Why was Elmer able to knock off early today?

_____

3. Do you ever knock off early?

_____

4. What would you say if your teacher wanted to knock off before your class ended?

_____

Move Up   Be promoted

Does not take an object

> You may hear it used like this: She is **moving up** fast. She might become a vice president soon.

It's time to meet some of our characters. Read these conversations aloud.

Edgar (46, the dad): "Hi, Kendall. Did you enjoy work at the car wash today?"

Kendall (20, the son): "Oh, I had a great time. My boss told me I could **move up** next week. Then, when I dry the cars I can use towels instead of just blowing air on them."

A while later . . .

Henrietta (42, the mom): "So, Kendall, Dad tells me you'll be **moving up** at the car wash. What will you be doing?"

Kendall: "Well, why don't you stop by next week and see? The van could definitely use a wash. I don't think you've washed it since last year."

Let's perform the skits. Take roles, add your ideas, and practice the phrasal verbs.

Skit 1   The following week, Henrietta visits the car wash and sees Kendall drying a car using some nice *monogrammed* towels. She tells Kendall she's very proud of him for **moving up** to such an important position. He smiles and says he hopes to **move up** even higher. Henrietta asks what other jobs he could do at the car wash. He tells her there are a lot of opportunities to **move up**. For example, he could work in the Soap Department or even the Wheel Washing Department. Then, Henrietta asks him why he's using her monogrammed towels at work. He says that his new job requires him to use towels from home. He says he just remembered that the monogrammed ones were her favorite.

Skit 2   A few weeks later, Ms. Washington (40, Kendall's boss) is asking Kendall if he likes being part of the towel *crew*. He says he has been enjoying his new job but would be interested in **moving up** again if Ms. Washington wants to promote him. Ms. Washington says that one of the employees is **moving up** to a management position, and she would like to offer his old job to Kendall. Kendall asks what his new job will be. She says he will be the new wheel washer. Kendall asks what kind of brush he will be using to clean the wheels. Ms. Washington says plenty of toothbrushes will be available.

Write sentences using the phrasal verb and bonus words in italics.

1. When Kendall moved up the first time, what did he use to dry the cars?

_____

2. When Kendall moves up the second time, what will his job be?

_____

3. Would there be a lot of opportunities to move up if you worked at a car wash?

_____

4. If you moved up but didn't like your new job, would you ask for your old job back?

_____

Put In For   Request (usually a raise, different job, or vacation)
Is followed by a noun phrase or pronoun

You may hear it used like this: She **put in for** extra vacation, but her boss denied the request.

It's time to meet some of our characters. Read these conversations aloud.

Helena (24, a bank employee): "Pietro, I've been thinking of **putting in for** a new job at the bank."
Pietro (25, Helena's husband): "Why? Aren't you happy dusting the money in the *vault*?"

A while later . . .

Helena: "Hello, Leslie. I'm thinking about **putting in for** the job that was advertised on the bank's
Web site. Can you please give me the application?"
Leslie (40, the personnel manager): "Which position do you want to apply for? We have openings in
the Penny Counting and Quarter Counting departments."

Let's perform the skits. Take roles, add your ideas, and practice the phrasal verbs.

Skit 1   Pietro and Helena are playing cards with Dominique (25, their friend). At the end of the
hand, Helena says she's going to sit the next few hands out because she wants to work on her
résumé. Dominique asks Helena why she's not happy with her job. Helena explains that she wants a
new job because people look down on her for working in the Dusting Department. Pietro adds that
Helena is going to **put in for** a job in the bank's Quarter Counting Department. Dominique asks
Helena why she chose to apply for that job. Helena explains that she **put in for** it because people in
that department work fewer hours than others in the bank. They work only a quarter of an hour at a
time.

Skit 2   Helena has been working in the Quarter Counting Department for two months. She is
asking Daniel (30, her co-worker) how much she can expect if she **puts in for** a raise. He says he
always gets a quarter more per hour whenever he requests one. She then asks him if he has always
worked in the Quarter Counting Department. He says he has but that he sometimes thinks about
putting in for a different job at the bank. She asks him why he hasn't gone through with it. He
answers that he likes the hours he works in the department. Helena says that if he ever changes his
mind about **putting in for** a new job, she recommends the Dusting Department. Although they
must work eight hours a day, they are allowed to yell, "Goodbye dust!"

Write sentences using the phrasal verb and bonus words in italics.

1. Why is Helena thinking of putting in for a new job?

_____

2. What kind of job did Helena put in for?

_____

3. If you put in for more time off, would your boss agree to your request?

_____

4. What happened the last time you put in for a raise? Did you get one?

_____

Write Up   Write a negative report/evaluation about an employee

Can take an object between the verb and the preposition

You may hear it used like this: He **wrote her up** because she was always late.

It's time to meet some of our characters. Read these conversations aloud.

Spencer (24, an employee of *Mask* World, which Mrs. Baum, 42, owns): "Jamie, I can't believe Mrs. Baum **wrote you up** for wearing a scary mask in the store!"

Jamie (21, Spencer's co-worker): "Neither can I. I was just trying to show the customers our most expensive mask."

A while later . . .

Jamie: "Spencer, has Mrs. Baum ever **written you up?**"

Spencer: "Yes, I got a bad review last month. Mrs. Baum was upset because I told her that the mask she was planning to wear one evening didn't *suit* her."

Let's perform the skits. Take roles, add your ideas, and practice the phrasal verbs.

Skit 1   Jamie is meeting with Mrs. Baum to go over her evaluation. Jamie explains why she wore the scary mask in the store and apologizes for putting it on. Mrs. Baum says she will **write Jamie up** if she does it again. Only Mrs. Baum is allowed to wear the masks. Jamie then asks if Mrs. Baum is happy with the rest of her work. Mrs. Baum says that except for wearing the mask, Jamie has been a perfect employee. Mrs. Baum then asks Jamie if she likes the bright green mask that Mrs. Baum has been wearing all day. Jamie asks Mrs. Baum not to **write her up** for saying that it doesn't match her pants.

Skit 2   Homer (43, Jamie's father) is asking Jamie if she likes her job at Mask World. She says she does but mentions that she has been **written up** already. Homer asks her to explain, so she tells him why Mrs. Baum **wrote her up**. Homer then asks Jamie if she *gets a discount* on masks in the store. He wants to buy Jamie's mom a mask but is not sure he has enough money to *pay full price.* Jamie says she gets fifteen percent off and suggests he stop by the store tomorrow after he gets off work. Homer says he can clock out at 4 p.m. Jamie says she will show him a really great mask that Mom will love. She describes the scary mask she was wearing when she got **written up.** Homer asks her if she will be able to model it for him.

Write sentences using the phrasal verb and bonus words in italics.

1. Why did Mrs. Baum write Jamie up?

_____

2. Why was Spencer written up last month?

_____

3. If your boss wrote you up, would you ask for an explanation?

_____

4. If you worked at a store, would you get written up if you gave your family members a big discount?

_____

Chapter Review Questions

Rewrite each sentence using the correct phrasal verb. Choices: **clock in/punch in/clock out/punch out, get off, knock off, move up, put in for, write up.**

1. I left work two hours early.

_____

2. Her boss gave her a negative evaluation.

_____

3. He left work on time at 6 p.m.

_____

4. I'd like to get a promotion.

_____

5. She started work at 8 a.m.

_____

6. Yesterday she asked her boss for some vacation time.

_____

7. My boss never lets me leave before my shift is over.

_____

8. She lost her timecard so she couldn't use it when she left work.

_____

9. She doesn't like giving bad evaluations because it puts her employees through a lot of stress.

_____

10. What time do you leave work tonight?

_____

11. He's thinking about applying for a managerial position.

_____

12. She's on her way up in the company.

_____

CHAPTER 20

OFF DUTY AND ON VACATION (RELAXING)

Check In (To)   Arrive (usually at a place where you need to register)

If not followed by "to," does not take an object; if used with "to," is followed by a noun phrase or pronoun

Check Out (Of)   Leave (often a hotel)

If not followed by "of," does not take an object; if used with "of," is followed by a noun phrase or pronoun

---

You may hear them used like this: The president was **checking into** the hotel just as I was **checking out**.

It's time to meet some of our characters. Read these conversations aloud.

Giorgio (27, a hotel guest who will *be in a wedding* tomorrow): "Hi, ma'am. My wife and I would like to **check in**. Oh, and could I borrow a needle and thread? I need to *hem* my tuxedo pants because they are way too long."

Emma (35, the hotel's front desk clerk): "I'm sorry, sir, but we don't have any needles. Would you like to borrow this stapler instead?"

A while later . . .

Deanna (23, Giorgio's wife): "Giorgio, your pants look terrible with these staples in them. Maybe we should **check out** and find a hotel that can lend us a needle."

Giorgio: "Dear, I don't think the groom will notice my stapled pants tomorrow. He'll be too busy trying to remember where he put the wedding rings."

Let's perform the skits. Take roles, add your ideas, and practice the phrasal verbs.

Skit 1   Matilda (39, a guest at the wedding) is sitting next to Deanna at the ceremony. Matilda asks Deanna what's wrong with Giorgio's pants. Deanna explains about **checking into** the hotel last night and borrowing the stapler. Matilda asks why Giorgio didn't take the pants to a tailor. Deanna says he probably should have. Deanna then asks if Matilda can recommend a local tailor because Giorgio will need help removing the staples. Deanna explains that she accidentally stapled his bright yellow socks to his pants when she was hemming the pants this morning.

Skit 2   Russell (54, a tailor) is at Deanna and Giorgio's hotel room trying to fix Giorgio's pants. Russell tells Giorgio it will be difficult to make the pants look better, but he'll try. Deanna then tells Russell they need to **check out** in about an hour. While Russell is working, Giorgio remembers that they need him to fix something else before they **check out**. He tells Russell that he stapled his pillow to the sheet last night because Deanna kept throwing it at him in her sleep. Could Russell fix that too?

Write sentences using the phrasal verb and bonus words in italics.

1. Why are Giorgio and Deanna checking into the hotel?

_____

2. Why does Deanna suggest they check out?

_____

3. Have you ever checked into a really expensive hotel?

_____

4. Have you ever realized you left something important in a hotel after you checked out?

_____

Eat Out   Eat in a restaurant

Does not take an object

> You may hear it used like this: She **eats out** every night when she's on vacation.

It's time to meet some of our characters. Read these conversations aloud.

Margaret (42, a hotel guest): "Sir, can you recommend a nice restaurant *within walking distance* of the hotel? My husband and I would like to **eat out** tonight and get some exercise too."

Serge (37, the *concierge*): "Sure. Our guests love the Exercise Café, which is fairly close. You order your meal and then try to catch up to the waiter, who runs through the restaurant with your food."

A while later . . .

Mr. Waite (28, the waiter, who speaks and then runs off): "Welcome to the Exercise Café, the most exciting place in town to **eat out**."

Margaret (who has to shout as she runs): "Wait! We'd like to sit down now! We've just walked two miles."

Let's perform the skits. Take roles, add your ideas, and practice the phrasal verbs.

Skit 1   Margaret and Virgil (48, her husband) are waiting for the Exercise Café's menu. Margaret asks Virgil how long it's been since they **ate out**. Virgil thinks they last **ate out** when they went on their honeymoon, three years ago. When Mr. Waite runs past their table, he throws them a menu. Margaret and Virgil each order a special. When Mr. Waite tells them their food is ready, Margaret and Virgil chase him around the restaurant. Mr. Waite gets away at first, but they finally catch up to him. Virgil grabs the food, and they both enjoy their meal. When it's time to pay, Virgil puts some cash in his back pocket and makes Mr. Waite chase him through the restaurant.

Skit 2   Margaret is thanking Serge for recommending the Exercise Café. Serge says he's glad she enjoyed **eating out** there. Then Serge asks if Margaret would tell his supervisor that he did a good job. He explains that he was recently written up and wants his boss to know that the hotel guests appreciate him. Margaret tells him she'd be happy to do that. She says she'll recommend that the boss let him knock off early today. Serge thanks her and asks if she needs another restaurant recommendation. Margaret says she would like to **eat out** again tonight because it's so nice to have someone else cook. Serge recommends that she and her husband try the Cook It Yourself Cantina.

Write sentences using the phrasal verb and bonus words in italics.

1. At what kind of place does Margaret want to eat out?

_____

2. Who recommends that Margaret eat out at the Exercise Café?

_____

3. Do you always eat out when you're on vacation?

_____

4. How often do you eat out when you're not on vacation?

_____

Fly In (To)   Arrive somewhere in an airplane

If not followed by "to," does not take an object; if used with "to," is followed by a noun phrase or pronoun

Fly Out (Of)   Leave somewhere in an airplane

If not followed by "of," does not take an object; if used with "of," is followed by a noun phrase or pronoun

> You may hear them used like this: We **flew into** London, took a train to France, and then **flew out of** Paris.

It's time to meet some of our characters. Read these conversations aloud.

Mrs. Lafayette (53, a schoolteacher): "Hi, class. Our trip to the *archaeological site* begins tomorrow. Be sure to turn in early because we are **flying out** at 6 a.m."

Bartholomew (16, a student): "Mrs. Lafayette, I can't wait to get on the plane! I'm really looking forward to eating the airplane food!"

A while later . . .

Bartholomew (who is on the phone): "Mom, we just **flew in**, but my luggage got lost. What should I do?"

Yolanda (41, Bartholomew's mother): "Well, I'm sure the airline will find your bags soon. Until then, why don't you borrow some clothes from Mrs. Lafayette?"

Let's perform the skits. Take roles, add your ideas, and practice the phrasal verbs.

Skit 1   Bartholomew is telling Kyle (17, his classmate) he is looking forward to visiting the archaeological site. Kyle asks how they will be getting there. Bartholomew thinks they will **fly out** on a small plane. Kyle says he usually throws up on small planes, so he's *dreading* the flight. Bartholomew says that Kyle will want to laugh, not be sick, tomorrow. Kyle asks him what he means. He replies that his bags were lost and that he has been borrowing Mrs. Lafayette's clothes. Tomorrow he'll be borrowing a shirt with flowers on it.

Skit 2   Bartholomew is calling Yolanda to tell her he has just **flown in**. When Yolanda gets to *Baggage Claim*, she looks around but doesn't see her son. When she finally *spots* him, she asks him why he's wearing a very large flowered shirt. He explains that just as he was checking out of the hotel, his lost bags arrived. He didn't have time to take off the clothes he had borrowed from Mrs. Lafayette because they were going to be **flying out** within the hour. Yolanda asks him if he enjoyed the trip. He says he and his friend Kyle enjoyed eating out at a restaurant near an archaeological site they visited. They both loved the fried lizard soup.

Write sentences using the phrasal verb and bonus words in italics.

1. Is Kyle looking forward to flying out to the archaeological site?

2. When Bartholomew flies in, where does Yolanda meet him?

3. What airport did you fly out of when you last took a trip?

4. When relatives fly in, where do you usually meet them?

Run Up (A Bill)   Accumulate charges

Is followed by a noun phrase (almost always a "bill" [often for food/telephone] or a "tab" [often for drinks])

> You may hear it used like this: They **ran up** a huge bill at the luxury resort.

It's time to meet some of our characters. Read these conversations aloud.

Clyde (46, a man looking at a credit card receipt): "How did we **run up** such a large bill when we ate out last night? We ate only ice cubes for dinner."

Christine (42, Clyde's wife): "Well, we had to pay for all the dishes the waiter broke when you accidentally tripped him."

A while later . . .

Monty (24, Clyde and Christine's waiter last night): "So, Ike, I had some really good customers last night. They **ran up** a huge bill and left me a really big tip."

Ike (57, Monty's boss): "That's good, but I'm afraid you may need to put in for a job somewhere else. We might have to close the restaurant because almost all of our dishes got broken last night."

Let's perform the skits. Take roles, add your ideas, and practice the phrasal verbs.

Skit 1   Monty is having a job interview at the Delicious Deli. Miss Delly (32, the restaurant's owner) asks him why he needs a new job. Monty tells her that the restaurant where he used to work had to close. He then explains about his customers who **ran up** a huge bill because they broke almost all of the restaurant's dishes. Miss Delly asks him what kind of job he wants. Monty says he'd like to move up from a regular waiter to *maître d'*. She then asks him what he needs to improve about himself. He admits he often spills drinks on customers, especially those who **run up** a *substantial* tab.

Skit 2   Clyde and Christine are eating out at the Delicious Deli. They notice that their waiter (who is Monty) looks familiar. Monty accidentally spills ice cubes on them. As he is cleaning up the mess, Christine asks him where they might have seen him before. Monty reminds them that they **ran up** a large bill at the restaurant where he used to work. Clyde apologizes for breaking the dishes. Monty apologizes for spilling the ice cubes and admits he does it a lot. Christine then asks Monty if his new boss gets mad at him for spilling so many ice cubes. Monty answers that Miss Delly doesn't get angry, although she does **run up** a pretty large ice cube bill.

Write sentences using the phrasal verb and bonus words in italics.

1. How did Clyde and Christine run up such a big bill?

_____

2. Why does Miss Delly run up a large ice cube bill?

_____

3. Have you ever run up a substantial bill at a toy store?

_____

4. If you ran up a large tab at a restaurant, would you pay by credit card?

_____

Sleep In   Sleep late

Does not take an object

You may hear it used like this: They **slept in** until noon every day while on their honeymoon.

It's time to meet some of our characters. Read these conversations aloud.

Fiona (40, Lyle's wife, who is on vacation with her family): "Lyle, why did you **sleep in** so late today? You usually get up at 5 a.m."

Lyle (43, Dennis' father): "Well, I stayed up late last night helping Dennis get ready for the cake-decorating contest at the resort today. I had to teach him how to open a can of *icing*."

A while later . . .

Fiona: "Dennis, why didn't you **sleep in** this morning?"

Dennis (11): "Oh, I had a nightmare that I was eating some icing but it was mustard flavor. You know how I hate mustard."

Let's perform the skits. Take roles, add your ideas, and practice the phrasal verbs.

Skit 1   It's 11 a.m., and Lyle and Dennis are walking to one of the hotel's conference rooms to participate in the cake-decorating contest. When Dennis says he's sleepy, Lyle assures him he can **sleep in** tomorrow. Dennis says he thought they were flying out tomorrow at 10 a.m. Lyle says he's right and apologizes for *misleading* him. When they get to the conference room, Dennis is amazed to see fifty cakes and forty-nine big bowls of icing. Lyle says the hotel must have run up a huge bill buying so much icing. Then Dennis notices that one bowl of icing is missing. He approaches Mr. Holt (42, the judge of the contest) to tell him. When Mr. Holt turns around, he is holding tightly onto the missing bowl, and his face is full of yellow icing.

Skit 2   Mr. Holt has cleaned himself up and is getting ready to explain the cake-decorating rules to the contestants. He looks around the large room but sees only Dennis and Lyle, and another pair of contestants. Odette (35, the mom) says that the other people must have **slept in**. Kylie (9, the daughter) says she's glad they **slept in** because now she can eat more cake and icing. Mr. Holt asks Lyle and Odette if they want to cancel the contest. Odette suggests that, instead, they have a contest to see who can guess what kind of icing is in the bowls. Mr. Holt says that's a good idea, but he already knows that the icing is mustard flavor.

Write sentences using the phrasal verb and bonus words in italics.

1. Why didn't Dennis sleep in today?

___

2. Why can't Dennis sleep in tomorrow?

___

3. How often do you get to sleep in?

___

4. If you accidentally slept in and missed class, what would you tell your teacher the next day?

___

Take Off   Leave (in an airplane)

Does not take an object

You may hear it used like this: The plane **took off** on time.

It's time to meet some of our characters. Read these conversations aloud.

Alison (33, an ESL teacher): "Oh no! I accidentally slept in! I have to hurry and *catch my plane* to the National ESL Awards."

Jonathan (37, Alison's husband): "Don't worry. Last night, I set the clocks ahead by two hours. You still have plenty of time until your plane **takes off**."

A while later . . .

Ira (25, a taxi driver): "So, ma'am, what time does your plane **take off**? Do I have time to take the *scenic route* to the airport?"

Alison: "No, I'm leaving for the National ESL Awards in an hour. I'm winning the Silliest ESL Teacher Award."

Let's perform the skits. Take roles, add your ideas, and practice the phrasal verbs.

Skit 1   Alison has just checked into her hotel and is calling Jonathan. He asks if her plane **took off** on time. Alison says it **took off** two hours late. Jonathan then asks her what she did while she waited. She says that she chatted with some other ESL teachers who were going to the awards. He asks if she met anyone interesting. She says she became friendly with Cecil (30, an ESL teacher). Cecil was going to win the Tallest ESL Teacher Award. She says she felt sorry for him because once they got on the plane, Cecil hit his head on the ceiling whenever he stood up.

Skit 2   Mr. Ward (55, president of the National ESL Teacher Association) has just called Alison's name at the awards. At the *podium*, Alison thanks the association for giving her the Silliest ESL Teacher Award. Mr. Ward then announces a surprise for Alison. Pauline (12, one of Alison's ESL students) comes onto the stage and thanks Alison for teaching her so many phrasal verbs. Pauline says she will show Alison how much she has learned by using **take off**, take off, and take off in two sentences. Pauline says, "Right after the plane **took off**, I took off my shoes. However, my brother started tickling me, so I took off down the aisle." The audience claps. Then Alison and Pauline start to pretend they are airplanes **taking off** (they make an airplane noise). Then they take off their shoes and take off down the aisle of the auditorium.

Write sentences using the phrasal verb and bonus words in italics.

1. Does Ira have time to take the scenic route or will Alison's plane take off soon?

_____

2. Did Alison's plane take off on time?

_____

3. Do you prefer to take off or to land?

_____

4. When you're on an airplane, do you take your shoes off after the plane has taken off?

_____

Chapter Review Questions

Rewrite each sentence using the correct phrasal verb. Choices: **check in (to)/check out (of), eat out, fly in (to)/fly out (of), run up (a bill), sleep in, take off.**

1. We took a plane into Philadelphia.

_____

2. He left from a small airport.

_____

3. They ate in a fancy restaurant.

_____

4. When I left the hotel, I accidentally left my toothbrush.

_____

5. She charged a lot of money on her credit card.

_____

6. He likes getting up late while on vacation.

_____

7. The airplane left on time.

_____

8. My family and I eat at a restaurant every Saturday night.

_____

9. I didn't set the alarm, so I accidentally slept late.

_____

10. Before you leave, perhaps you should buy a souvenir at the airport.

_____

11. We got to the hotel and then took a nap.

_____

12. She had a lot of drinks at the restaurant.

_____

GLOSSARY OF BONUS WORDS

Chapter 1
Behind the Wheel (Driving)

Behind the wheel: When you sit in the driver's seat in a vehicle

Break Down

To be stranded: To be unable to continue going somewhere, usually because of a transportation problem

To run errands: To go to various shops to buy/do things, such as buy stamps at the post office or get groceries

Hard of hearing: Cannot hear well

Quack: The sound a duck makes

Cut Off

Jerk: Someone you don't like; someone who is behaving badly

Soufflé: A French pudding that puffs high when baked in the oven

Puffy: Big; contains a lot of air like a cloud

Drive Around

To be tired of doing: To not want to do anymore

Bat: A small furry animal that flies at night

Darn: Something you say instead of a rude word when you are a little upset

Waste of time: Not worth spending time doing

Fill Up/Gas Up

Ninth annual: For the ninth year in a row

Convention: A gathering of people interested in the same hobby or business

To have a long day: To be tired after working hard

Pump: A machine that contains gas at the gas station

Run Over

On purpose: Intentional; not by accident

Dalmatian: A white dog with black spots

Woof: The sound a dog makes when it barks

Support group: A group of people with the same problem; they help each other by talking about the problem

Speed Up/Slow Down

Get out of my way: Another way to say, "Move away from me"

Backseat driver: An annoying passenger who tells a driver how to drive

Chapter 2
On Foot (Walking)

On foot: When you go somewhere without a vehicle

Catch Up (To)

To hop: To jump on one foot

To fall flat on my face: To hit the floor face first

Paramedic: A person who gives medical help before someone goes to a hospital

Clumsy: Falls down and drops things a lot

Head Out (To)

Diapers: What you put on a baby's bottom to keep it clean and dry

Wipes: Wet towels you use to clean a baby's bottom

Fruit stand: A place where farmers sell fruit

Hurry Up

I don't have all day: I'm in a hurry

Three-legged race: A race where two people stand side by side and tie their inside legs together; they then run with "three" legs

To catch your breath: To be able to breathe at a normal rate

Double feature: When two movies are shown one after the other

Run Off (With)

Suspect: Someone that the police think committed a crime

Polka-dotted: With spots/dots on it

Accomplice: Someone who participates in a crime with another person

To get stung: To be injured by a bee or wasp

Take Off

Chore: A task that you must do at home, like vacuum or load the dishwasher

Folks: People; also, *my folks* means "my parents"

To make small talk: To discuss unimportant topics, like "how are you?" and the weather

To be/get fired: To lose your job

Walk Up (To)

Bug: An insect

Weirdo: A strange person

Roach: A kind of insect (cockroach)

Tongue-tied: Unable to speak normally, as when you are nervous; shy

Chapter 3
At the Top of My Class (Studying)

At the top of your class: When you are the best student in your class

Be Up On

Special: Another food in a restaurant that is not always written on the menu

Snail: A small animal with a hard shell that you find in the garden

Sushi: A cold Japanese dish of rice with raw or cooked seafood/vegetables

Allergic to: Sensitive to something that makes you sick

Pail: A bucket; a container

Go Over

PJs: Pajamas; the clothes you wear to bed

To drain: To let the water go out

To lure: To make someone go to a certain place

Llama: An animal that lives in South America

Hand In/Turn In

Home Ec: Home Economics; a class in cooking, sewing, and other home-related topics

Peel: The skin of a vegetable or fruit

Leftovers: Food or other items that you didn't eat or use; extra

Gil: A man's name (short for Gilbert); a *gill* (same pronunciation) is what a fish uses to breathe

Look Up

Baldwin: A common last name; *bald* means having little or no hair

Hairpiece: A piece of fake hair

Shiny: Reflects light (as a bald head would)

Neon: A very bright color, such as "hot pink"

Read Up On

Brochure: A few pages that advertise something

Neat: Slang for "interesting"

Pirate: An evil sailor on a ship who steals valuable things from other ships

Tropical: Very warm; near the Equator

Sit In On

Geology: The study of rocks

A ton of: A lot of

To sell like hotcakes: To sell very well (hotcakes, or pancakes, are eaten for breakfast)

Chapter 4
In the Prime of Life (Youth)

In the prime of life: When you are young and have your whole future ahead of you

Break Out (In)

Pimples: Acne/spots on your face you get when you are a teenager

Yummy: Very delicious

Rash: Redness or other marks on your skin

Carry On

Earplugs: Things you put in your ears when you don't want to hear something

To have a tantrum: To become very upset and carry on loudly

To yell: To shout

Look Up To

Barefoot: Without shoes

Starving: If you're being serious, dying of hunger; if you're not, very hungry

To console: To try to make someone feel better

Put Up With

Field trip: When school children visit somewhere interesting with a teacher

The big cheese: Slang for "a very important person"

Quesadilla: A Mexican dish with cheese and a tortilla (flat bread)

Chunky: A *chunk* is a big piece of something; *chunky* can mean with big pieces or can describe an overweight person

Take After

To bang: To hit

Heavy sleeper: Someone who sleeps very deeply and doesn't wake up despite loud noises

To snore: To make loud breathing noises while sleeping

Runs in the family: When a lot of people in the family have the same characteristic

Tell Off

Crayon: A stick of colored wax used to draw pictures

To not mind: To think it's OK

To have a blast: To really enjoy yourself

Chapter 5
Around the House (At Home)

Around the house: Within the home

Clean Off

Messy: Not neat; when a lot of things are where they don't belong

Company: Guests

Super neat: Really tidy

Then again: On the other hand

Clean Out

Real estate agent: Someone who helps you buy or sell a house or other property

Junk: Items that are no longer useful

Walk-in closet: A closet large enough to walk into

Cubicle: A small square-shaped office space

Clean Up/Straighten Up/Clean Up After

To gossip: To talk about other people in an unfriendly manner

Oink oink: The sound a pig makes

Pig: Slang for someone who leaves a mess

To carpool: To share the driving so you use less gas

Run Out (Of)

To wipe: To clean using a rubbing motion

How come?: Why?

Grease stain: An oily mark

Load: A big pile; a lot of

Throw Away/Throw Out

Rags: Old pieces of fabric sometimes used for cleaning

Swap meet: A place where people sell used items; also called a *flea market*

Business is slow: When not many customers visit a shop

To get rid of: To throw away/discard

Wash Up

Nutty: Has nuts in it; silly

To pick weeds: To remove unwanted plants from the garden

To lick: To move your tongue over the surface of something, such as ice cream

Worm: A long, thin animal that lives in the earth

Chapter 6
On Sale (Clothing)

On sale: At a lower price than normal

Break In

Amateur: Not professional

Raft: Logs tied together to make a simple boat

Flippers: Footwear worn while swimming to make you go fast

Ow: Ouch; something you say when something is painful

Dress Up (In)/Dress Down (In)

Costume: Special clothes to make you look like someone/something else

Black tie: A very formal event where men wear tuxedos and women wear fancy dresses

In a panic: In a very worried manner; not calm at all

To go trick-or-treating: On Halloween, October 31, to dress up in a costume, visit the neighbors, and get candy

Hang Up

Teeny: Really small

Shower rod: A pole on which you hang a shower curtain

Rumpled: Wrinkled; not pressed

Shopping spree: When someone buys too much when going shopping

Put On

Long johns: Long underwear to keep your legs warm

Sloppy Joe sandwich: A messy meat and tomato sauce sandwich

To compromise: To change your point of view a little so you can agree with someone

Oops: Something you say when you do something by accident, such as drop your keys

Take Off

To pour: To rain really hard

Grand opening: A celebration when a business has just opened

Filthy: Very dirty

Nap time: Time to sleep for a while (during the day)

Try On

Maid of honor: The most important bridesmaid at a wedding

Flattering: Makes you look good

Reception: The party after the wedding ceremony

To have bad taste: To like things that others think are ugly

Chapter 7
In Sickness and in Health (The Body)

In sickness and in health: Something usually said at a wedding to mean "no matter what happens"

Come Down With

Sleeping sickness: A serious disease you can catch in Africa

Infectious diseases: Diseases that you can catch very easily from other people

Stage fright: Fear of talking in front of a large group of people

Food poisoning: When you get sick from something you ate

Come To

Prom: A formal dance for students

To reminisce: To talk about what happened a long time ago

High school reunion: An event where classmates meet again after many years

The good old days: A long time ago when life was good

Give Out

To crawl: To move on hands and knees like a baby

Beat: Really tired

Marathon: A race that is 26.2 miles long

Banana split: A dessert of ice cream, chocolate syrup, and whipped cream over a halved banana

Knock Out

To duck: To lower your body to avoid being hit

Aw: A sound you make when you see something cute

Round: How a boxing match is divided

Throw Up

Parrot: A bird that can sometimes be trained to talk

Blind date: A date with someone you have never met or talked to

Vet: Veterinarian; a doctor for animals

To peek: To look quickly

Work Out

Mentor: An older, experienced person who helps a younger person with sports, school, or work

Ping-Pong: Table tennis; a game like tennis that you play on a table instead of on a court

To get in shape: To exercise so you are in good physical health

Chapter 8
At First Sight (The Senses)

At first sight: When you see something for the first time

Come Across As/Come Off As

Loan officer: Someone in a bank who helps customers with loans

Witch: An imaginary woman who is mean and flies on a broom

Peephole: A small hole in the door that allows you to see who is outside the door

Give Off

Au lait: A French term indicating there is milk in something, as in café au lait

Coffee grounds: The small bits of coffee left in the coffee maker's filter after you make coffee

Sour: Not fresh, as when cream is old and smells bad

Aroma: A smell/odor (usually a good one)

Listen Up

To leap: To jump really high

Missing: Cannot be found

Look Around

To browse: To look at many things in a shop

By the way: Something you say when you want to mention something

Thrilled: Really happy or excited

Put Off

Block party: A party in the street attended by all the neighbors

Deviled eggs: A dish of halved hard-boiled eggs with a filling

So-so: In between good and bad

Watch Out (For)

Automotive: Relating to cars

Fatal: Causes death

To swerve: To turn sharply to avoid something

Chapter 9
On the Tip of My Tongue (Communicating)

On the tip of your tongue: When you are thinking of something but you can't quite remember what it is

Bring Up

Drive-in: An outdoor movie theater where people watch movies from their cars

Plot: The main points of the story

Gift certificate: A coupon you can exchange for merchandise in a store or for services

Tip: Extra money you voluntarily give to someone who gives you a service, such as in a restaurant, where you usually give a fifteen percent tip

Drive At/Get At

Handy: Good at fixing things

Thingamajig: Something you say instead of a noun when you don't know what something is called

What on earth . . . ?: Something you say instead of just, "What?" when the other person seems to be doing/saying something strange

Get Across

Home stay: When a student of a foreign language goes to another country and stays in someone's home to practice speaking

Lox: Smoked salmon

Homonyms: Words that sound the same but that have different meanings (such as to, two, and too)

Run By

Landscaper: Someone involved in designing and planting various gardens

To have a strong opinion about: To believe something very strongly

Speak Up

Obnoxious: Very annoying and inconsiderate of others

To mumble: To not speak clearly

To go on a break: To take a rest while at work

Talk Into/Talk Out Of

To hike: To walk outdoors as exercise

Park ranger: Someone who works at a state or national park

Cub: A young bear

Chapter 10
On My Mind (Thinking)

On your mind: When you have been thinking about something for a while

Come Up With

Personalized: Something that is made specially for one person

License plate: The metal identification plate on the back/front of a car

Figure Out

To talk in your sleep: To say words or make sounds while you are asleep

To count sheep: To try to go to sleep by imagining lots of sheep jumping over a fence, one by one

To have a hard time: To have difficulty

Stressful: Makes you feel worried and not calm

Look Into

Comedy act/routine: A performance of something funny in front of others

Retirement home: A place where senior citizens live

Hilarious: Really funny

Make Up

Sleepover/slumber party: When children sleep at a friend's house and have fun

Gingerbread men: Cookies that are in the shape of little men

To yawn: To open your mouth wide and breathe deeply when you are tired

Sleep On

Spectacular: Amazing or really great

To sue: To bring legal action against someone

To warn: To tell someone to be careful about something

Think Through

Talent show: A show at a school where people perform and are judged on how good they are

Aspirin: A white pill you take when you have a headache

Chapter 11
In Love (Dating)

In love: Romantically attached to

Ask Out

Laps: When you swim from one end of the pool to the other

Skinny: Very thin

To shave: To remove hair with a razor

Fall For

Manicure: When you go to a salon and someone paints your nails

To get your nails done: To get a manicure

Fix Up (With)/Set Up (With)

Thanksgiving: An American holiday in November when you give thanks and eat turkey and pumpkin pie

Loser: A person who is not "cool" and fun to be with

To poke: To hit someone quickly with your finger

Go Out (With)

Food fight: When people (usually children) throw food at each other as a game

Double date: When two couples go out on a date together

Vegetarian: Does not eat meat

Make Up (With)

Bangs: Short hair that covers the forehead

To dye: To make something a different color

A bad hair day: A day when your hair looks bad although you try hard to make it look good

To change the subject: To start discussing a new topic

Take Out (To)

Afraid of heights: Fearful of being in a high place

Bake sale: A sale of homemade sweets to raise money

Lemon meringue pie: A lemon pie with a fluffy topping

Orange marmalade: A jam made of oranges

Chapter 12
On the Rocks (Hating)

On the rocks: When a couple is having problems

Be Over/Get Over

To have something in common: To be interested in the same thing as someone else

To make a crank call: To phone someone as a joke (not a good thing to do)

To be made for each other: To belong together romantically

Be Through (With)

To smooch: To kiss

Romantic getaway: A vacation you take with the person you love

With everything on it: With onions, pickles, olives, and anything else available

Break Up (With)

To get on my nerves: To annoy me

Personally, I think: In my opinion

Brunch: A combination of breakfast and lunch that's usually eaten in the late morning

To get the point: To understand what someone meant to express

Have It Out (With)

To be a disaster: Slang for "to not go well"

To nibble: To eat small amounts of food

Kick Out/Throw Out

Garage sale: A sale of used household items from your garage or front yard

To apologize profusely: To sincerely say you're sorry for a long time

Prized possessions: Items that are very important to you

Walk Out On

Your place: The place where you live

Kitty litter: Sand in a cat's box

To have second thoughts: To think that a decision you made was not the right one

To get back together with: To become romantically involved again after breaking up

Chapter 13
Through Thick and Thin (Friends)

Through thick and thin: When you are loyal to someone during good times and bad

Come By/Stop By
Mechanic: Someone who fixes machinery

To take a look at: To examine

Get Along (With)
Spring Break: A vacation from school around March or April

To frown: To do the opposite of smile

Hang Out (With)
Nosy: When you want to learn personal or private information about someone

Report card: A list of grades that the school gives a student

Woodshop: A class where you learn how to make items out of wood

To carve: To create something (such as a statue) out of wood or other material; to slice meat

Keep Up (With)
To get up the nerve to: To become brave enough to

Business is booming: When many customers visit a shop

To elope: To get married in an untraditional manner (sometimes secretly without your parents' permission or knowledge)

Look Up
The big day: A very important day

Beach bunnies: A slang term for ladies who like to get a tan at the beach; here, a joke on Dave's last name and the pet store, which sells rabbits (bunnies)

Run Into
You're bound to: You will probably

To take someone's advice: To do what someone suggests

To hiss: To make a "sssss" noise like a snake

To make a fool of yourself: To do something that causes others to laugh at you

Chapter 14
On Good Terms (Nice)

On good terms: When you get along with someone

Go Along With
To charge double: To make the price twice as much

Sign language: A language of hand signals used by the deaf

Look After
Unicycle: A vehicle (like a bicycle) with one wheel

Grumpy: In a bad mood

Invalid: Someone who is sick or injured and unable to move

Crutches: Medical devices that you lean on when your legs are injured

Look Out For
Earmuffs: Warm things you wear on your ears in winter

Bully: A child who is mean to other children

Recess: A short break at school when children play outside

To make friends: To become friendly with others

Put Up
Exchange student: A student who lives with a family in another country

Jet lag: The tiredness you feel after you have traveled a long time and there is a time change

See To
To ask someone a favor: To ask someone to do something nice for you

New paint job: A new coat of paint

Rusty: When metal becomes red after being outside a long time

Stand Up For/Stick Up For
To hum: To make sounds (usually like singing) without opening your mouth

National anthem: The song that represents your country ("The Star-Spangled Banner" in America)

Patriotic: When you express love for your country

Assertive: Good at standing up for yourself

Chapter 15
Up to No Good (Crimes)

Up to no good: When you are doing something bad or illegal

Break In (To)

VCR: Video Cassette Recorder; a machine that videotapes programs or plays tapes

911: The phone number you dial to get help quickly if there is an emergency

Break Out (Of Jail/Prison)

Fish sticks: Frozen breaded fish (usually in the shape of a rectangle)

To be stuck: To be unable to get out

Get Away

Thorn: The sharp point on a rose or other plant

Nursery: A place where you buy plants; also, a baby's room

To be under arrest: To be captured by the police and taken to jail

Get Away With

To tickle: To lightly touch someone to make the person laugh

To direct traffic: To stand in the street and tell drivers when to start and stop (often when a traffic light is broken)

Hold Up

To be out on bail: To be temporarily released from prison after you pay money

To plead guilty/not guilty: To tell the judge you are guilty/not guilty

Eggplant Parmesan: An Italian dish of baked eggplant, cheese, and tomato sauce

Turn In

Spot: A common name for a dog

Dog groomer: A person who washes dogs

Miss Demeanor: A joke on the word *misdemeanor*, which is a crime that is less serious than a *felony*

Chapter 16
On Bad Terms (Mean)

On bad terms: When you don't get along with someone

Beat Up

Mime: A person who performs by using actions, not words

ER: Emergency Room; the section of the hospital you visit when you need care quickly

Hang Up On

Door to door: When you knock on every door in the neighborhood (often to sell something)

Gallon: A liquid measure (milk and gasoline are often measured in gallons)

Look Down On

Janitor: A person who cleans a business or school

Snobbish: When you act as if you are better than another person

To give it a shot: To try something

Pick On

Mayonnaise: A white egg-based sauce you spread on sandwiches

Super: Really good

Put Down

Gravel: Little rocks that are sometimes found on hiking trails

Open-minded: Not critical of others, not *closed-minded*

Put Through

Travel agent: Someone who arranges trips for others

Booked: Reserved/already taken

Insect repellent: Something to keep insects away

Beekeeper: A person who raises bees and collects honey

Chapter 17
Up and at 'Em (Action)

Up and at 'em: Something you say when you want someone to get out of bed and get to work

Be Up For/Be Up To

Pet shelter: A place where animals live while they are waiting to be adopted

Piranha: A fish from the Amazon River known for eating meat

Triathlon: A three-part race of running, swimming, and cycling

Do Over

Mother's Day: A holiday in May when mothers are celebrated (fathers are celebrated on *Father's Day* in June)

Mischievous: Naughty

Get On With

To make cookies for Santa: A Christmas tradition where children make cookies for Santa on Christmas Eve and leave them near the Christmas tree

Batter: Unbaked cookie dough

To procrastinate: To delay doing

Rudolph the Red-Nosed Reindeer: One of Santa's reindeer

Go For

Couch potato: An inactive person who likes to sit on the couch and watch TV

Three days straight: Three days in a row

To concentrate: To think really hard

Go Through With

Raise: An increase in the amount of money you earn

The Blues: A style of music where the subject of the song is often that you're sad (blue)

Keep At

Skateboard: A piece of wood with four wheels that youngsters like to ride

Tip: A useful piece of information

To get your balance: To hold your body so you don't fall down

Chapter 18
At a Standstill (Inaction)

At a standstill: When nothing is happening

Get Out Of

Recital: A performance of music or dance

Ridiculous: Something silly that makes others laugh

Yo-yo: A round toy that moves up and down on a long string

Out-of-date: Not current, not *up-to-date*

Give Up

Fourth of July/Independence Day: A holiday (July 4) when Americans celebrate their independence from England

Grilled cheese sandwich: A cheese sandwich you usually cook in a toaster oven, not on a gas grill

Hardware store: A store that sells tools

Put Off

To wait until the last minute: To do something at the last possible moment/to procrastinate

Optician: Someone who makes or sells eyeglasses

Frames: The rim of a pair of glasses

Sit Around/Stand Around

Flat: Has no air in it

To have a crush on: To like romantically

Lobby: The waiting/reception area of a large building such as a hotel

Sit Out

Windbreaker: A thin jacket you wear when it's windy (not when it's really cold outside)

To have a ball: To have a really good time

Turn In

Lion tamer: Someone who trains lions to perform

Housekeeping: The people in a hotel who clean rooms

Air bed: A mattress you blow air into

Mane: The hair around a lion's head

Chapter 19
Up the Corporate Ladder (Working)

Up the corporate ladder: When you get promoted at work

Clock In/Punch In/Clock Out/Punch Out

Timeclock: At your workplace, a machine that stamps your arrival or departure time on a timecard

Donkey: A long-eared animal that looks like a small horse

Get Off

French toast: A breakfast dish of bread dipped in egg and then fried in butter

Flip-flops: Open summer shoes with a strap between the toes

Soggy: Contains too much liquid

Lint: Little bits of fabric or fuzz

Knock Off

Shift: A certain number of hours you are supposed to work

To juggle: To rapidly throw and catch multiple items (often balls)

Emporium: A store

The woman of his dreams: The ideal woman for him

Move Up

To monogram: To put the first letters of your names (your initials) onto something

Crew: A team of workers

Put In For

Vault: A secure place in a bank where money and valuables are kept

Hand: A game of cards

Résumé: A list of your work history and accomplishments

Write Up

Mask: Art in the shape of a face (usually paper or wood) worn at Halloween or in ceremonies in some cultures

To suit: To look good on

To get a discount: To pay a lower price

To pay full price: To pay the asking price

Chapter 20
Off Duty and On Vacation (Relaxing)

Off duty/on vacation: Not working

Check In (To)/Check Out (Of)

To be in a wedding: To be a bridesmaid or an usher at a wedding ceremony

To hem: To shorten clothing using a needle and thread

Eat Out

Within walking distance: Close enough to walk to

Concierge: An employee at a hotel who helps guests and answers questions

Fly In (To)/Fly Out (Of)

Archaeological site: A place where you can see old buildings and art made by ancient people

To dread: To not look forward to/to fear

Baggage Claim: The place in the airport where you collect your luggage

To spot: To notice

Run Up (A Bill)

Maître d': The head waiter

Substantial: Quite large

Sleep In

Icing: The frosting on a cake

To mislead: To try to make someone believe a lie

Take Off

To catch a plane: To arrive at the airport in time to take an airplane

Scenic route: A pretty, but slow, route

Podium: A place where you stand to give a speech

ANSWER KEY

Chapter 1 Review Questions

1. Instead of slowing down, the driver cut me off.
2. Laurie needed to fill up/gas up.
3. The baseball players couldn't play their game because the bus broke down.
4. My boss wanted me to speed it up.
5. The ice cream truck drove around the neighborhood.
6. The mailman ran over the dog by accident.
7. The driver slowed down because she saw a police car.
8. She sped up because she thought the truck was going to run her over.
9. The policeman cut off the criminal.
10. He needed to fill up/gas up his van.
11. My car broke down in the middle of the street.
12. Angie drove around because she was bored.

Chapter 2 Review Questions

1. As I headed out to the museum I remembered to get the discount coupon.
2. Hurry up and get dressed or you'll miss the school bus.
3. The spider tried to catch up to the roach but it couldn't.
4. I wanted to take off when my mom told me she was unhappy with my grades, but we were in the car.
5. The hostess walked up to the guests and asked them how they liked the dinner.
6. The homeless man ran off with my sandwich.
7. Hurry up!
8. The girl ran off when she saw the ice cream truck.
9. My new shoes prevented me from catching up to Matt.
10. She headed out to her boyfriend's house in her new dress.
11. I didn't like the lecture so I took off.
12. Joey walked up to Andy and gave him a hug.

Chapter 3 Review Questions

1. I wanted to go over the directions with my husband before we got on the highway.
2. Tanya sat in on her friend's conversation class.
3. The teacher counted how many essays she had and saw that three students hadn't handed them in/turned them in.
4. The scientist has been up on shells for the last seventeen years.
5. He looked up the information in his book but it wasn't there.
6. The tour guide suggested they read up on the university after the tour.
7. Graham wanted to learn about elephants so he looked up the information in the nature magazine.
8. I was late handing in/turning in my essay to the substitute teacher.
9. Marci read up on chemistry.
10. We went over the shopping list before I went to the store.
11. The triplets sat in on the lecture but they had to share the two remaining seats.
12. He wasn't up on the rules of sumo wrestling but he learned them when he watched a tournament.

Chapter 4 Review Questions

1. The boy carried on when his mother wouldn't buy him the toy.
2. I don't like it when the kids scream, but I put up with it.
3. The policeman told the girl off when she crossed the street without looking.
4. The 13-year-old bought some acne medicine when she broke out.
5. I hope my children take after me.
6. The teacher asked her students to write a report about someone they look up to.
7. I look up to my dad.
8. The boy told the dog off but it didn't understand.
9. He carries on when he doesn't want to do what his father asks.
10. She usually breaks out in a rash if she uses that particular cream.
11. Carlos takes after his mom.
12. They don't want to put up with that bad music.

Chapter 5 Review Questions

1. She threw away/threw out what she didn't need.

2. The waiter cleaned off the chair before I sat down.

3. The dishwasher is broken so you will have to wash up tonight.

4. The wife didn't want to clean up after her husband.

5. I ran out of garbage bags.

6. Please clean out your sock drawer.

7. This plant is dead so you need to throw it away/throw it out.

8. He ran out of matches.

9. Your desk has too many things in the drawers so I suggest you clean it out.

10. The woman cleaned off the table.

11. She needs to wash up.

12. Before the guest arrives, I need to clean up/straighten up.

Chapter 6 Review Questions

1. Although the dry cleaner always hangs up my clothes, they are always wrinkled.

2. She took off her bracelet because it was time for bed.

3. They dress down at work.

4. I need to break these shoes in even though they are uncomfortable now.

5. My mom tried on the dress.

6. She forgot to put on her glasses, so she couldn't take the driving test.

7. Her father is always a size extra-large, so he never has to try shirts on.

8. The boy had to put on a new shirt because he spilled soda on the one he was wearing.

9. The boss dresses up every day.

10. She broke in her new boots.

11. The kids took off their slippers and went to bed.

12. My wife hung up my clothes for me because I was too lazy.

Chapter 7 Review Questions

1. My legs were so tired I thought they were going to give out.
2. She felt like throwing up when she was pregnant.
3. A car ran over him, and when he came to he was in the middle of the street.
4. They like working out at the gym.
5. I hope I don't come down with the flu this year.
6. She was knocked out by a baseball.
7. He likes working out in the morning before work.
8. The boxer was knocked out when the other man hit him.
9. She came down with a cold last week.
10. My legs gave out after I swam across the big lake.
11. After surgery, she came to in the hospital.
12. The cat threw up on the carpet so we took him to the vet.

Chapter 8 Review Questions

1. She looked around but she couldn't find her checkbook.
2. Watch out! There's a big piece of glass on the carpet.
3. OK everyone, listen up and don't speak.
4. That man comes across as/comes off as very friendly.
5. I like the aroma that your perfume gives off.
6. Women who wear too much perfume put him off.
7. She comes across as/comes off as very smart.
8. The old man is put off when old women color their hair purple.
9. Everyone please listen up because the president is about to give a speech.
10. Watch out for the lion that's coming toward you.
11. They looked around for the perfect gift.
12. That candle gives off a great smell.

Chapter 9 Review Questions

1. I'm not sure what you're driving at/getting at.
2. His dad tried to talk him out of eating all the fudge.
3. Speak up.
4. When Grandma brought up that my room was messy, I offered to clean it up.
5. He needs to run it by his wife.
6. I tried to explain it to the doctor, but he didn't understand what I was trying to get across.
7. I talked my husband into going shopping with me.
8. What are you driving at/getting at?
9. She couldn't get it across.
10. At dinner, he brought up that he wanted to study abroad.
11. Mom needs to run it by Dad.
12. Could you please speak up?

Chapter 10 Review Questions

1. She can't figure out her math homework.
2. He made up a good recipe.
3. They thought it through.
4. I came up with a good name for my dog.
5. She needs to look into it a little more.
6. I'll sleep on it and let you know tomorrow.
7. Before she accepted his marriage proposal she thought it through.
8. He can't figure out how to open the wine bottle.
9. He'll sleep on it.
10. Toby's mother looked into the baseball camp before she let him go.
11. Dickens was good at making up interesting characters for his books.
12. She came up with ten reasons why she didn't want to do her chores.

Chapter 11 Review Questions

1. They had a fight but then they made up.
2. She took him out to the movies.
3. They fell for each other on their second date.
4. He asked her out to the museum.
5. My friend fixed me up/set me up.
6. The couple has been going out for three years.
7. Her aunt usually fixes her up/sets her up with nice men.
8. My boyfriend and I made up.
9. She went out with him only once.
10. I'd like to take you out to the ballpark.
11. I'm too shy to ask the boy out.
12. He fell for her immediately.

Chapter 12 Review Questions

1. She broke up with him.
2. He had to find a new apartment because she kicked him out/threw him out.
3. They had it out in the middle of the night.
4. He walked out on her.
5. The young lady was over/got over the young man.
6. The couple decided they were through and got a divorce.
7. They had it out.
8. I am not over him/haven't gotten over him.
9. He kicked her out/threw her out.
10. I suspected we were through when my girlfriend never answered my phone calls.
11. I don't like breaking up.
12. When she walked out on him, he became sad.

Chapter 13 Review Questions

1. My friends and I like to hang out with each other on weekends.
2. I didn't expect to see him, but I ran into him at the store.
3. She and her sister did not get along.
4. They didn't keep up with each other.
5. The plumber will come by/stop by the house at 3 p.m.
6. He decided to look up his old friend.
7. She ran into her grandpa when she was shopping for his Christmas present.
8. I hung out at home last night.
9. May I come by/stop by your house tomorrow evening?
10. I was curious about what she was doing, so I looked her up.
11. She was very good at keeping up with old friends.
12. I get along with my classmates.

Chapter 14 Review Questions

1. My older brother looked out for me in the playground.
2. She needs to learn to stand up for/stick up for herself.
3. They put her up.
4. Although she didn't want her husband to have a pet lizard, she went along with it.
5. I'll see to it.
6. We had to look after our sick aunt.
7. When the boy made fun of her hairdo, her friend stood up for/stuck up for her.
8. My mother saw to everything, so the wedding was perfect.
9. She looked after him while he was ill.
10. When I went to college, I was sad because my family wasn't there to look out for me.
11. She went along with the idea although she didn't like it.
12. The airline put me up at a nice hotel.

Chapter 15 Review Questions

1. The criminal got away.
2. I turned the robber in to the police.
3. Someone broke into the house and took the stereo.
4. The man got away with robbing the bank.
5. The woman broke out of prison.
6. The robber held up the store and stole some money.
7. I saw my neighbor steal the car, so I turned him in.
8. The two thieves held up the restaurant and stole some beer.
9. She saw him commit the crime, but he got away.
10. In the middle of the night, someone broke into the store and took some jewels.
11. She was usually late but always got away with it.
12. The criminal didn't want to stay in jail, so he tried to break out.

Chapter 16 Review Questions

1. The rich man looks down on poor people.
2. She put me through a lot of stress.
3. He hung up on her.
4. The little boy picked on the little girl.
5. When the man tried to break into my house, I beat him up.
6. She always puts her roommate down.
7. The doctor put me through a lot of worry because he didn't tell me the test results for a long time.
8. I didn't like it when other children picked on me.
9. The children beat each other up.
10. Every day, she puts me down.
11. The salesman called late at night, so I hung up on him.
12. The actress looked down on the waiter.

Chapter 17 Review Questions

1. Her mom always encourages her to go for it.
2. You should get on with it.
3. He decided to keep at it.
4. He isn't up for cooking dinner for ten relatives.
5. He planned to hold up the grocery store, but then he couldn't go through with it.
6. Please do your assignment over.
7. Please get on with it.
8. If you keep at it, you'll improve.
9. I'm not sure I am up to it.
10. You should go for it.
11. The teacher told me to do my homework over.
12. I was thinking about walking out on him, but then I couldn't go through with it.

Chapter 18 Review Questions

1. They like to sit around on the couch all day.
2. I usually put off doing my homework.
3. She doesn't want to work, so she's trying to get out of going.
4. He wants to turn in early.
5. I tried to learn how to dance but then I gave up.
6. She will sit this game out.
7. I usually turn in at 11 p.m.
8. He was supposed to mow the lawn before noon, but he put it off until the last minute.
9. They usually stand around outside the mall on weekends.
10. I was able to get out of taking the test because I was sick.
11. I was too tired to play the game so I sat it out.
12. She tried to break out of prison but then she gave up because it was too difficult..

Chapter 19 Review Questions

1. I knocked off two hours early.
2. Her boss wrote her up.
3. He got off work at 6 p.m.
4. I'd like to move up.
5. She clocked in/punched in at 8 a.m.
6. Yesterday she put in for some vacation time.
7. My boss never lets me knock off early.
8. She lost her timecard so she couldn't clock out/punch out.
9. She doesn't like writing her employees up because it puts them through a lot of stress.
10. What time do you get off work tonight?
11. He's thinking about putting in for a managerial position.
12. She's moving up in the company.

Chapter 20 Review Questions

1. We flew into Philadelphia.
2. He took off from a small airport.
3. They ate out at a fancy restaurant.
4. When I checked out of the hotel, I accidentally left my toothbrush.
5. She ran up a large credit card bill.
6. He likes sleeping in while on vacation.
7. The airplane took off on time.
8. My family and I eat out every Saturday night.
9. I didn't set the alarm, so I accidentally slept in.
10. Before you fly out, perhaps you should buy a souvenir at the airport.
11. We checked in and then took a nap.
12. She ran up a big tab at the restaurant.

OTHER MATERIALS AVAILABLE FROM JAG PUBLICATIONS

Comics and Conversation

More Comics and Conversation

New Comics and Conversation

Foreign Students' Guide to Pronunciation
        and Audio Cassette

Begin in English, Volumes 1,2, and 3
        and Audio Cassettes

Motivational Strategies: Text and Transparencies in Composition and Grammar

From the Beginning: A First Reader in American History

Rhythm and Role Play

Rhythm and Role Play: Audio Cassette

Decision Dramas—Real Language for Real Life

Americana—Historical Spotlights in Story and Song

Americana—"Easy Reader" Historical Spotlights in Story and Song

Americana—Historical Spotlights in Song, Audio Cassette

47% American—Coping with Cultural Issues in Middle School
        Teacher's Guide Including Complete Student Text

47% American—Coping with Cultural Issues in Middle School
        Student Text

A Different Angle: Co-operActivities in Communication

The Talking Edge: Co-operActivities in EASY Communication

The Complete Listening-Speaking Course: Student Centered, Teacher Guided

The Complete Listening-Speaking Course
        Audio Cassettes and CDs